"Go on now. Give your wife a kiss."

Gus elbowed the stranger in the ribs good-naturedly. The man's eyes flashed like lightning, but he moved toward Lottie.

Wife? Lottie's heart contracted and ceased to beat for a moment as she was buffeted by emotions. A frisson of fear coursed through her, but there was a stronger ripple of excitement and sexual awareness that stunned her.

Suddenly the dark-eyed man Gus had called Shayne scooped her up and wrapped her in a hard embrace that took her will and her breath away.

"Hello, darlin'."

With a wicked gleam in his eyes, he drew her tighter to his chest. She felt the plane of muscle and the thud of his heart while he held her against him in a punishingly hard grip.

"Did you miss me?" His voice was a threatening purr in her ear, his eyes bleak and wintry as ice.

Lottie swallowed. She was unable to speak or look away. The impossible had happened. Shayne Rosswarne had come to McTavish Plain. And he was staking his territory in front of God and everybody in her shop.

Dear Romance Reader,

Last year, we launched the Ballad line with four new series, and each month we'll present both new and continuing stories set everywhere from medieval England to the American West—the kind of passionate, romantic stories you love best, written by the most gifted authors. At the back of each book, we'll tell you when you can find subsequent books in the series that have captured your heart.

This month, Cindy Harris returns with the second installment of her celebrated *Dublin Dreams* series. When a penniless miss decides to become a "modern" woman, she must decide if the dashing sea captain who agrees to help her is a **Wolf at the Door**—or the man of her dreams. Next, travel back to the lush intrigue of Georgian England with Maria Greene, as a man returning from war with no memory of his past faces the alluring woman who was his wife with **A Stranger's Kiss.**

In the third entry of the century-spanning *Hope Chest* series, talented Karen Fox introduces an art historian hired to restore a royal portrait—until she travels back in time to meet the prince himself. Is love part of the **Grand Design?** Finally, reader favorite Linda Lea Castle concludes the uproarious *Bogus Brides* trilogy with **Lottie and the Rustler,** as the cowboy one woman chose as her "husband" from a wanted poster arrives in town with mischief in his heart—and temptation on his lips. Enjoy!

Kate Duffy
Editorial Director

Bogus Brides

LOTTIE AND THE RUSTLER

Linda Lea Castle

ZEBRA BOOKS
KENSINGTON PUBLISHING CORP.
http://www.zebrabooks.com

ZEBRA BOOKS are published by

Kensington Publishing Corp.
850 Third Avenue
New York, NY 10022

All Kensington titles, imprints and distributed lines are available at special quantity discounts for bulk purchases for sales promotion, premiums, fund-raising, educational or institutional use.

Special book excerpts or customized printings can also be created to fit specific needs. For details, write or phone the office of the Kensington Special Sales Manager: Kensington Publishing Corp., 850 Third Avenue, New York, NY 10022. Attn. Special Sales Department. Phone: 1-800-221-2647.

Zebra and the Z logo Reg. U.S. Pat. & TM Off.
Ballad is a trademark of Kensington Publishing Corp.

First Printing: August 2001
10 9 8 7 6 5 4 3 2 1

Printed in the United States of America

To the many readers who have written and e-mailed me about Bogus Brides, I hope this one is a cherry on top for you. To the Trois Riviere Fiction Writers, you were an anchor. And to the gambling women of Monday night, you provided inspiration when it was needed.

Prologue

Shayne Rosswarne adjusted the gun belt at his waist. He fastened the thin leather thongs of the tie-down around his upper thigh. The holster snugged down to a comfortable fit. The weight of the gun and the fancy buck-stitched belt felt good and tight on his hipbones. After all the years he had spent in prison shackled, herded, and confined, having a holstered gun was like a badge of honor. It signified freedom and power and all the things he had missed while behind bars. He had lived for this day when he could strap on a holster and seek his revenge.

He was finally free to begin the long journey that would allow him to go home.

He put on the flat-crowned black hat, pulling the brim down low in front. By bits and pieces Shayne was reclaiming himself, trying to find the soul of the man who had been wrongfully sent to prison, if any part of that man still existed. But today he found himself choosing clothes suited to the creature prison had wrought. Each piece was black, grim as the death he contemplated.

A little man wearing thick spectacles popped up from behind the counter of the dry-goods store. "Will you be wanting garters for those sleeves?"

"Yep. Give me a red satin pair—something real flashy," Shayne drawled. "Where I am going I want them to see me coming."

The diminutive proprietor blinked owlishly behind his glasses as he searched until he located the preferred color. He shuffled around the counter and picked up a split-leather vest. Dyed black as a raven's wing, he held it while Shayne slid his arms into the holes. Then, with the practiced care of a man long used to dressing other men, the proprietor slid the garters up, gathering the cloth of each long sleeve loosely above Shayne's elbows.

"Sir, if I may comment without giving offense, in this suit of clothes you look like a gunfighter straight out of a dime novel."

Shayne looked up and cocked a brow. How shocked would the storekeep be to learn how close to the mark he was on that observation? Would he be stunned to know that only a week ago Shayne had been breaking rocks in prison?

"Would you care to take a look, sir?" The man asked in a monotone while he gestured to a dim corner of his shop. A filmy, dust-covered narrow mirror was propped amid boxes and rolls of brown paper.

Shayne walked over, delighted by the harmonious music of his spur rowels—another sweet melody of freedom.

He stared at his reflection in the neglected-looking glass. Years had gone by since Shayne had stood in front of a mirror of any kind. Every one of those hard-spent years was etched into his face now. He was severe, hard, mean-looking, and years older than he remembered. Hell, he *was* mean—he'd had to turn mean just to survive his confinement with thieves, murders, and rapists.

The black Rosswarne eyes that stared back from the glass held no warmth, no humor; there was no good-natured mischief winking in their depths. Now only cold, dark fury glowed in the narrow-eyed reflection.

Shayne gave himself a sad half smile when he remembered the playful prankster he once had been: reckless, carefree, and wild as a young colt. Maybe if he had taken life a little more serious he would not have ended up in prison.

"I also need a rain slicker, a shearling coat, and an extra pair of saddlebags," he said, turning away from the grim image and self recriminations in the mirror. Too many sad memories and regrets were in that reflection.

"Better throw in some chaps as well." He forced himself to focus on his quest. The desire for revenge had kept him alive in prison. He had lived for it and now it was at hand.

"Where are you going, if you don't mind my asking?" the shopkeeper asked conversationally.

"Heading up north," Shayne said, adjusting the gun belt as if to assure himself this was not a dream brought on by too much heat, too much work, and too many beatings by cruel guards.

"Ah, north," the little man said with a sigh of longing. "I always wanted to travel and see a bit of the world."

"I'm headed to a town named McTavish Plain. Have you ever heard of it?" Shayne was growing ever more curious about the town since he had heard the name and realized that was where his quarry had gone.

"No, sir, I can't say I have. Do you have business there?"

Shayne did a quick draw, pointing the gun at his own grim reflection in the dusty mirror. "Yes, long overdue business. I'm going there to kill a man."

One

"Dear me, Lottie, your head must just be swimmin'
with the way Mattie and Roamer got married so soon
after her husband's death," Marilee Walker exclaimed.
Her daughter-in-law, Corabeth Walker, fidgeted on the
stepped platform that Lottie had built to elevate her
customers and ease the strain on her lower back as
she pinned hems and basted on dust ruffles. Lottie
was pinning a row of tatted lace to the bottom edge
of Corabeth's long corset today while the women of
McTavish Plain traded recipes and gossip among
themselves.

"Isn't that French corset cut a bit high over the
bosom?" Marilee asked, squinting through her thick
square lenses at her daughter-in-law's full bosom.

Lottie Rosswarne's dress shop was full this morning,
and as usual, all of the women were eager to assist in
Corabeth's corset fitting or any other task Lottie was
turning her hand at.

"No, I think it is about right, Marilee. If it gets any
lower she will be tumbling out of it," Lottie chuckled.
What would the women of McTavish Plain think if
they knew their fashionable small clothes were being
patterned after garments worn by the painted ladies
and soiled doves of St. Louis?

The deep-cut corsage and the frilly, almost naughty, mode of decoration was straight out of a French sporting house, courtesy of Mattie. She had brought more than a dozen French pieces back. Lottie had copied their unusual and somewhat risqué design. Now the new-style corsets were the rage in McTavish Plain. Every female with a bosom had to have a corset made by Lottie Rosswarne. Now her shop was full every day as she took measurements and fittings.

"I think it's wonderful that Roamer and Mattie have married. It's the luckiest thing ever happened to the rest of us. That rascal Scout has been downright quiet since they got back," Sue Perkins said with a sunny grin, bringing everyone's thoughts back to the recent wedding.

"I ain't going to be lulled into no false sense of security. I still open my privy door and use the broom to make sure it's empty afore I go inside," Gert said with one brow arched. "You never know when that young'un might take a notion to strike again. I don't intend to get caught with my drawers down—so to speak."

All the women giggled at Gert's outhouse humor, but there was also a collective sigh of relief among them. Scout had put the fear of God into the whole town before Mattie got him straightened out properly.

"You can relax a bit, Gert. Scout went with Roamer to Miles City to see about a new anvil for his forge. You are polecat worry-free for at least a month." Lottie grinned before she put the straight pins into her mouth, holding them with her lips as she worked on her knees.

"I am glad Roamer took the boy. I think Mattie deserves a little quiet time. Wasn't it awful about her being abducted and taken to that *place?*" Sue shivered. "I thank the Lord that Roamer found her before . . . before she was *violated.*"

"Amen." All the women said at once. Their eyes were wide with fear, but Lottie didn't understand how they could overlook the wonderful and thrilling adventure that Mattie had experienced.

"That Roamer is a lot of man," Gert sighed, and rolled her eyes toward Lottie's ceiling. "I never would've pegged Mattie as a woman who could handle that much man."

When Mattie had told the women the story of going down the river and being held prisoner in the cathouse, Lottie felt a twinge of envy so sharp it was downright painful. Mattie had not only managed to rid herself of her silly pretend sea-captain husband, she had done something exciting and daring to boot. In fact, she had been elevated to heroine status by her bold actions and her inspiring exploits. Every woman in McTavish Plain was a little jealous of her for having captured Roamer's heart. Lottie was envious for very different reasons. While most of the women in town thought Roamer's coming to the rescue and professing his love to the new "widow" was romantic, Lottie envied Mattie her *enterprise.*

She wished she could have such an escapade. She wanted something completely unexpected and exciting to enter her life. But things like that didn't happen in real life. Dangerous men only came riding into town or striking out on a quest of honor in Mattie's storybooks.

"This lace is itching real bad," Corabeth complained, pulling Lottie's concentration back to the task she had been doing by rote. She might yearn for excitement, but she earned her living by sewing. Every tiny stitch was like a link in a chain—a chain that bound her to McTavish Plain.

"Hold still or you'll have a pin in your upper limb," Lottie said with raised brows. "If you want the trim to lay correctly I have to pin it on before I sew it. Unless you want to leave off the extra row of black lace. We could do that but your corset would be a bit plainer—"

"No!" Marilee cried before Corabeth could say anything. "Corabeth, you keep still," Marilee chided. "Don't you do nothin' to spoil that French corset. We want it low-cut and decorated just like the one your sister brought home, Lottie."

Lottie grinned. Her business had doubled since Mattie returned with the new French corset. Lottie's money, hidden in the coffee tin in her kitchen, was growing quickly. In fact, she might be able to afford passage to Europe by spring if the rage for corsets continued at the same frantic pace. She had resigned herself to the fact that no irresistible scoundrel was going to come walking into her life and sweep her into a web of intrigue or take her in search of an illusive prize.

"Lottie, I do declare, you can work magic with a needle. Corabeth has never looked so womanly." Marilee Walker's expression was pure approval. Her daughter-in-law was all gussied up in a black corset with the deep-cut cleavage and the high-cut legs. Her white lawn drawers flared out from beneath the bottom edge, giving her an exaggerated hourglass shape. Lottie had worked a row of soft pink lace at the neck of the chemise and a matching row at the legs of the drawers for contrast. The entire ensemble was provocatively sexual and more than a little wicked. It was certainly daring for the likes of McTavish Plain.

"If I don't get me a grandchild outa' that corset, then I think my son needs to be fitted for one of John Tubman's wooden coats," Marilee announced boldly.

"Mama Walker!" Corabeth blushed fiery red. "How can you talk like that about your own son?"

"I believe in speaking plain. I want a grandchild. I think I'd have me a grandbaby if Corabeth knew how to be more alluring—more womanly."

"You are speaking way too plain, Marilee, and mortifying the girl and some of the rest of us old hens in the bargain. I think we'd best change the subject before her cheeks catch fire," Gert said with a chuckle, casting a sympathetic gaze at the young woman on the platform. "Did you happen to read the paper today?"

Marilee didn't respond; she just kept looking at Corabeth with a speculative smile on her lips.

"Mr. Jones's paper carried a piece about the government hacking off a chunk of the territory to make Colorado," Sue Perkins provided. "Who knows what they'll do next? Maybe take a big hunk north between us and the Northern possessions and give it some wild Indian name?"

"I doubt the government will be paying any mind to us while the conflict of secession is going on," Corabeth said reasonably, her cheeks still flushed with embarrassment. She had been married for more than five years without conceiving a child, much to Marilee's sorrow. Lottie knew Corabeth was sensitive on the subject, but her mother-in-law was more than willing to discuss it with anyone who would listen. And she usually did it within earshot of Corabeth herself.

Lottie glanced up at Corabeth and smiled. She sympathized with the young woman, having spent her own entire life with her two sisters telling her to how to behave. She knew exactly how Corabeth felt when Marilee accused her of not being alluring enough. Lottie had spent her life hearing that she was not ladylike enough, or that she was too impulsive or wild.

"What's the latest news, Gert?" Lottie prompted, hoping to keep Marilee distracted with the news until she finished Corabeth's fitting.

"In Mr. Jones's printed essay he mentioned the number of men needed in the war. They need more volunteers for the fighting."

"You mean for the dying," Gert snorted.

"Lands, I thought when President Lincoln called for those forty-two thousand volunteers back in sixty-one it would be enough," Sue agreed.

"I guess there are never enough men to die in war," Gert said sadly.

"What other news is there? Isn't there anything less grim?" Lottie asked. "I have been so busy I haven't had a moment to read the paper."

"Well, let me think. Soldiers are being pulled out of many forts and sent back east to fight," Sue recounted with her brow furrowed.

"My George says he fears what may happen with the Indians hereabouts without the soldiers," silver-haired Molly Cuthbert interrupted. Shy as a mouse, it was unusual for her to add much of anything. Today her hands trembled while she pulled embroidery floss through the taut, fine linen caught in her oval hoop. She had commissioned a Sunday dress from Lottie but was doing the handiwork for the collar and cuffs herself.

"Now, Molly, don't go getting yourself all worked

up." Marilee went to her and patted her shoulder. "Remember your delicate constitution."

"You're right. I am as nervous as a cat in a roomful of rockers. Ever since George told me about the soldiers heading east to war and the forts being decommissioned, I haven't had a wink of sleep. Can you believe there will be dangerous criminals set amongst us God-fearing folk?"

Molly gulped so loud, Lottie heard the sound of her throat working in her skinny, age-lined neck. She was worried the old woman might faint or have a seizure of the heart right in her shop. And though that would be exciting, it wasn't the kind of excitement she had in mind.

"All done, Corabeth. You can go slip into your wrapper before we begin the fitting for your day corset." Lottie was anxious for a break and eager to do something to ease the strain in Molly's face. "I have tea ready."

"Oh, good." Corabeth made her way down from the stepped platform. "I could use a cup."

"So could Molly."

Lottie stood up straight, put her palms in the small of her back, and stretched. She had been working without a break for the better part of the morning and she had not yet heard one *juicy* bit of gossip about a single resident of McTavish Plain. She did not count her sister Mattie's venture as gossip, since she and Addie were the only ones in town who knew the real story behind her recent marriage anyway. Only the three Green sisters knew that Mattie hadn't been married and that her husband was a fake, or that Lottie's husband was only a name plucked from an old, faded "wanted" poster.

"I think you should have some tea too, Lottie," Gert said. "You seem a little melancholy today."

"You do seem a little tightly wounded up, Lottie. And Molly, you know how you get the vapors when you get worried." Marilee settled herself and waited for Lottie to pour out. "It's silly to worry about the soldiers leaving. We have all been just fine here in town, what with Ian's good graces with the Salish."

Corabeth stepped from behind the linen-lined screen with a calico wrapper secured from throat to waist. Her cheeks were still flushed.

Lottie settled herself in an armless chair. She did feel strange today. She was restless and sad and dissatisfied in a peculiar way. She busied herself with the cups, having laid out cookies and all the fixings for a proper ladies' tea on a low oval table, but the nagging feeling of wanting more in her life remained.

"Corabeth, have some tea," Lottie offered, pushing her annoying thoughts aside. "Tell me more news, Sue."

"Mr. Jones said that some of the more civilized criminals will be receiving early releases and pardons." Sue's eyes rounded as she talked. "Others that are too violent"—at this Sue shivered theatrically—"well, those men will simply have to be sent to other prisons."

"My, my," Lottie breathed. "Desperadoes, bank robbers, and gunslingers roaming the land again. Imagine that." She heard excitement sneaking into her own voice and was glad her sisters were not here. They would be taking her to task for her careless words.

"I swan, Lottie Rosswarne, the way you go on!" Marilee chuckled. "I think you are just getting itchy for that husband of yours to get here. Are you anxious to hear harrowing tales of the perils of driving cattle to market, or is it just needing to do what pretty young women do with husbands that have been away too long that has you jumpy as a frog on a griddle today?" Marilee waggled her brows, the smallish glasses bobbing comically on her narrow nose.

Her words sobered Lottie. "Marilee, how does Joe keep up with you?" Lottie asked with a smile. The last thing she needed was Marilee asking about her husband. And Marilee's thoughts were uncomfortably close to the mark.

"Who says he does keep up?" Marilee asked suggestively without a pinch of shame. "I keep him worn down to a raw nubbin."

Corabeth's breath caught and she ducked her head, concentrating on her teacup.

"Marilee, you could make a sailor blush," Gert chided with a shake of her head.

Marilee and Joe had married late in life, both being way past twenty-five. There had been more than a little curiosity and speculation about what profession Marilee might have been in before they married, due to her gutsy way of speaking about relations between men and women. But if she had been a lady of questionable virtue, it was not an issue in McTavish Plain. This was a town where people were judged on present character, not past mistakes. Still, Lottie did find Marilee's preoccupation with her missing husband a bit amusing—and more disquieting. She didn't want anyone asking questions. She wanted to go on as she was until she had the money to travel far away from McTavish Plain.

Marilee's assumption that Lottie was lonely for her husband was surely based more on Marilee's disposi-

tion than on anything Lottie had ever said. She never
spoke of her husband if she could avoid it. The truth
was that Lottie was enjoying every bit of her independence. She never felt deprived for not having stumbled into a romance. In her opinion her sisters had
gotten themselves into a pretty pickle by creating
make-believe men to be their "husbands." Lottie had
risked no such foolishness. She had seized on the name
of a real, flesh-and-blood man, but a man who would
never bother her.

In Gothenburg, while delivering new shirts, Lottie
had seen an old, tattered "wanted" poster in the sheriff's office. The drawing on the poster had shown a
handsome cuss, dark and dangerous as a stormy night.
She had asked the sheriff about him and found out
the luckless cattle rustler had been sentenced to many
long years in prison. It was a waste of a good-looking
man, no doubt about it, but Lottie had turned his misfortune to her advantage. She had picked that rustler
to be her so-called husband, conveniently confined
where he would never present an unexpected problem
to Lottie. She had taken his name as her own.

Yes, she had been clever—the cleverest of the
Green sisters in her humble estimation. Her lies
couldn't trip her up because good, strong iron bars
kept Shayne Rosswarne far away from McTavish Plain.

". . . Is that what you are going to do, Lottie?"
Marilee was asking with a knowing smile and a wag-
gle of her brows.

"What? I'm sorry, Marilee, I was wool-gathering.
What were you saying?" Lottie asked.

"I said, the first thing you'll do is plant a big old
kiss on that man's face when he gets here. Then the
two of you will test the ropes on your bed."

The ladies all giggled at Marilee's continued randiness. It was whispered that her husband, Joe, could barely keep up with her passionate nature. Lottie didn't know if that was true or not, but Joe did smile and yawn a good bit more than most men in town.

"Now, Marilee, don't you go getting all hot and bothered. You know it takes a good long time to gather a herd, put together drovers, and then trail them to market. I don't think I'll be kissing my husband anytime soon," Lottie said bluntly, determined not to be reduced to blushes the way Corabeth always was when Marilee got started on the topic of bedroom sport.

Blushing fiery red, Corabeth abruptly launched a new topic of conversation.

"What is Sarah Sampson going to do with that wild son of hers? I heard he rode to Belle Fourche, got liquored up and was arrested for dancing naked on the roof of the Imperial Hotel."

Lottie's attention perked right up. Now *this* was juicy gossip and a heap more interesting than a husband that would never show up. "I hadn't heard. Tell me all." she sipped her tea and settled down to listen.

"You all know I am the last one to spread gossip," Sue allowed. The women all nodded in agreement. "But I heard it from Mazie, who heard it from Jules Mank, who has it from someone quite close to the family, that it wasn't the first time the boy has done something like that."

Marilee's eyes twinkled with interest. "What part? The dancing or being naked on the roof?"

Sue shot Marilee a scowl but didn't rise to the bait, smoothly continuing her story. "And I heard there was a touch of madness back in their family. Seems Sarah had a great-great-uncle who thought he was George

Washington. The poor man near bit his tongue off when he tried to wear wooden teeth."

The room erupted into gales of laughter. Cups clattered; tea was spilled. This was what Lottie enjoyed the most about her day, the tea and the good-natured gossip. Her friends were not cruel, just a little nosy. They never hurt anyone with all their chatter and repeating and embellishing of stories. Surely no truly married woman could enjoy such freedom as she enjoyed.

For a few moments the group discussed nothing more important or dangerous than the weather. They emptied their cups and refilled them once again. Lottie settled back to listen contentedly while Sue and Marilee compared tales about the Proctor twins, a pair of closemouthed, leggy men who had recently come to town. But soon the talk turned to the drudgery of being a wife. The cooking, cleaning, and mending each woman struggled to keep up with repulsed Lottie.

This was why she preferred being alone. There was no man clomping in wanting to be fed when she didn't feel like cooking. No children were shrieking through her pretty parlor at home, dirtying up her braided rugs or cluttering her house with toads and old wasps' nests the way Scout always did at Mattie's place.

If Lottie wanted to kick off her shoes of an evening and do nothing, then she could. And if her life was a tad staid and boring, she also had the unique pleasure of it being *her* life.

Lottie made her own decisions, lived her own way. And until she managed to stuff enough money into that coffee tin to finance a grand adventure, this was the way she planned to continue.

Alone, independent, and on her own. She answered to no one.

Her position here in McTavish Plain was just about perfect. And she had her brother-in-law Ian to thank for it. If he knew the truth, she would shake his hand and tell him what a service he had done for her. His rule about unmarried women had given her an opportunity for independent living that few women could ever aspire to having. Of course, he didn't know. Only Mattie and Addie shared her secret and her little white lie.

Yes, Lottie was well satisfied with her life and felt fine about the lies she had told to get here. She had nothing to be sorry for—nothing at all.

She was happy and safe and nobody could ever reveal her secrets.

Nobody but a luckless rustler spending the rest of his days in a faraway prison.

TWO

"Good journey, Addie." Lottie hugged her sister, taking care not to crush the pink-wrapped bundle in her arms. "And take good care of little Kathryn."

"I will." Addie smiled, but there were tears of joy in her eyes.

"Addie, don't you overdo," Mattie said sternly, casting a withering look at Ian. He looked almost civilized in his tailored traveling suit, courtesy of Lottie's stitchery and Addie's good taste.

"We wilna' travel hard. I promise. You needn't worry on your sister's account." Ian frowned darkly.

"I just don't understand why you have to go at all." Mattie glared up at Ian. "If you wanted to travel, why didn't you just go with Roamer to Miles City? I am sure he and Scout would be happy for the company."

"I dinna want to go to Miles City," Ian said bluntly. "Adelaide didna have a proper honeymoon. This will be our wedding trip. I wilna be riding with Roamer and Scout." Ian deposited a kiss on Addie's upturned face and grinned. "I am taking my wife and my daughter on a *private* journey."

"At least tell us where you are going," Mattie pressed.

Ian shook his head at her. "Nae. You wilna know where we are going or when we will be returnin'. I am devoting myself to Adelaide and Katie and wilna be drawn back before I choose. And you two meddlin' sisters will just have to live wi' my decision."

"Meddling sisters are we?" Lottie's head snapped back as if she had been slapped.

Mattie pursed her lips, but she said no more. Ian handed Kathryn to Lottie while he helped Addie into Gert's finest buggy. He checked the top covering and the harness buckles. Then he gently took his daughter from Lottie and deposited her into his wife's loving arms.

"We will be back when it suits us. Take good care of my town," Ian said with a smile as he levered himself into the seat beside Addie. A sturdy trunk was strapped to the back of the buggy struts. "And you two try not to stir up too much trouble while I am gone." Ian snapped the buggy whip in the air and the horses moved out. The pair were well trained and smooth-moving. The yellow wheels sang on the packed earth while everyone in town lined up along the road to wave good-bye and wish them merry.

"Oh, the nerve of that man!" Mattie cried with a stomp of her foot.

"Hurry back," Lottie said sweetly. She was just as insulted as Mattie, but she was determined not to let it show and give Ian that satisfaction.

"If the size of that traveling trunk means anything, I think they will be gone until Kathryn is walking," Lottie added in a tone that she hoped Ian heard. "My niece will likely need fitting for a pinafore and pantalets before that stubborn Scotsman brings them home."

"Oh, don't say that," Mattie wailed. "I couldn't bear it if they were gone too long."

"Their departure ensures this will be the most boring summer ever recorded in McTavish Plain. Not even Scout is here to liven things up," Lottie grumbled to herself. She shook her head in disgust. "Oh, well, at least I will have my ladies and their gossip to keep me busy; Lord knows there will be little else to do in this quiet town."

Shayne stared up at the stars. He had never expected to see them again, but here he was bedded down on the Great Sand Hills of Nebraska, staring up at a sky wrought by the hand of God. Suddenly a streak of light blazed across the black expanse above. He let out a tense breath of air as the shooting star disappeared somewhere far to the north.

Did the star fall on McTavish Plain? Had Ian seen that same star?

Shayne's eyes burned and his gut twisted as he stared into the night. He needed to rest, but sleep brought haunts and specters from his past. The thirst for revenge had ridden with him every mile he had traveled since getting out of prison.

With a disgusted snort Shayne changed position and closed his eyes. Instantly the sights, sounds and memories of prison flooded his brain.

How long would it take before he could sleep the whole night through without nightmares? Would the scars and voices from years of living like an animal come to torture him for the rest of his life?

Would he ever know peace of mind again?

Only by evening the score can you regain your self-respect. He could almost hear his father saying it.

Shayne's horse whickered and stamped his feet restlessly. The line-back dun stallion was strong and tough, but he had a strange need to be touched and petted like a child's mount. Shayne had ridden him hard, but the horse had never come up sore and had never been so tired that he didn't nudge Shayne's arm or nip at his cuff until he stroked his head.

"It's all right, Little Bit; in a few more days we will find McTavish Plain. And after I kill the man that betrayed me I'll sleep without the past haunting me. And then we can go home."

Dawn found Shayne riding north. A herd of antelope had kept pace with him since the first pink fingers of morning pulled back the curtain of night. He looked beyond the sandhills to the far horizon and wondered what McTavish Plain would be like.

Shayne couldn't puzzle out how a man could swindle the government, leave Indians to starve through the long winter, and then go on and start a new life.

"While I rotted in jail for a crime I did not commit," Shayne added between clenched teeth. His gloved fingers tightened on the reins. He lightly touched his spur rowels to Little Bit's side.

Need clawed at Shayne's gut. He lived for one thing and one thing only: to reach McTavish Plain and exact his own brand of justice for the years that he had lost—the years that had been stolen from him. The years he had not been able to contact his family.

Lottie set the table with tatted doilies and five cups. The teapot was under the embroidered cozy Lottie had done on the long journey here. It was one more reminder of how she struggled to keep her wildness under control. A breeze rushed through her open window. It stirred her hair and tugged at her soul.

It had been too quiet since Addie and Ian left. And Lottie missed Scout and his pranks.

She was restless—itchy in a way that was a little frightening. Sometimes in the dark of night Lottie allowed herself to imagine for a moment what it might be like to let her steely self-control slip—to do something shocking and wild—but the very thought was so overwhelming that she tamped down those feelings.

It was comforting to do the proper thing, the safe thing every day.

But today her soul was rebelling. She found her gaze returning again and again to the open window. Her mind wandered free over the hills and valleys to the big world beyond. It beckoned to her like a siren's song; that big expanse of the unknown promised adventure outside the small town of McTavish Plain. Lottie wanted it, and she feared it.

Suddenly the bell over the shop door jingled. In bustled Harriet, Gert, Corabeth, and Marilee. They were all bright-eyed and smiling. They were part of her safe, proper, predictable world.

"Now don't you all look like cats in the cream," Lottie said as they removed their bonnets, hung their shawls, and found their usual places amid her bolts of cloth and worktable. She was grateful they had arrived. It made it easier to ignore the restlessness inside her.

Safer to cling to her old habits.

"Hop right up here, Harriet. Let me get started with the skirt measurements." Lottie assisted Harriet up the steps. The minister's wife wanted a new dress for services since her old one had taken on a worn shine that could no longer be hidden by dying it in strong tea, and the cuffs had been turned so many times that Lottie no longer recalled in which direction they began life.

"Miley brought news of Ian and Addie last evening," Gert said with a toothy grin. The teamster's wife settled herself in one of several soft-padded armchairs and took a deep breath. The other women leaned toward her in anticipation, their eyes glittering with interest.

"Miley was in Belle Fourche and he saw them having a steak dinner in the Imperial Hotel." Gert smiled with satisfaction and happily settled herself, having revealed her plum of information to the eager clutch of women.

"Is that *all?*" Lottie and Corabeth said in unison. "They ate a steak?"

Gert shrugged, looking sheepish enough to be part of Ian's woolly flock. "Miley said Addie looked real pretty in that peach colored frock you sewed up for her, Lottie." Gert swallowed hard when Lottie's eyes narrowed.

"And—and—he said the baby was quiet and sweet as a summer rain," Gert said, in a desperate rush to give the demanding women what they wanted.

A thick silence descended over the room. Lottie had been hoping for more. She had been hoping for some juicy tidbit, or perhaps word of where Ian and Addie were going and how long they planned to be gone. Now the bubble of her temporary happiness had burst and she felt even more melancholy and restless than she had before.

It was a terrible letdown. Her mood darkened as the fidgety humor returned even stronger than before.

"Well, that's all Miley told me," Gert said sullenly. "I cain't very well go making things up, now can I?"

Lottie sighed and turned her attention to Harriet's skirt hem while the other ladies poured themselves a cup of tea. She secretly wished somebody would make something up to ease the boredom that had settled over the town. She prayed for something to happen to sooth the itchiness inside her mind and body.

Surely something would happen soon. It just had to. Or the tight rein Lottie had on her own wild soul would surely snap.

The town was more than Shayne expected—much more. There were thriving businesses and level, dry streets. Instead of soddies and tents, proper frame houses and storefronts lined the wide avenues. Neat kitchen gardens were in every lot, and at the end of town a whitewashed steeple thrust into the seemingly endless expanse of blue sky.

"I wouldn't have thought a low-life, backstabbing bastard would have much use for a town like this," Shayne said, watching the dun's ears work back and forth at the sound of his voice. "Most especially a church."

Shayne took a cross street and headed for the livery stable from the back side. He had no desire to tip off anyone about his intentions or even announce his presence until he had a chance to size up the place and see what they had in the way of law and lawmen.

Shayne wanted revenge, not a shortcut back into a cage or a quick trip to the nearest hanging tree. He intended to walk soft until he knew where he would find his quarry. He turned a corner and came up an alley. He found the livery being tended by a balding man with beefy arms while a slat-thin youth mucked out an empty stall.

Shayne nodded at the man. He wore no side arm, but a hog-leg revolver rested on a ledge against the back of the barn. The livery keeper wasn't looking to cause trouble, but it was obvious he could handle any that had the misfortune to find him.

"Help you?"

"I need to stable my horse. I want him brushed, grained, and his feet checked. If he needs new shoes, see to it fast. I'm not sure when I'll be needing him again." Shayne was still mounted and ready to ride if need be.

"Brushing and graining we can manage. Can't do anything about shoes; our smith is out of town." The man took a small step nearer the gun.

"Fine, then see to the rest." Shayne flipped a coin into the air. It landed with a thud at the man's booted feet. The livery man barely glanced at the coin.

"And do you have a name?" With a frown he looked Shayne over, sizing him as a troublemaker, if Shayne was any judge of the way his eyes narrowed. It was plain he was not overly fond of strangers in general and Shayne in particular. He slid a bit closer to the hog-leg.

"Shayne—Shayne Rosswarne."

The man's face transformed like the sun coming from behind a thin cloud. His eyes widened as quickly as his smile broadened. The tension evaporated. The hog-leg was forgotten while he walked up to Little Bit, reached up, and grabbed Shayne's hand as if they were old friends. He jarred Shayne in the saddle as he began pumping his arm up and down.

"Shayne Rosswarne. Why didn't you say so? We didn't know, that is to say, Lottie did not tell us. She must've been keeping it a secret, eh? I'm Miley Thompson and I am right pleased to meet you—at last. Doggone it, boy, I thought you were some troublemaking drifter."

"Miley," Shayne said cautiously. His arm was still being levered up and down, up and down.

"Miley Thompson, I own the livery stable here in town."

Miley took a deep breath and continued palavering fast and furious. "The whole town is going to be pleased as a weevil in tall cotton. Come on, we've got to go see Gus. He ain't going to believe it. Finally. After all these months. Who'd have thought you'd just come walking in?"

"Gus?" Shayne repeated dumbly as he dismounted. His belly tightened with uncertainty and confusion. The hair on the back of Shayne's neck rose up. He certainly hadn't been anticipating any sort of a welcome.

Had they been warned of his release?

But though he was off balance and wary, Shayne found himself being pulled along to meet the mysterious Gus. The skinny youth that held Little Bit's reins looked at Shayne with something akin to hero worship glowing in his honest brown eyes. Shayne was being treated like a favorite uncle come to visit instead of a hate-filled man intent on vengeance and murder.

And just who was this Lottie? And who was Gus? And why did Miley think this Lottie woman had any notion that Shayne was coming? Up until a few weeks back, Shayne surely hadn't expected to see freedom again until he was too old and gray to care. His release had been a complete surprise, so how could a woman he didn't know have been expecting him?

Something was mighty out of joint in McTavish Plain. All Shayne's survival instincts were working at fever pitch. He wasn't about to let his guard down until he figured out what in hell made Miley treat him like the prodigal son as he walked beside him grinning and talking fast as a scatter-gun would belch shot.

"Yep, old Gus ain't a'goin' to believe you are here," Miley said again.

"I can hardly believe it myself," Shayne said softly. A voice inside his head told him to run. But he didn't put up a fight; he just kept walking along, listening in trap-jawed silence. Miley regaled him with tales of the town and its inhabitants, pointing out each store-front and providing a history of every proprietor until Shayne's head was spinning.

"And this is where John Tubman builds the coffins. We've been real fortunate not to need him for that service, but he turns out right nice furniture, so he has little idle time with all the newcomers we've been getting."

Shayne shivered. The places he'd seen had over-worked coffin-makers who couldn't keep up with the demand, which was usually violent, unexpected, and bloody. Like as not, a dead man would be rolled in a tarp or just dumped in a hole deep enough to keep the coyotes from digging him out overnight. If McTavish Plain hadn't needed the bone-layer's ser-vices, it was even more remarkable than Shayne had first thought.

Or was this some sort of deception? Was Gus wise to Shayne? Was this all a lie?

"Right over there is John Holcomb's stationery

store. He handles the mail. I bring it in from Belle Fourche year-round in all weathers. Even in winter. I just slap the runners on my wagon when the snow gets too deep for the team to manage. Yep, we are right proud of having good mail delivery here in McTavish Plain. We are far from anywhere but we ain't without civilization."

Shayne paused to stare at the building before him. The shop, like most of the others, had a tall false front constructed of lumber. Nothing looked out of the ordinary at first glance, but something must be wrong with the water in this place—or it was populated by a collection of loonies. It was the only explanation for why Miley was acting so pleased to see Shayne. It just didn't make sense . . . unless someone had warned them that someday a man named Shayne Rosswarne would come to town seeking blood and a man's life.

But if that was the case, it was more likely Shayne would be staring down the barrel of a gun than examining storefronts and being escorted though town like some sort of highfalutin dignitary on close inspection.

"I suppose when you were on the trail you found few towns with going-out mail," Miley said with complete sympathy.

"Yep," Shayne agreed in confusion. He felt like the butt end of a joke with the big hee-haw yet to come. Questions hammered at his brain as he tried and failed to come up with any explanation that wasn't full of holes.

"Right here is Gus's mercantile." Miley halted in front of a well-stocked store. "He will be plumb thunderstruck to see you. He has taken a real shine to those girls and thinks of 'em like family."

Girls? What girls? Was this Gus the local whore-monger and storekeep?

Shayne stepped inside, his spurs playing an awkward tune with the bell over the door. He kept his hand near the butt of his shooter.

"Gus, you'll never guess who this galloot is," Miley said with a grin. "It's Shayne. Shayne Rosswarne. He's finally arrived."

Gus came round the counter and grasped Shayne's arm.

"Shayne. You finally came."

Shayne was unable to find his voice while the thin, balding man pumped his arm much as Miley had done. Shayne couldn't have drawn down on the man if his life depended on it, so firm was the grip on his hand. He began to wonder if he'd be able to draw again after all the punishment his arm was taking with so much glad-handing going on.

"I 'spect Lottie will be pleased as a pig in mud to see him," Miley said.

"You haven't seen the little lady yet?" Gus asked, all winks and grin.

"I haven't seen her yet."

"She doesn't know anything?"

"No, not a thing," Shayne said suspiciously. He had decided he had no choice but to play along until he found out what was going on and got a bead on the man he was looking for.

"Well, let us walk you over to Lottie's place. By golly, it will be a treat for us to see her reaction," Gus said while Miley nodded his agreement.

"You can't be any more anxious to see the look on

her face than I am," Shayne said truthfully. He couldn't wait to meet the lady and find out what the hell was wrong with the people of McTavish Plain.

Lottie was down on her knees pinning the dust-ruffle lining to the bottom of the fine black watered silk that Harriet had shipped from New Orleans. The ladies were all talking quietly in between sips of tea and bits of shortbread when the jingle of the bell over Lottie's shop door brought their murmuring to a halt.

She turned and looked up from her crouched position. Miley, Gus, and a man Lottie didn't know were standing at the threshold of her storefront. Gus and Miley were grinning like a pair of foxes in a well-stocked hen house. Lottie's eyes, however, were drawn the silent stranger with them.

Not so tall as Ian, or so heavily muscled as Roamer, the dark-eyed man was all lean sinew and raw angles. His body spoke of strength, agility, and an animal grace. Well dressed but covered with a fine powder of trail dust, he looked like he had been on the road for a while. Hard muscle and tendons bunched and corded in his arms as he flexed his right hand, encased in black leather gloves, near the butt of his side arm. Lottie sensed he was holding himself tightly in check as if he might draw that gun at any moment.

A shiver of excitement rippled through her. Was he here to rob her?

Her eyes flicked back to his face. He was handsome and vaguely familiar, though Lottie was certain-sure she had never made his acquaintance. He was not a man a woman would soon forget. This hard-eyed stranger was someone other men would envy and women would want to know better. This was a man that could move like lightning and hold his own.

Her body twitched with interest. A warm flush moved across her skin.

"Go on, Shayne, don't be shy."

Shayne?

His black eyes focused on Lottie's face. One corner of his wide mouth twitched.

"Go on, now. Give your wife a kiss." Gus elbowed the man good-naturedly in the ribs. The man's eyes flashed like stormy lightning, but he moved toward Lottie.

Wife? Lottie's heart contracted and ceased to beat for a moment. She was buffeted by a collection of emotions. A frisson of fear coursed through her, but there was a stronger ripple of excitement and sexual awareness that stunned her.

Suddenly the dark-eyed man Gus called Shayne was moving toward her. He scooped her up from her position on her knees beside the stepped platform. He wrapped her in a hard embrace that took her will and her breath away.

"Hello, darlin'."

With a wicked gleam in his eyes, he drew her tighter to his chest. She felt the plane of muscle and the thud of his heart while he held her against him in a punishingly hard grip.

"Did you miss me?" His voice was a threatening purr in her ear, his eyes bleak and hard as wintry ice.

Lottie swallowed. She was unable to speak or look away. The impossible had happened. Shayne Rosswarne had come to McTavish Plain. And he was staking his territory in front of God and everybody in her shop.

Lottie was trapped in his arms and trapped in full

view of her friends. Her clever web of lies collapsed around her in a gossamer whirl. She couldn't refuse or deny him without bringing her sisters' lies to light along with her own.

She was trapped—forced to remain silent.

"I can't wait to hear you explain to me why it is I can't remember marrying you," he whispered as he nuzzled her ear, nipping the soft lobe with his teeth. "And I would lay money that these fine folks would enjoy the story too."

He squeezed her a little tighter when she tried to pull away.

"So why don't you tell me, darlin', just how I came to be your *husband* when I've never laid eyes on you in my life?"

Three

"Kiss me, you fool," Lottie hissed.

"What?" Shayne blinked at her. "Who are you calling a fool, lady? What are you up to?"

"I don't have time to explain now. Just kiss me. And act like you mean it. Act like a man anxious to kiss a wife he hasn't seen in a while."

Shayne gave her a crooked grin that was equal parts wild threat and boyish tease. His face was rife with raw sex appeal. He obeyed as if he really did want to be pressing his lips across her own. His mouth was firm and insistent, his lips slightly dry and tasting of trail dust, his tongue a hot bolt of sensuous lightning that seared her soul.

Suddenly the restlessness inside Lottie's soul exploded into a shower of sensation. It was no longer contained beneath the surface. It fought its way free.

Shayne kept her bosom smashed against his chest. He plundered her mouth, not once but twice, as if he were thirsty and her lips were sweet spring water. His tongue did a wicked dance along her own. When she feared she might expire from lack of breath, he finally raised his head and their eyes met.

He raised one brow. "Was that enough of a kiss, or do you want me to do more?" He whispered. "I think I can manage a bit more if you require it of me."

Lottie was jolted by his kiss and his words. This was not a man to trifle with. He was more than a little dangerous; she could see it in those unreadable black eyes and the set of his stern jaw. And it was obvious he didn't find her innocent little lie the least bit amusing—he had proven that much with his forceful kiss. Now, with a twinkle in his eye, he was just daring her to say they weren't married—just daring her to push him away in fright, or indignation, or both. But Lottie had no intention of doing either.

She wanted to press her fingertips to her bruised lips, to see if the kiss was real or imagined, for surely no man could make a woman feel all that she was feeling with just a single kiss. Her toes had darn near curled inside her shoes, and her heart was doing a little jig.

She wouldn't give him the satisfaction of knowing that his lips beckoned to her or that she wanted him to kiss her again. And she wasn't going to blush and simper, either. She wasn't some little shrinking violet. Lottie had more spine than a lot of women—certainly enough to match this man, this drifter who claimed to be Shayne Rosswarne.

Didn't she? Some inner voice told her that if she showed one tiny bit of fear he would be on her like a puma on a helpless fawn. He would gobble her up whole.

But in spite of Lottie's determination to be strong and fearless, she began to do something she had never done in all her life. She began to tremble. It started in her hands and soon her whole body was afflicted. She stood before her "husband," quaking like an aspen in a strong northerly wind.

It was not fear of the dark-eyed stranger that made

her shake; it was some hot, reckless *thing* that had wakened inside her soul the moment his lips touched hers. Her breasts were taut, so sensitive she felt the rasp of the fine lawn of her chemise against them with each shallow breath she sucked into her lungs.

Her hands itched and burned with wanting to test the flesh on the nape of his neck just beneath the cape of obsidian black hair, to see if he felt as powerful and sleek as he appeared.

Lottie had never gone silly over any man before, much less one who appeared as dangerous as this one. Shayne Rosswarne was a rambler and a rogue if ever she saw one, and she could well believe he had just gotten out of prison.

But how? There was something hungry in his eyes, his touch, his very being that spoke to the wildest part of her—the feral part she had fought to control since she had been no older than Scout.

His soul spoke to her reckless nature, and it wanted to answer.

For a moment Lottie's childhood flashed in her mind. She had been an untamed force of nature when her parents died. The preacher and his wife who ran the foundling home had a difficult time trying to curb Lottie's natural inclination to mischief. Being a godly pair, they had seen wickedness and sin in most everything she did.

It terrified them. It frustrated her. It saddened her sisters.

Lottie remembered many, many long hours spent in solitary contemplation of her escapades. That was how she had learned to sew. Every tiny, uniform stitch represented an hour of repentance. Every cross-stitch and fancy needleworked garment marked another shackle on Lottie's free spirit. Idle hands were the devil's playground, or so she had been taught—and so she had stitched and tamped down her own nature. Every stitch was another manacle on her wild soul.

And those shackles had held, for the most part.

Until now. Until this man touched her.

Shayne Rosswarne had roused the sleeping beast that dwelled in Lottie's heart and restless soul. With only a kiss and a flash of his eyes, he had made her tremble. A frisson of fear rippled through Lottie—fear of her own self—fear of the beast he had unleashed.

"Why, look at that," Gert cooed, bringing Lottie's mind back to the moment. "The little thing is so happy that she's quivering all over."

Lottie hated herself for trembling and hated Shayne for possessing the power to destroy her control. She had worked hard to appear cool and composed, but he had ruined her act, cracked the delicate surface of her facade.

Everyone in the shop, including Shayne himself, thought she trembled because of *him*.

Damn him for a rounder! Damn him for a handsome rogue.

Shayne's lips twitched at the corners, as if he found her discomfort amusing. She glanced around the room while she tried to control her emotions.

Miley and Gus still stood in the doorway, watching with benevolent smiles on their lined and seamy faces.

Lottie stiffened and prepared to free herself from this stranger's mystical grip, both real and imagined. But Shayne must have anticipated her intent. He dipped his head low, his warm breath fanning like a butterfly's kiss over her earlobe.

His whisper was soft and yet full of dark, drugging power.

"I don't know what your little game is, darlin'. This looks like a nice little town and those seem like real decent people. How would they react if they knew we weren't really married? What would they do?"

A shiver danced up her spine. He was close enough so that only he would hear her answer.

"You wouldn't dare," she hissed.

His grin was feral and fraught with malice. "Where I've just come from, rising to a dare is a way of life. I am real curious to find out what kind of trickery you're pulling on these good citizens, and why you claim to be my *wife*. Maybe they would be as curious as I am, but would they be as forgivin'?"

Forgiving? This is what he called forgiving? Holding her captive in front of an audience while he made subtle threats and kindled a fire in her belly with his sultry kisses?

"We need to get out of here and give them a little privacy," Gert murmured with an embarrassed cough.

Privacy? Alone—the two of them alone?

"Oh, no—" Lottie feared her own tenuous control would snap if they were alone. She might give into the hunger growing inside her if everyone left.

"Tell me, Lottie, darlin'," Shayne drawled, focusing on her face. "Did you miss me?" He never took those hard, dark eyes off her. He did, however, let her slide from his grasp, slowly, deliberately, making sure to let her know he was *allowing* it. And though he no longer had his hands on her, there was no doubt he had control.

While Lottie watched him in angry, conflicted silence, he smiled and nudged a bunch of frothy lace

from his path with the toe of his boot. He flopped down
in a softly padded chair. It was about half a size too small
for his too-tall frame, and it brought home how much
he did not belong in Lottie's shop or her life.

"I cannot find the words to tell you how I have
missed you, darlin'," Lottie said with a brittle smile.

His own smile was predatory when he answered.
"It warms a man's heart to know he has a devoted
woman waiting for him." Shayne glanced around at
the dress shop, his gaze lingering on the sign swaying
in the breeze outside the window.

LOTTIE ROSSWARNE, DRESSMAKER. *Rosswarne*. His
name.

The place was full of feminine fripperies and ells
of expensive cloth. This woman, his "wife," was doing
all right for herself—that was plain as the perky nose
on her pretty face. This would be a right comfortable
spot for Shayne to rest up, plan his revenge, and wait
for his quarry to show himself.

He propped one booted foot across the other knee
and smiled at Lottie. Even at this distance he could
feel the sting of her anger and the heat of her passion.
The lying little cheat looked like an angel with that
wealth of golden curls and those innocent blue eyes,
but he had felt the devil inside her when they kissed.

Shayne let his eyes roam over her body, taking no
care to hide his assessment since everyone in town
believed he was her husband. He had a right to gaze
at her bosom and grin in appreciation at her curves.
She had used his name—stolen his name. Now he intended to get something in return.

"I'm right tickled to be home. What say you close
up the shop for the afternoon, darlin'?" He cocked
his head and silently dared her to refuse him.

Gus and Miley grinned behind their gnarled, work-hardened hands. A couple of the old biddies gasped and blushed. But to Shayne's delight, they rose and obligingly started for the door with surprising speed.

Lottie's eyes rounded for a moment. Shayne expected her to blush like the other women, to ask them to stay, to try and leave with them—to do anything but remain with him.

But she didn't. She tilted up her saucy little chin and glared at him. Her blue eyes sparked with defiance.

She had sand, he would give her that. She gave him a stiff smile and said, "Yes, why don't I just do that? I think we have some catching up to do—*darlin'*."

Gus and Miley coughed and grinned, their cheeks bright red now. Shayne couldn't wait to hear why she had taken his name and why she was in this particular town—the town where his enemy waited.

When Gus and Miley had led everyone down the street and she was sure no one could overhear, Lottie turned to Shayne.

"My advice to you, cowboy, is that you get on your horse and head straight of town while you can."

"Trying to run me out of town? That is no way for a wife to speak to her husband." Shayne took off his hat, turning it around and around as if he were carefully inspecting the brim. "That is what you told all these folks, isn't it? That you are married to me? So if you run me out of town, I think you might be coming right behind me, and maybe with a tar-and-feather coat on that curvy body of yours."

He never lifted his head, but his gaze drifted up to lock with Lottie's. A shudder rippled through Lottie's body as his words penetrated her anger. He was right.

She had lied; she had created a fictional life with this man. At the very least she would be branded a fallen woman. Her business would be ruined; her sisters would be shamed. Ian would never forgive her for bringing pain and humiliation to Addie's door.

And what about little Kathryn? There was her niece to consider in all this now.

His eyes continued to roam over her body without contrition or restraint. She folded her arms over her bosom to shield herself from his gaze, but it didn't help. Her own body betrayed her. Her heartbeat quickened; her breasts grew heavy. She lifted her chin and tried to pretend she was in control of herself, but in truth she felt as if she were standing on quicksand.

"What exactly do you want from me?"

He chuckled but no humor lit his eyes. "From you? Why, nothing, darlin'."

"Then why are you here? Why did you come to McTavish Plain?" Lottie started to tremble again. He did things to her that she had never believed were possible. She felt all fluttery inside each time he looked at her. His eyes were so dark and bottomless that Lottie fancied she could see forever inside them—could fall forever inside them.

"I'll tell you why I'm here if you tell me why you stole my name," he bargained with a sneer.

"I did not *steal* your name," Lottie said indignantly.

"Really? Then what exactly is the meaning of that?" Shayne jerked his thumb toward the sign waving in the breeze outside the dress shop.

"I—I didn't steal it. I just sort of . . . well, I borrowed it for a while. Besides, you weren't going to be needing it in prison," she blurted out in a rush.

He stood up with a speed and grace that astonished

Lottie. She tried to back away, but he had her wrist in an iron grip before she could even react.

"I suspected you knew I had been in prison, but I wasn't sure. Now, darlin', this is the way we're going to play this hand. I'm going to stay here. You are going to go right on telling everyone that I'm your husband."

Lottie jerked her hand free, rubbing the spot where he had gripped her. If she had any doubts about him being Shayne Rosswarne, they were gone now. She took a deep breath to steady her nerves.

"What do you want here in town if you didn't come for me?"

Shayne shrugged. "I'm looking for a man. I didn't know about you until I met Gus and he spilled the beans. But now that I am here and you have been expecting a husband named Shayne Rosswarne, I may as well oblige you."

"What makes you think you'll find the man you're looking for in this town?" Lottie challenged. "This is a mighty big country in case you haven't noticed."

"Oh, I know I'll find him here," Shayne said with an ugly twist of his lips. "I'm downright certain about it."

"And how can you be so sure?"

"Because the bastard owns the place. I'm here to kill that lying bastard Ian McTavish."

Four

"You want to kill Ian McTavish?" Lottie repeated in a whisper.

"Just as soon as I clap eyes on him," Shayne said coldly. "But that can wait; right now I want another kiss."

He bent his head and kissed her hard. The power and heat of his lips surged through Lottie's body like a molten wave. Once again her blood heated and trilled, singing a wild, untamed song, matching his violence—his hunger. Finally he pulled away and released the invisible grip he had on her soul.

She slapped him. Her hand stung and the room echoed from the impact.

"You bastard!" She stepped away from him, her heart pounding inside her corset so hard she was sure the laces would burst. Shayne's words hammered at her; his kisses tempted her.

"What do you mean you're here to kill Ian McTavish?"

"Just what I said." Shayne rubbed the reddening print on his lean cheek. "Why? What is it to you? Is he your lover? Is that how you knew I was in prison? Are you and Ian in this together?"

"I knew you were in prison because I took your name off a 'wanted' poster." Lottie's mind was whirling, racing, trying to process this information and the way Shayne made her feel. It was too much—too raw and naked.

"When did you get out of prison?" Lottie heard herself ask. This man did have the hard, cold eyes of a killer.

"A few weeks back." He stopped rubbing his face. "Don't ever raise your hand to me again or I may be forced to return the favor, and since we're married, I would be within my rights."

"Don't push your luck, cowboy." Lottie began to pick up pieces of pink ribbon, rolling them on her hand while she tried to think. If he was after Ian she had to stop him—but how?

"Why do you want to kill Ian McTavish?" she asked softly.

"The bastard framed me for rustling and got me sent me to prison."

She glanced up. The hatred and fury in Shayne's face was frightening. Eyes that had been cold and hard were now ablaze with the hunger for revenge.

She shuddered. She had to keep Shayne here. . . . She had to find out what was going on and save Ian. Addie and Kathryn needed him, needed a husband and a father.

Lottie looked up at Shayne and smiled. "Fine, you can stay here. You can run tame around my house and pretend we're married."

She saw a slow, satisfied grin creep across Shayne's face. "Now you're talkin', darlin'."

And as she watched, Lottie realized her body was humming with sinful anticipation.

The news of Shayne Rosswarne's arrival went through town with all the speed of a prairie fire. Lottie was not surprised when, less than an hour after the dress shop had been shuttered and locked tight, Mattie burst through her kitchen door.

"Oh my God, Lottie, I just heard." Mattie's eyes were round as saucers. "*He* actually came here looking for you?"

"Shhh, *he* is in the parlor. And he didn't exactly come looking for me," Lottie said with a frown, cleaving the pullet in two with the meat clever. She had already hacked her way through a summer squash and two melons. During her attack on the food, she had decided she would keep Shayne's deadly reason for being here from Mattie. There was nothing her sister could do. Roamer was out of town, and even if he were here, it was obvious Shayne Rosswarne was a man who knew how to use a gun and wouldn't hesitate to do so. Lottie was not about to get Roamer or any of the other men in town shot up or killed when there was a chance she could outsmart him, trick him, or do something to stop him before Ian returned to town.

"What are you going to do?" Mattie whispered.

Lottie paused in her chicken chopping to stare at her sister. "Right now I am going to feed him. Then I am going to use my wits and do whatever needs to be done. But whatever happens, don't tell him Ian is married to our sister."

"But why, Lottie?" Mattie fidgeted with the small cameo at her throat. She kept casting nervous, furtive glances toward Lottie's front parlor.

"I don't have time to explain right now. Just promise."

"All right, I promise. But what are you going to do?"

"For now he wants me to act like we're married." Memories of his sizzling kiss made Lottie shiver. She forced herself to forget the enchantment that had enveloped her when he touched her body.

"Married? You mean he's willing to go along with your lie? Do you really believe him?" Mattie wrung her hands, the fingerless mitts straining with the effort.

"It isn't like I have much choice. If he opens his mouth and tells everyone in town the truth—"

"Lottie, darlin', you didn't tell me we were expectin' company." Shayne's voice hit Lottie like a blast of northern wind. He strolled into the kitchen as if he owned it, looped an arm around her waist, and kissed her soundly. She put her fists against his chest to keep a space between them, but not before her own body heated up two degrees. She hated herself for responding to him. Hated herself for responding to the man who had threatened Ian and had the power to ruin her perfect lie.

"Lands!" Mattie exclaimed, her eyes going round with alarm.

"You can save the playacting, Shayne. This is my sister—*your* sister-in-law, Mattie Tresh. She knows we're not really married, so you can let me go now and stopping kissing me every chance you get." Lottie yanked free, but some deep part of her was almost sorry for it. Her body liked his touch, his scent, his very essence.

"My mama didn't raise no fool," Shayne chuckled with a lewd wink. "I'll steal a kiss whenever I can, darlin'."

He moved toward Mattie and his eyes narrowed. A strange sense of disappointment buffeted Lottie when he didn't put up any argument about leaving her alone. Maybe he didn't feel the same electric pull she was experiencing.

"So you're my sister-in-law?" He asked.

Mattie flicked a quick glance at Lottie before she nodded. "Ye-Yes."

He gave her a slow grin, then leaned close and kissed her cheek. "Pleased to meet you, Mattie. I'm Shayne Rosswarne. Now if we expect to pull off this charade, then I think you and I had better get acquainted. Who are you married to?"

"Roamer Tresh, the blacksmith," Mattie said stiffly.

"And are there any other brothers or sisters I should know about?"

"Addie," Mattie blurted.

"Ah, three sisters. And where is Addie?" Shayne asked, his soft voice almost hypnotic.

Lottie's heart was in her throat when she stepped in front of Shayne. She looked him square in the eye.

"Addie is out of town, so you won't be meeting her." Lottie whirled toward Mattie. She hoped her stern gaze would seal Mattie's lips. "Mattie, of course you'll stay to supper."

Mattie nodded, and Lottie felt a burst of relief. She knew her sister had understood. She would make no more mistakes. But what could Lottie do about the rest of the town? How could she prevent them from talking to Shayne?

How long would it take before one of them said something that revealed all to him. How long would it be before he learned that Ian was his wife's brother-in-law?

It had been too long since Shayne had been around a woman. He had lost all his charm, or maybe it was his foolish admission that he was here to kill Ian

McTavish that made golden-haired Lottie glare at him with murder in her own eyes. Whatever the cause, she was prickly as a porcupine. For some strange reason a small part of him wished it were otherwise.

"I think you and I should get a few things straight," Lottie said abruptly, pulling Shayne's gaze from the bottom of his empty coffee cup. She sat on a striped settee by the curtained window, looking cool, serene, and entirely too pretty for such an accomplished liar.

"Such as?" Shayne asked.

"You can stay here, but don't expect me to fetch and carry for you."

"Fair enough." He grinned but she just arched one slender brow. Yep, he had definitely lost his touch with the ladies.

"And about the sleeping arrangements—"

"Now you have my attention." He leaned forward in the rocker. It had been way too long since Shayne had a woman in his bed. The prospect of that warm, curvy body beneath him made him hard as a post.

"My bedroom is off limits to you. I have a rifle by my bed, and I can shoot the eye out of a prairie dog from my back door. Don't be sneaking up on me. Don't startle me. If you need the privy, then walk soft and stay away from my door and my window."

Shayne raised his brows. "Thanks for telling me. I'll be real careful about hanging around prairie dogs—on my way to the privy that is."

Her eyes widened and her face flushed with indignation. Then she gave him a look that was guaranteed to curdle milk.

"Go ahead; act like a fool, but I'm warning you. You may have the upper hand now but I won't be prodded or threatened or backed into a corner."

"Yes, ma'am." Shayne was careful not to laugh. Hell, she might just shoot him. The way her eyes were crackling with blue lightning, he could well believe she would do it.

"At least you're not thinking of poisoning me. That was a damned fine meal." Shayne leaned back and rocked gently.

"Watch your language and don't give me any ideas," she said with the annoying realization that his compliment was oddly satisfying. "I just might try and do it. In fact, a little poison on your eggs in the morning or in the coffee might do the trick. I wouldn't be bothered with you anymore."

He laughed aloud. "Well, darlin' I have to say I've been threatened by worse, but never by anybody prettier."

"Hogwash." Lottie shook her head and tried to shrug off the glow of another compliment.

She stood up abruptly. The fatigue of the day weighed heavily on her shoulders and her mind.

"I'm going to bed. And remember I have that rifle." Lottie walked across the parlor, but she turned and lingered near her bedroom door. She didn't want to look at him, and she sure didn't want to be *aware* of him; but she did and she was. She allowed her gaze to travel over his body.

Shayne Rosswarne was by far the most dangerous-looking man she had ever seen in her entire life. And knowing that Ian was his intended target only made things worse. She had told Mattie she would explain later, and for once, thank God, her sister had not argued.

But what was Lottie going to do about Shayne? He was lethal as a rattler, meaner than a grizzly.

Just the way his brows slanted across his forehead, and the way the little creases in his lean jaw deepened when he grinned spoke of power, maleness, and a deadly streak a mile wide.

Shayne Rosswarne was trouble on the hoof. He knew her secret, and though he was unaware of it, he had the ability to crush the life out of Addie, Mattie, and little Kathryn with one cruel word.

She had to find a way to get rid of him before Ian returned to town.

"Why don't you just take a good, long look, darlin?" Shayne said softly.

"What?" Lottie jumped. "What do you mean?

Shayne leaned back in the rocking chair and met her gaze. His heavy-lidded eyes were dark and swirling with amusement. "I mean you've been sneaking peeks at me all through the meal and while we've been talking. Why don't you just take a good, long, slow look?" His lips curled into the most sensuous, wicked, and inviting smile. "I don't mind—not a bit."

"I have not been peeking at you." Lottie turned and put her hand on the doorknob. "I would never do such a thing."

"Yes, you would, darlin'," Shayne said reasonably. "And I would too."

Her head snapped around. "You would?"

"Sure. I'm just as curious about you as you are about me. It's only natural."

Lottie stiffened even more. Was anything natural about her reaction to the man who threatened her brother-in-law?

Shayne rose from the rocker. He moved like a cat, quiet and smooth. "Do you want to start now or when we get ready for bed?"

"What?" Lottie squeaked. She stepped backward, but the closed door at her back halted her retreat.

"The very best way to take a good, long, slow look at a body is in the altogether. I am willing—and able."

She wished she had the rifle in her hand right now, but could a gun stop the way her heart hammered in her chest? Or the way her eyes kept returning to his mouth while she remembered those kisses?

"I never." Lottie leaned against the door, but there was no give in it or in the man before her.

"Then maybe, Lottie, darlin', it's high time you did."

"I am going to *my* room. You can make up the bed in the spare room; there are linens in the chest. And if I hear so much as a board creak tonight, I am shooting until I don't hear anything."

Shayne watched her go, all swirling petticoats and iron-willed indignation. A strange conflict of feeling rolled over him. The last thing he needed was his pretty little "wife" getting under his skin. She was dead serious about putting a bullet in him if need be. And yet—

Whoa, hoss. You don't need to get tangled up with a pretty little liar, he told himself. Not until Ian McTavish was dead and buried. Then maybe there would be time for that golden-haired vixen before he headed back to Texas and his old life.

Five

Lottie was tempted to wring the neck of the big red rooster in the coop down the street. His proud crow had woken her from the only sleep she had known all night.

Cursing the cock and all his progeny for the next decade, Lottie flopped over in her bed, pulling the pillow over her face. All night she had been assaulted by fear, doubt, and a wild restlessness that she had not felt since she was a girl budding into womanhood. She had thought of every possible way to thwart Shayne—even entertaining the notion of brewing some horrible concoction into his coffee. And the realization that she could entertain murder chilled her. Now she was tired, cranky, and . . . was that coffee she smelled?

Lottie pulled the pillow from her face. She opened one eye and squinted toward her bedroom door. It was still shut, the chair she had wedged beneath the handle firmly in place.

It was coffee. But how?

She sat up and pushed the tangled hair from her face. Sniffing suspiciously, she slid from the bed and padded barefoot to the door.

With infinite care she managed to slide the chair from under the knob without making a sound. Then, ever so slowly, she turned the doorknob and eased the door open toward her.

"Mornin'." Shayne waggled his brows at her over the rim of a cup of steaming brew. "I found the makings in your kitchen. I thought you might like a cup. I heard you tossing and turning all night long."

"I was not tossing and turning. I am a . . . restless sleeper, that's all," Lottie said indignantly, feeling foolish that he had been waiting for her right outside the door while she took pains to open it silently. He glanced at the chair and grinned.

"Thanks." She took the cup from Shayne's hands. It was hot and she had to shift it from hand to hand.

"You're welcome." His gaze flicked over her body, lingered on her bare toes peeking from the lacy edge of her night rail, then slid back to her face. She was hotly and suddenly aware of the fact she was wearing very sheer lawn on her body.

He drew in a deep breath and backed up a step, as if he didn't trust himself to be near. His nostrils flared like a stallion's scenting a mare in heat. "I am going to fry up some of that bacon I found in your larder. How do you like your eggs?"

"I—I like them scrambled," Lottie said hesitantly, feeling her body react to his maleness while her mind processed his words. "You can cook?"

Once more those dark, unreadable eyes skimmed over her thinly clad body like wildfire over dry grass. She could actually feel heat in that gaze—scorching, unrelenting, tempting.

"Darlin', there isn't much I *can't* do."

While she was trying hard not to moan with desire, Shayne turned on his boot heel and left her standing there, quivering with physical yearning.

Lottie had seen something in his eyes, but surely she had been wrong. And yet . . . for a moment she thought she witnessed a gleam of attraction and his attempt to hide it.

"I knew he was dangerous the minute I saw him. I just didn't know he was lethal."

Lottie held her breath and jerked the laces on her corset. It was one of the new French design and was an armor of sorts. Not only did it keep Lottie straight and tall and properly upright; it also kept her *in*. When she wore her corset all her wild, free, rebellious thoughts were contained—under control and tied down. Usually she found a certain stiff, oppressive security in putting on her boned undergarments. Today it pinched, cinched, confined, and squeezed her in a most uncomfortable manner. And the repression seemed as much emotional as physical.

"I need to be under control now more than ever," she told her reflection as she tied the laces into a taut bow and ran her hands over her nipped-in waist.

Having Shayne Rosswarne in the house was a frightening situation. Not only did Lottie fear what would happen when Ian returned; she feared what Shayne did to her. Each time she looked into his eyes there was a hot, swirling awakening of passion deep inside her. Strange emotions fought to be set free. And those hot, reckless feelings were trying to claw their way out.

"Why him?" she asked herself. Why did the man who vowed to kill her brother-in-law, the man who would wreck her sister's life and leave her niece father-less, have the power to make her feel such overwhelming hunger? Why did her heart pound and her mouth go dry when she looked into his dark eyes?

"I have to get him out of town—permanently."

She brushed out her hair and wound the curls into a severe coil. Then she used long tortoiseshell pins to make a chignon at the nape of her neck. One or two stubborn tendrils refused to submit and curled defiantly at her temples, but for the most part she was laced up, cinched in, and tied down. And that was exactly how she intended to remain. Lottie was going to keep herself and this hard-eyed killer under control—if it killed them both. And the way her knees kept shaking, she was convinced it just might.

Shayne was turning strips of browning bacon when Lottie walked into the kitchen with her empty cup in her hand. He barely glanced at her, but her image sizzled through his brain and his body. His jaw worked convulsively as he fought to keep his passion and his expression under control.

"Ready for a refill?" He picked up the pot. "Yeow!" He dropped it and jerked his arm back. "That wire is hotter'n the gates of hell." She was getting to him, making him careless, making him lose his focus.

"Here, let me do it," Lottie said impatiently. She used one of the quilted squares of cloth she had made for grasping the wire handle of the pot. She filled her cup and one that was sitting empty near the dry sink. While she was returning the pot to the back of the stove, she accidently brushed against Shayne.

And froze when her body reacted.

It was like walking through a garden of herbs. A million scents and sensations filled the air. She was assaulted by a clean, outdoorsy smell and the languid wash of heat that surrounded her, rushed through her, and filled her mind.

Shayne Rosswarne was hotter than the gates of hell, and just as sin-filled. He awakened something inside her.

Lottie's head swam. She let the pot go awkwardly. It landed on the stove top with a dull metallic clunk. A little coffee sloshed out the spout and sizzled on the black iron lid.

"Are you all right?" Shayne asked, taking her by the shoulders and running his hand down her arm until he grasped her hand. He held her palm up and inspected it. Then he looked into her face with eyes deep and velvety as summer night.

His hands held hers lighter than a whisper, and yet she could feel the rapid thump of his pulse. Beneath his fingers her flesh tingled and heated in response.

A strange, hot coil started to unwind in Lottie's middle. In spite of her boned corset it grew, crowding her heart, stealing her breath. She sucked in a startled breath because she knew what the coil was: it was the loss of all her hard-won discipline; it was her lost cool demeanor; it was her slipping sanity.

She jerked her hand away with an effort and forced herself to stop drowning in his eyes.

This was madness. He was a convict. A man who vowed to kill Ian. She found herself wondering how many he had killed already. He said he'd been framed for rustling, but was he on the wrong side of the law long before that?

He was dangerous.

She was in danger of falling into a pit from which

she could never return. And it was not only her in jeopardy but her sisters and niece as well.

"I think I must be light-headed from hunger," she lied.

His gaze narrowed. He nodded stiffly. "Yes, that must be it. I feel . . . hungry too." He returned his attention to the bacon sizzling in the pan. He seemed calm and unruffled, but Lottie felt as if the whole world had suddenly shifted and tilted beneath her feet.

All Lottie's life she had craved adventure and excitement. In truth, she had a secret fascination with the dark side of life. Her foster parents had tried to turn her from it. Her sisters' love had kept her from it. Now Shayne's magnetism threatened to lead her to it.

He was a man who could give her all the dark sin she ever fantasized about and more. She knew it instinctively in the marrow of her bones. There was something wild and untamed—*untamable*—about Shayne Rosswarne. But Lottie dare not even consider it. If—*when*—Shayne Rosswarne learned that Ian was married to her sister, there would be a price to pay. Lottie needed to keep a clear head so she could save her sister, even if the price Shayne demanded was her own soul.

Six

"I was thinking you might want to see some of the country around McTavish Plain," Lottie suggested over the rim of her cup.

"You want to show me around?" Shayne said, abruptly pushing himself up from the table. "Why?" The one word was heavy with suspicion. His eyes narrowed and they were wary.

All through the breakfast he cooked, which was remarkably good, she had thought of ways she might get him out of town. She wasn't sure what she was going to do then, but at least she could keep him away from Gus, Miley, and anybody who would inevitably let it slip that Ian was her brother-in-law. For a while she could breathe easily and think of some way to get rid of him.

"Don't you think people in town will think it strange if we go riding off?" Shayne asked.

"Uh . . . no. Not at all." Lottie swallowed. Her mind was racing, trying to latch onto a plausible reason why a trip would be reasonable so soon after her husband's arrival.

And then she had it.

"And why is that, darlin'?" Shayne drawled lazily. He leaned back in his chair and stared at her as if he could see into her lying heart, which started beating in double time under that sultry gaze.

"Because I have been wanting to see the Devil's Tower since we arrived here in McTavish Plain. It would be only fitting that my *husband* accompany me on such a trip."

"Devil's Tower?" Shayne's eyes glowed with interest, but he was still suspicious; she could sense it in the taut line of his wide shoulders. "What is the Devil's Tower, darlin'?"

"It is a wonderful place, or so I have heard." Lottie found herself being caught up in the web of her own deception. Excitement bled into her voice. "There are stories about it stretching back in time."

"Tell me one of them," Shayne said. "I got nothing better to do but listen to a story."

"You think I'm making it all up, but I'm not. There is the legend," Lottie said sullenly, somehow wounded by his obvious doubt in her.

"So, tell me about this legend of yours." He cocked one brow. "Convince me—if you can."

"It isn't my legend; it's an old Indian tale. One day a tribe was camped beside a beautiful river. The children of the tribe were playing and seven little girls wandered away from the main camp. A grizzly bear saw them and started to chase the children. The little girls ran and ran but when they grew tired they had no choice but to climb on a boulder and pray to their pagan gods. Suddenly the rock heard their prayer and decided to help. . . ."

Shayne watched Lottie and became mesmerized. Her face glowed; her expression was animated. Her cornflower blue eyes sparkled with an inner fire that blazed from the inside out. His gut clenched while a pool of heat simmered in his crotch.

". . . the rock got bigger and bigger. But the bear didn't give up. He clawed and clawed but the rock continued to grow. It reached upward to the sky—"

"That is a mighty fanciful tale, darlin'," he interrupted.

"You don't believe me. You think since I lied about being married to you that I'll lie about everything." Her voice was flat, but Shayne thought he heard a tiny ring of hurt. Could his opinion matter to her? Could this pretty woman with the quick tongue care what he thought about anything?

"I guess you'll just have to show me the damned rock and prove it," Shayne said with a crooked grin.

"Do you mean it?" Lottie heard the pleasure in her voice and cringed a little. "I mean—of course I'll prove it."

"How long will it take to ride out there and come back?" Shayne asked.

"I—I don't know. It's around fifty miles at least, or so I have been told." Lottie realized her knowledge of the world was painfully limited. She knew the dusty, long trail from Gothenburg to McTavish Plain and not much more. Once again the call to explore and wander nipped at her resolve. How wonderful it must be to know the distance and scenery of places. And how fulfilling to learn new things as one traveled.

"Two or three days should do it, then," Shayne said. He wondered why it didn't much bother him that he would be taking in the sights for two or three days when he should be formulating his plan to kill Ian McTavish.

"Two or three days. That means we'll have to camp

on the trail." Lottie swallowed hard. Her heart was doing a jig in her chest. She was finally going to see the Tower.

"You don't have to be afraid of me. I wasn't in prison for rape—in case you were worried." His black eyes blazed with rage.

She blinked in the face of his fury. How could she tell him that it wasn't him she feared, but the effect he had upon her? Or that she was jittery with anticipation, not terror. She could see spikes of amber and forest green in the depths of his dark, hard eyes. The hot, manly scent of him filled the room, and she blinked with the heady brew of the journey she was going to make—finally.

She was giddy with the thought. "I am not afraid of you," she said finally.

"Maybe you should be, darlin'. A woman as pretty as you should be more careful who you keep company with."

She thought he might kiss her. For a moment he did stare at her lips, his nostrils flaring again as he breathed in the scent of her. Then he grinned abruptly, the tension of the moment evaporating.

"Do you own a horse?"

"No."

"Get ready to ride, darlin'. I'll be back in a while with two horses ready to go."

Shayne's spurs jingled as he walked down the hard-packed street. He chided himself for agreeing to this trip. He should be marking every building, every shadow, plotting his exit from town while he waited for the moment he would meet Ian McTavish—planning his escape. He wanted to have his revenge, not to commit suicide.

He reached the livery before he even realized it, so caught up in his thoughts had he been. When Miley saw him, the man's face was a study in friendliness. It made Shayne's nerves prickle. He had never been made to feel so welcome, not since he had left home and Texas. There was something eerie and unnatural about all this cordiality. It made him even more determined to keep his guard up.

Shayne had stopped trusting anybody a long time ago, and he wasn't about to trust anyone again—especially in a town bearing Ian McTavish's brand.

"Mornin', Shayne. By golly, I didn't expect to see you for a while." Miley clapped a hand to Shayne's shoulder in a gesture of male kinship. "Figured you and Lottie would be . . . well, you know . . . getting to know each other again."

Shayne fought the imagery that ripped through his mind. "I thought I might have her show me around and take a little side trip to that Devil's Tower." Shayne lied smoothly, wishing he didn't want to do exactly what Miley had suggested.

"Ah." Miley grinned. "I should've known."

"Should've known?" Shayne's neck hair prickled. He hated not knowing what his "wife" had told people. He was reluctant to say much or ask many questions until he found out.

"That Lottie has been itching to go to the Devil's Tower since she got here. She 'bout drove me crazy with questions about the legend, asking how far it is, how hard the trip. I should've known that's where you'd be headed." Miley grinned. "Your horse is ready, and I got a real nice little saddle mare that

Lottie will love. Are you taking a picnic lunch or camping rough?"

"Uh, I'm not sure." Shayne hadn't thought of such things, but he realized he should. A married man would concern himself with the comfort of his woman.

"Just give me a minute. Gert butchered some rabbits yesterday. I bet she could have them fried up in a wink. And I think Gus has some canned peaches and odds and ends. You leave it to me, Shayne. I'll send young Toby to get things together. Then he can bring it back here and I'll pack it in your extra saddlebags and put them on Lottie's horse. You got bedrolls?"

"I have mine and some extra clothes in my saddle bags." Shayne admitted hesitantly. "I hadn't thought . . ."

"Don't give it another worry. I got one for Lottie and a slicker for her in case the weather in the mountains builds. I see you got a side arm, and I'm sure you can use it." Miley nodded at the gun on Shayne's hip.

"What makes you say that?" Shayne asked, his body going still from the inside out.

"A man that trails cattle has to know the business end of a side arm, ain't that right?"

"That's right." The raw knot of suspicion eased inside Shayne's chest. He couldn't afford to slip up and let anyone discover his secret—anyone besides his "wife." Lottie could ruin him, but it wasn't likely she would say a word to anyone—not when it meant exposing herself as a liar and a fallen woman. But he wouldn't rest easy until he knew why she had taken his name in the first place.

* * *

Lottie was adjusting the split and draped skirt and short jacket when she heard the sound of horses outside her door. Her stomach was doing a lively jig, but she knew she had to do this. She told herself she had to find a way to get Shayne Rosswarne out of town and keep him out, and this was the first step; but she was secretly so excited that she could hardly stand still.

The sound of the back door opening set her teeth on edge. Shayne didn't even knock. That small intrusion on her autonomy annoyed her. She didn't like him settling into *her* life.

"But then how would that look if Harriet or Sue saw him knocking on a door that was supposed to be his own?" She recognized she was going to have to relinquish some of her independence, at least for a little while.

Shayne Rosswarne had her backed into a corner with her own lies, but that was not important now. What was important was finding a way to get him to leave before he met up with Ian.

"Then I can tell folks he deserted me—ran off with a floozy," she murmured.

"Who ran off with a floozy?" Shayne drawled behind her.

She whirled to find him lounging in the doorway of her bedroom. His eyes roamed over her as if he had every right to do so, and though she was loath to admit it, she didn't mind his scrutiny at all.

"I don't like you sneaking up on me," she snapped, though what she really wanted to say was: *Why do I feel these things that I feel each time you come near me?*

"Darlin', I've been accused of a lot of things, but never of being sneaky." His eyes lingered on her waist and slid over her bosom. "Kind of fancy duds for taking a ride, ain't they?"

"I'm the town seamstress. I have to dress well so the women of the town will want me to design and make clothes for them," Lottie explained reasonably while every inch of her flesh warmed under Shayne's gaze. His eyes seemed to take in the tight fit of her jacket. A slow, lazy grin kicked up the corners of his mouth.

"It doesn't look very comfortable, but it sure as hell is interesting."

"Women's fashions are not based on comfort." Lottie tugged the edge of her jacket and pulled on her matching gloves, all the while wondering what it would feel like to have a man like Shayne undress her.

He gave her one last, sizzling perusal and then he shrugged. "Suit yourself, but I wouldn't be surprised if you get saddle sores on that round backside."

He turned and sauntered away while Lottie's eyes drank in the sight of him: broad shoulders, narrow hips, long legs ending in boots and spurs; and, she noticed with a hitch of breath, *his* backside wasn't bad to look at.

"No, I don't suppose anybody ever accused you of sneaking," she whispered. How could they? Shayne Rosswarne gave off heat and sparks like a bolt of summer lightning. In one instant his cold eyes could lay down a frost as quick as a blizzard, and half a heartbeat later he was melting her bones. He was a man who ran hot and cold. Lottie prayed that she would soon learn to master this ridiculous infatuation with him. He was poison—death and destruction rolled up into the form of a long-legged man. She had to break free of his spell before it cost Ian his life and Addie her happiness.

They were mounted and headed out of McTavish Plain. Shayne halted. "What is that place?" he asked, nodding his head in the direction of a shadowy structure that sat on the lee side of a craggy mountain.

"That's where my sister Addie lives," Lottie said, not even looking at Ian's castle. If it was the last thing she ever did, she needed to keep him from finding out that she was related to Ian.

"Where is she now?" he asked with a frown, still staring at the stone house with a glow of interest in his eyes.

"Gone on a trip with her husband." Lottie continued to look west, not allowing herself to glance at Shayne or the house on the hill. She was afraid he would see her unease if she so much as looked at him.

"You aren't going to make this easy for me, are you?" He demanded.

"I don't know what you are talking about," Lottie said, settling herself firmly in the saddle.

Shayne reined his horse around and stopped in front of her mount. She had no choice but to look at him. Her eyes met his and her stomach dropped.

"I mean you are not going to give me any information except what I pry out of you—are you, darlin'?"

"I have answered all your questions. What more do you want?" Lottie stared into his bottomless black eyes and her heart galloped wildly. Why, oh why did it have to be *him?* Of all the men she could have developed a craving for, why did it have to be this man, this bringer of death? This killer with lightning in his touch?

"I want you to tell me things about this place. I want to know where Ian McTavish goes, who he sees, how his life has turned out," Shayne said harshly. "I want to know how a bastard like Ian ended up in a nice town like this one."

Lottie stared at Shayne's face, now a mask of bitterness and rage, and her heart ripped a little. Shayne had suffered; that was obvious. But Ian, the man she knew, the man who had carved out a town and married her sister, was hard, rigid, and opinionated—but surely not capable of treachery. Was there a side to Ian she didn't know? Could he be a man who would inspire this kind of hatred? She had to find out.

"Fine, I will tell you about Ian McTavish as he is now, on one condition."

Shayne's jaw twitched as his teeth grated together. It was painfully apparent that she had made him angry.

"I don't think you're in much of a position to bargain about anything, darlin'."

"I'm in as good a position as you are," she snapped. "Or have you forgotten that I could just reveal your plans?"

His eyes narrowed. "And ruin yourself in the process."

"Perhaps I'm prepared to do just that."

She could see he was battling with himself. It was taking a toll on him to give in to her request.

"What is your bargain?" he asked coldly.

"I will tell you about Ian McTavish and you do the same. You tell me what he did to make you want his life."

"Done," he agreed with a stiff nod.

Lottie extended her gloved hand to him. "Will you give me your hand on it?"

"What's the matter, don't you trust me?"

"No, I want your hand on it."

"Sure, darlin'." Shayne stuck out his hand and leaned far over the saddle, but instead of shaking her hand, he grabbed her forearm and pulled her to him. She was stretched awkwardly across the saddle and the distance separating their horses, and she was unable to fight in such a position.

His mouth was hot and demanding. The world swirled in a haze of bright sunshine and muted colors. Her heart kicked roughly in her chest. Against all reason, she returned his kiss. Her tongue mated with his.

Slowly he pulled away from her and her eyes focused.

"Now our bargain is sealed proper."

They rode side by side in a westerly direction. Lottie tried hard to keep herself contained and under rein, but with every mile they put between them and McTavish Plain, she felt her control slipping.

The scent of summer was heavy in the air. Every hillock brought a new sight and sound. Rabbits, antelope, and even a small herd of buffalo had been seen since they left the isolated town. Now Lottie's heart was thumping and she felt itchy again. This is what she had hungered for—this discovery. She wanted to see it all, to experience every possibility beyond the little town.

"If you squirm much more on that horse you're going to have a sore on your back end," Shayne said dryly.

Lottie turned to him, ready to show him the rough side of her tongue, but the sun put an inky blue shine into his hair and cast seductive shadows along his lean, angular face. The words stuck in the back of her throat.

"Since you aren't going to flay my skin off with a reply, I guess we might just as well get it over with now," Shayne said while dismounting.

"Get what over with now?" Lottie found herself recalling his kisses, reliving the sweet, sensual, drugging effect.

He walked toward her mount.

"Come on, get down. It's too hard to do it properly on the back of a horse. A body cramps up and I can't get proper purchase." He took the reins from fingers that had gone suddenly limp.

"What . . . what did you have in mind?" Lottie stammered. She couldn't quite muster up the indignation that would be proper at his suggestion. "I am not that kind of woman," she finally managed to say but her words lacked any fire or conviction. She kept getting mental pictures of his hard body stripped bare.

Shayne turned to her and raised one dark brow. "What kind of woman would that be, darlin?"

"The kind of woman that would allow you liberties," she said softly as he moved closer, slipped his hand around her neck, and slowly pulled her head down until their lips touched.

The world shifted and tilted crazily, and all Lottie could do was hang onto Shayne's shoulders. He was the only solid thing in a swirling, hot world of sensation. She was suddenly thrust into a world without control and restraint, a world that beckoned her. A world that Shayne offered.

Lottie fought it. She tried to pretend his mouth was not warm and sweet. She tried not to notice that he tasted faintly of the morning's strong coffee. She tried to deny that her breasts were sensitive and heavy against his chest, or that her legs went a little weak.

She tried and she failed.

Once again Shayne Rosswarne had taken a kiss—taken her will—and this time, like all the other times, Lottie felt a little more of her control sift through her fingers like hot sand. Her hands curled into his shirt as if she could hang onto the illusion of being able to resist him. But she heard a sound . . . a moan. It was a soft sound of passion and surrender. Her failure to resist him.

A strange combination of sorrow and desire flowed through Lottie's veins. She wanted Shayne and she hated herself for wanting him.

He lifted his head and looked at her. "You are a strange woman, Lottie." He frowned and laughed ruefully. "Since we aren't really married, I can't call you Lottie Rosswarne. What is your real name?"

"Green. I'm Charlotte Green."

"Well, Lottie Green, let's you and me have a peek in this basket those crazy galoots packed for us. And when we're finished, I want you to show me that rock called Devil's Tower."

"You brought a picnic lunch?" Lottie's head was still swimming from Shayne's kiss. "I didn't expect you to do so. I brought bacon, coffee, and biscuits."

"We sure won't starve on this trip. I ended up bringing us a few things so Miley and Gus would quiet down and let me go." Shayne reached for the saddlebags while Lottie dismounted.

Had they told him that Addie was married to Ian?

But if that was true, he wouldn't be grinning at her now . . . would he? He was cagey and sly. Maybe he was trying to trap her.

"What did they ask?"

"They wanted to know where I was going and why."

"And what did you tell him?"

"As little as possible. That's a nosy bunch back there." Shayne slung the bags over his shoulder and looked at her. "Why, did you think they told me something special?"

She glanced up to find Shayne studying her with a pensive expression. He looked good enough to eat.

"No."

"That getup of yours has got to be the most god-awful uncomfortable thing to ride in."

Lottie sighed in relief. She was hot, her nape was damp with sweat, and her corset was pinching her ribs. Her mind was spinning from Shayne's magnetic appeal and her determination not to surrender.

"It's not like I have any choice in the matter," Lottie said with no small amount of impatience in her voice. What she wanted was to strip herself bare and let him have his wicked way with her, but she couldn't very well lie down with the man who had vowed to kill her sister's husband. Funny thing, though: her heart and body weren't listening to the logic of her mind.

He grinned and flipped the saddlebag to the ground. Then suddenly Shayne was up and moving toward her again. He took her by the arm and led her back to where he had ground-tied Lottie's horse.

"I can't stand this another minute." He said, digging deep into the saddlebag. He brought out a plaid shirt and a pair of men's trousers.

"Go put these on before you melt away."

Lottie stared in shock at the clothes he held out to her. "Those are men's trousers. My . . . uh . . . limbs would show."

"Uh-huh. All four of them." Shayne raised his brows. "But in my clothes you can sit without worrying about spoiling the pretty cloth. You can take a deep breath without me waiting for you to swoon at any moment. And you'd be a deal more comfortable." He grinned wickedly. "And a whole lot more interestin' to look at."

Lottie looked at the clothes. She looked at Shayne. His lips curved into a sensual leer. His dark, sin-filled eyes beckoned to the wildest part of her spirit.

There was no way Shayne could know, but she had always wondered what it would feel like to have the freedom of trousers—to be able to flop into a chair without being mindful of her petticoats and bustle and all the other baggage women carried around. All her life she had craved that freedom.

And Shayne was offering it to her as if he had read the deepest, most secret parts of her.

"There's a nice fat bush right over there. I'll even promise to turn my head." His sensuous grin turned playful. "Unless of course you need help getting out of that rigging you wear—"

"Of course I don't need help," Lottie interrupted. "Turn your head and keep it turned until I tell you."

She carried the clothes behind the low, scrubby shrub. When she removed her jacket, she relished the cool air that drifted through her damp blouse. When she dragged off the heavy split skirt, she felt ten pounds lighter. And when she peeled off her blouse, a refreshing draft of cool, unfettered air caressed her shoulders.

Standing in her stockings, half-boots, drawers, corset, and chemise, she felt like a complete heathen. She still wore half a dozen garments and yet she felt almost free.

She peeked over the top of the bush to see if Shayne had kept his word. Sure enough, he had his back—his wide, straight back—turned to her. He was whistling a low tune, staring up at the cloud-dotted sky. She found herself wondering what thoughts ran through his head. Prison must have been hell for a man like him. He was as wild as the wind, being locked up would have been a slow death.

"You about done?" His deep voice jarred Lottie. She had been daydreaming about him, standing there in her underwear and thinking of Shayne and his past—but for how long? It could have been a second or minutes; she wasn't sure.

"Nearly," she said, quickly unlacing her corset. Her ribs expanded when she sucked in a breath of sweet mountain air. The breeze went right through the clinging cloth of her damp chemise, cooling her skin, causing her nipples to contract.

It felt wonderful!

Lottie told herself it was wrong to take pleasure in such a simple act, but she did. She felt wicked, rebellious, and younger at heart than she had in many long years.

She tugged the trousers on awkwardly over her half boots and gartered stockings. Then she slid into the shirt. Both the sleeves and the legs were much too long, but the rest of the fabric fit in a comfortable, snug way that made her spirit trill with excitement.

She flexed her legs and experienced a freedom of movement she had never known before.

But what would Shayne think?

"You can turn around now," she said softly.

Shayne did as she instructed. He turned and looked at her—really *looked* at her. His eyes skimmed over her form, processing it all, feeling the heat ratchet up inside his belly.

That corset must have bound Lottie tighter than a parson's sermon, because now her soft, round breasts nudged against the buttons of his shirt, filling the pockets from the inside out. Her hips were womanly, flaring wantonly from the tight waist of his pants. His heart kicked a bit and he swallowed a hot, dry lump. It had been a long, long time since he had buried himself inside a woman.

"Darlin', we'll need to roll up those legs so you don't break your neck." Shayne strode to her and went down on one knee. He picked up her foot and rested it on his thigh as he began to roll up the long pant leg. Her ankle was small and her calf nicely formed, with a firm little bulge of muscle that he wanted to caress and fondle. He allowed his fingers to linger at the hollow of her ankle, feeling her pulse.

It would be so easy to flip her on her back and pleasure her until she invited him inside.

"When you were a girl did you climb trees?" He trailed his fingers against her smooth flesh. He had to get control of himself. Hell, he couldn't seduce her . . . could he?

She shivered. It made the lust pool in his loins.

Lottie blinked as Shayne looked up at her from under the brim of his hat. How had he known she had been a rough-and-tumble girl?

"I climbed trees and skipped rocks," she admitted in a soft voice.

"Well, I'll be damned," Shayne said as he studied her face.

Lottie cringed. Now she would hear his thoughts on women who were not ladylike. Her soul withered a bit under the criticism she knew was coming.

"That is the first time I have ever seen you blush, Charlotte Green." He chuckled. "You never colored up like a pink posey when I kissed you that first time and at no time since—until now." He tilted his head and watched her with his head cocked, speculation in his dark eyes.

"Now tell me, darlin', just what is it about being a tomboy that causes you to be embarrassed enough to blush?"

"I—I—am not embarrassed, and I never blush." Lottie said stiffly.

"Uh-huh, you just go on tellin' yourself that." He chuckled, the sound a soft, husky purr.

Lottie's breath caught somewhere behind her breastbone. She experienced a slow igniting of her insides. His long fingers rested on her ankle in the most intimate, sensual fashion. She had never experienced anything so powerful or forbidden.

This went beyond his kisses. This went beyond the touch of his eyes. And with that probing question, he had touched a part of her soul that she kept hidden from the rest of the world—maybe even from herself. This was frightening and sinful, the way he could communicate with the wildest part of her without even trying. It seemed as though Shayne knew her, all about her, even the most secret things.

"There, now." He reached up and patted her thigh,

sending a jolt of heat through her body. "At least you won't trip. Next leg, darlin'."

Darlin' . . . The endearment flowed over her like warm honey and sweet sin. Lord, what was happening to her in the company of this man?

Lottie tried not to tremble while she lifted her other foot to place it on Shayne's hard-muscled thigh. The moment she raised her foot, she found herself off balance, both emotionally and physically. Her world and all she held dear was spinning, swirling, in danger of being lost. Instinctively she put her hands on his shoulders to steady herself and keep from falling.

He looked up at her. Their eyes locked. Lottie's heart kicked inside her chest and her temperature went up at least ten degrees. She was doing a slow burn beneath that gaze.

"Careful, darlin'. I wouldn't want you to fall," Shayne purred, and then he bent to the task of rolling up the other trouser leg.

Fall. The word had more than one meaning. For Lottie it described perfectly the weakness in her knees and the thump of her own pulse in her neck. She drew in a shaky breath of fresh mountain air, but along with that heady brew she drank in the very essence of the man at her feet.

He was strong, lithe, dangerous, and oh so tempting.

She wanted to knock off that hat and tangle her fingers in his hair. She wanted him to use those strong hands and long fingers to soothe the smoldering desire that pooled in her belly.

Damn it all to hell, she just plain wanted what she knew she couldn't have.

Getting tangled up with Shayne Rosswarne would

be like playing with fire. She knew it. She couldn't deny it.

He was a threat to her family and her sanity.

He was pure, raw male trouble.

She could not deny his threat, but out here far from town and her sisters the danger didn't seem so real—or so she told herself.

He set her foot on the ground and grinned up at her. "Now you won't go ass—er, excuse me—tail over teakettle." As he corrected his error in speech, his gaze went to her behind—and lingered there sinfully. "I would hate to see your backside all bruised." He licked his lips as if he were looking at something tasty.

A hot, trilling song flowed through Lottie's blood. And though she had teased her sisters about needing a man, at this moment she did feel a need. It was deep, and nearly impossible to ignore.

She backed up a step because she feared if she did not, she might actually reach out and pull Shayne's face against her belly and lower. She wanted him to take her in his arms, to lave kisses over her too-hot flesh, to yank her clothes off and touch her until she cried out in pleasure.

"Are you ready?" His voice washed over her. He was no longer kneeling in front of her. He was standing close, looking down at her with his dark, unreadable eyes.

"Y-yes, I'm ready." *For what you won't give and I can't accept.*

Shayne's sensuous mouth kicked into an unrepentant grin. "You know, sometimes when you look at me like that, darlin' . . . I never met anyone like you. I am not sure how to act around you."

Lottie closed her eyes. Every minute in Shayne's

company was like doing a slow dance without touching. Her pulse quickened. Her nipples became sensitive, her very soul seemed to *know* him—recognize him as if he were a part of her she hadn't known was missing.

"Lottie . . ." He reached out and slowly dragged his knuckles down the side of her face. "I can't figure you out, Charlotte Green," he said with an awkward catch in his throat.

"Then maybe you shouldn't even try," Lottie heard herself say as she stepped up to him, wrapped her arms around his neck, stood on her tiptoes, and kissed him.

Shayne was shocked, aroused, and just plain interested. Lottie was not what he expected—not in any way. This woman had fire and a hot current of desire that flowed right through her and into him. She was like a bolt of lightning, striking without warning. He could, if he allowed himself, fall right into her arms.

But he couldn't. He had lived hard and rough for too many years to simply put aside his revenge for a woman.

He couldn't trust her. She was a liar by her own admission.

With great effort he reached up and clasped her hands. Slowly, painfully he unwound them from his neck, hardening his heart as he did so.

"I'm hungry."

Lottie blinked and swallowed hard.

"Of course. I—I don't know what got into me." She reached down, scooped up her fancy riding outfit, and walked toward her horse, where she stuffed the clothes into one of her saddlebags.

Shayne tightened his jaw and tried to tamp down the myriad of feelings rushing through him.

He couldn't let himself go all soft over her.

He damned well couldn't. Not until he saw Ian McTavish dead and buried. Then, when his family honor had been restored, he could go home again.

That was all he wanted—to see justice done and be able to go home with his head held high.

His plans didn't include Lottie.

Seven

Lottie wouldn't allow herself to look at Shayne, but she was still overwhelmingly aware of his presence while they sat on the grass and ate.

No matter how she tried to deny it, he spoke to her soul in a way that no other human being ever had. When he looked at her, she *knew* he could see things that were hidden to other folks.

And when he touched her . . . Lord above, it was as if he were caressing her very spirit. She hungered for him, feared him, wanted him, and hated him all in the same shuddering breath.

Where did he come from?

What kind of life had he lived?

The sun slanted down on his black hat, casting shadows over his olive-hued skin.

What was his story?

Where were his roots?

"Why did you get sent to prison, Shayne?" she heard herself ask, finally giving in to the gnawing hunger to learn about this strange, fierce man who had vowed to kill Ian.

He swung his head toward her. It was only a flash, lasting no more than the time it would take to blink, but she saw pain in his dark eyes.

"I told you I was framed by Ian McTavish. I was

dry-gulched, robbed, and framed by a man I thought I could trust."

"Would you tell me about it? The details, I mean?"

She could see him weighing her request in his mind. He was not a man who acted impulsively. Every time she asked him anything, he turned it over in his mind, gave it due consideration, judging the risks before he acted.

She liked that about him—the way he was both quick and yet strangely thoughtful. It was the opposite of her rash personality. They were like two sides of the same coin.

Finally he flopped back, lacing his fingers to make a pillow for his head, acting for all the world as if he were happy, relaxed, and not about to lay open his most painful secrets.

"Sure, darlin', why not? In fact, you should know all about the son of a bitch that founded that perfect little town you live in."

He stared unblinking at the sky. Lottie found her own gaze following his. There were fluffy white clouds in a blue that seemed to go on forever. Far away, on the distant horizon, a curtain of gray mist was building over the mountains.

"I was young and green. Full of piss and vinegar. I couldn't wait to get out of Texas, from under my Pa's eyes, and see the rest of the world."

"Is that where you are from?" Lottie heard herself ask.

"Uh-huh. A native-born Texican," he said with no small amount of pride bleeding into his words. "My mother is the granddaughter of a Spanish don, my father a homegrown Kentuckian who had itchy feet. He's been everywhere, seen everything—been his own man since he left home at an early age."

"I always wanted to see Texas. I heard it was wild and beautiful," Lottie murmured, trying to visualize the parents who had bred this strange, intense man. Surely Shayne had his mother's eyes and his father's spirit. But the core of raw sensuality was his alone.

"Oh, it is, darlin'. Wild and free as the wind. A man can ride a fast horse for days and never see the sun set on Texas. It's paradise on earth."

"Why did you want to leave?" Lottie nibbled on the fried rabbit Shayne had brought. There were also blueberry corn muffins and jerky in the bag.

Shayne's head turned toward her. His eyes narrowed. "A young man has more get-up-and-go than sense. I had grown up hearing tales of my father's youth." Shayne rose on his elbows and stared full into Lottie's eyes. "Did you know he once rounded up all the cats in Galveston, crated them onto a ship, and took them to San Francisco?"

"Whatever for?" Lottie giggled at the notion.

"It was during the forty-nine gold strike on the American River. Rats were eating everything quicker than the hungry miners could. Somehow or other my father heard about it. He sold those mangy Texas cats for ten dollars apiece."

"I never heard the like!" Lottie mused.

"Well I did, stories like that and more from the time I was out of nappies. I was itching to get away from my father's name and reputation to make my own mark. I made it, all right. I made my mark breaking rocks all day in the hot sun while a guard waited for an excuse to break my skull."

Lottie watched Shayne's eyes fill with longing and

regret. His voice tugged on her heart. This man, this convict, touched her in ways she had never believed anyone could.

"What happened?" Her curiosity was endless. She wanted to know everything there was to know about him.

"I met a man in Texas. He had been all over this land and back again. He had a notion that if we partnered up, gathered cattle, and sold 'em to the Army that we could get rich."

"So you agreed?"

"Yep, I was more than eager. I brought a little stake of my own, worked like a fool gathering cattle from every scrub farm and ranch along the way, and arranged to meet my partner in the Indian country. I contacted the Army; I made the promise to provide beef to one of the reservations. I was happy to be the man they talked to, the man in charge. I was a glory hog."

"What happened?"

"I woke up with a bullet in my leg, no horse, my stake stolen, and the cattle all gone." Shayne's face was hard, his eyes stony.

"How did you survive?" Lottie barely resisted the urge to touch him, to soothe him by rubbing her fingertips on his temples, to kiss away his pain and the disappointment in his eyes.

"I survived on my hatred. I vowed to live and find the dirty coward, Ian McTavish. I lived to make him suffer."

How could Ian have done such a thing? Or did he? Could Shayne be lying? But why would he bother to lie to Lottie? He did not know Ian was Addie's husband. He had no stake in telling her lies.

Or did he?

"I crawled for five miles. A strange old man found me. It took a couple of months before I was able to leave. He pointed me to the nearest town. But instead of receiving a fair shake when I went to the law, I soon found myself staring at a wanted poster with my likeness on it. I skinned out of there fast, but it didn't take long for a bounty hunter to find me."

"But why? I don't understand."

"The cattle had never been delivered to the Army as promised. They didn't care to hear my sad story. They wanted the money back or the cattle. Since I had neither, they decided my hide would be a fair trade. I had a trial of sorts, and the Army locked me up for a good long time for rustling and fraud."

"Surely with your wounds and the old man's testimony—"

Shayne's brows arched in anger. "You haven't been listenin', darlin'. I was framed. Ian McTavish shot me. He dry-gulched me and took the herd to sell elsewhere. Or maybe he used them to start the herd for that perfect little town back there. And while I was laid up with a bullet hole in my leg there were other rustlings. In fact, *any* rustling that took place for the next six months was attached to my name—except they had given me a fancy name to go with my new occupation. Colorado Jack they called me."

Lottie's mind was in turmoil. She believed Shayne's story. She had taken her own name from a poster that bore his face and name as well as the alias, Colorado Jack. The sheriff in Gothenburg had taken the poster and tossed it away, telling her the man on it had been convicted and would serve many, many years for stealing other people's stock.

How silly she had been to think of that incident as fortunate, but she had done just that. She had thought it a lucky break for her, because the man who owned the name Shayne Rosswarne would be behind bars where he could never cause her any trouble.

A hot tide of shame washed through Lottie. She had been petty and foolish, never considering that every face on a wanted poster had a story, a life, a family.

"Why didn't you return to Texas when you were released?

"I can't go home until I settle up with Ian. My pa taught me that a man's honor is worth more than anything. When I'm square, then I can go home with my head held high, and not until.

"Well, darlin', as much as I love reminiscing about my colorful past, the day is melting away," Shayne said with a rusty chuckle. He got to his feet. Lottie blinked to clear her head. She was surprised to see that the sun was indeed lower in the sky.

Trying to reconcile what she had just heard with what she knew about Ian McTavish, she began clearing the remains of the meal, wrapping everything back into oilcloth and sheets of brown paper. Shayne had eaten little, but then it was probably hard to choke down bitter memories and food.

But how could Ian be so different now? It didn't make sense to Lottie, but she was certain that Shayne was telling her the truth. There was too much pain in his voice for it to be a lie.

She watched him now and marveled at the man. Though he was motionless while he stood surveying the far horizon, he was never really still. There was a restlessness about him that she could read in every taut line and tense sinew of his body. His fingers flexed; the muscles bunched in his arms; his jaw twitched.

He was like a river. Though he appeared calm on the surface, there was a deep current running swiftly beneath. Lottie understood that the current was full of dangerous eddies.

Shayne Rosswarne spoke to her soul. And she nearly wept because she could not answer the call.

"Darlin', either that rock is a lot farther than everyone says, or we've been jawing too much and riding too slow." Shayne stopped his horse. He propped his forearms—his lean, muscled, forearms—on his saddlehorn and grinned devilishly at her.

Lottie had never been one to see the beauty in a man before, but she could see it in Shayne. It was not a soft, gentle kind of beauty; it was more like a bank of thunderclouds, dark with power and the promise of savagery. He was more like a cleansing wind that swept down from the mountains than like a gentle breeze. He was primal, strong, and so male that it took her breath away just to look at him.

"Are you up to making camp here?" he asked lightly.

Lottie glanced around. They were in a sheltered hollow with a ring of tall pines and short scrub bushes providing a natural windbreak. There were wild blackberry vines, and swarms of honeybees working a hive on a lightning-scarred tree. A flash of light on water marked the location of a nearby stream.

It was a good place to make camp. The sun was dipping low and washing the western sky with a crimson glow. And she was tired.

"How much farther do you think it is?" she asked, gazing at the horizon as if she could make the Devil's Tower appear by wishing.

"We'll probably run smack into it before noon. Unless this was all just some crazy story to get me out here where you would have me all to yourself." Shayne swung his leg over the horn and slid lightly to the ground.

"Why on earth would I want to get you out here alone?" she said as her belly clenched. Did he suspect her of luring him from town? Could he read every thought in her head?

He closed the small distance between them. Though she was still mounted and high above him, she felt small, feminine, and oh, so vulnerable when he gazed upon her.

"I thought—hell, I actually hoped you might want more of me than just the use of my name." He winked at her and tipped his hat off onto his palm.

She nearly swooned with relief and . . . something more.

Surely he wasn't . . . no, he couldn't be . . .

"Are you offering yourself to me, Shayne Rosswarne?"

"Hide, bone, and hair, honey."

He grinned and threw his arms wide, as if embracing life, welcoming her to sample all there was of him. He stood before her with his hat in his hand, offering himself like some sort of pagan sacrifice for her pleasure.

"Well, I never!" Lottie gasped.

"Then, darlin' Lottie, like I said before, it's high time you did. It's time you had a taste of sweet sin."

And before she had time even to think, he had swept her off her horse and into his arms. His lips were soft and insistent as they claimed her mouth. His hands were strong and rough as he rubbed her body through the worn fabric of his own clothes.

In her mind she saw Addie and Ian and little Kathryn. But they were far away, safe, secure. Lottie was here in the arms of a man she could not ignore, and whom she would be a fool to trust. With the greatest effort she did try to resist one more time.

"I . . . I appreciate your offer, cowboy, but we had better make camp. The Indians have been pretty tolerant so far, but I would hate to be caught out here in the middle of nowhere—"

"With your pants down, so to speak?" Shayne interrupted impishly.

Lottie swallowed hard. Images of Shayne and her locked in a hot, passionate coupling flashed through her mind. She was not a prude, nor was she frightened of the prospect of sharing her body with this man.

In fact, as Lottie looked him over from head to boot, she knew she would lie with him in a heartbeat if not for Ian and Addie. But love and loyalty had to come first.

Didn't they?

The air in the tiny camp crackled with lust. Each time Lottie glanced at Shayne across the campfire, she found him watching her with a mixture of desire and humor in his dark eyes. He was different tonight—different out here beneath the stars and the velvet black sky.

Or was it because he had told her his story that she now saw him differently? Perhaps he had not changed at all, and only her perceptions of him were altered because of her own compassion.

And lust.

She didn't want to admit it, but there it was. Just below the surface of their fleeting glances or conversation or the most mundane of chores, there was hot, needy, unquenched passion. It was seething, simmering nearly at the boiling point.

Lottie was put in mind of a great, hungry wolf lurking in the darkness. The firelight kept the hungry creature at bay—barely. But if the fire should go out . . .

She could so easily succumb to the charms of this strange dark-eyed man. And if she did, it would be the ruin of all she held dear.

"I think it's time, darlin'." Shayne's voice broke the taut sexual silence.

It's time. . . .

Lottie closed her eyes for a moment, grateful in a foolish way that he was going to take the decision from her hands. Now she would not be torn between wanting him and wanting to save Ian and Addie. He had decided. It took all the burden from her.

She took a deep breath and waited, anticipating his touch. He would be a wonderful, experienced lover; she was certain of that.

"You've heard all about me. Now tell me about yourself." His voice ripped through her fantasy like a sharp knife.

"T-tell you about *me?*" she squeaked, and she sat up. "That's what you meant about it being time?" she blurted, her guard down due to her shock and her own naughty thoughts.

"Uh-huh." His grin widened and warmed. He tossed another stick into the fire. "Now what did you think I meant, darlin'?" He slanted a quick look in her direction.

"Nothing. It isn't important." She rubbed her palms on her thighs nervously. "Why would you want to hear about me?"

"Oh, I don't know. Maybe I might be a tad curious about the woman who *married* me."

Lottie glared at him as he laughed, deep, low and a little too charmingly.

"I have two sisters; you know that. My father was a bit like yours. He had itchy feet. Seems like we were always pushing a bit farther west every year or so. My mother didn't like it, but she loved him—or at least that's how I remember it."

"You were young when they passed?" Shayne's voice was soft with compassion. "It must've been real hard."

"I had my sisters. Addie's tough and strong, and since she was the eldest, she shouldered most of the hardest parts," Lottie said honestly. "I'm beginning to think I have too much of my father in me."

Shayne smiled and rose. He came around the campfire and squatted next to her. "The wanderlust bred true?"

"Too true, I'm afraid. I've always wanted to see more, do more, *feel* more. I've managed to keep it under control until now. . . ."

"I can help you, Lottie. I can help you set it free." Shayne reached out and slowly trailed his fingers down her jaw and neck and along her collarbone.

She sighed and leaned into his caress. "I can't let you."

"Sure you can. What's the harm, Lottie darlin'? To the world we are man and wife. And who will ever know but us two all the way out here, alone, 'neath the stars?"

Lottie was falling, falling, but she didn't care. Shayne's touch was as gentle as rain, as powerful as a waterfall: tumbling, bringing her down into the depths of sensation, passion, and desire.

She leaned back, his hand cushioning the back of her head as he slid nearer to her. His mouth tasted, tested, tutored.

It was sinful—it was sweet, dark passion that drugged, beckoned, and lulled the last shred of Lottie's reserve.

She had no inhibitions; truth to tell, she never really had. Addie and Mattie thought she was like them, but she wasn't. She had only restrained herself all these years because no man had ever awakened this kind of drunken desire in her before.

But now the wolf of her lust was roused. The great, ravening beast was fully aware. He was hungry and wanted to be fed.

She wanted Shayne. She had to have him.

Damn the cost to them all.

Eight

Shayne knew he was a fool. The last thing he needed was to get sidetracked with a woman. But here he was with more woman in his arms than a man had a right to hold in two lifetimes. And his body was reacting to her just as God intended when he created Eve.

Charlotte Green, the beautiful liar with golden hair and flashing eyes, had done something to Shayne. She had gently pried and prodded at his reserve and his distrust until he had told her things, secret memories and emotions he had kept hidden deep in his heart. He was not the kind of man who shared himself. He had never needed or wanted a bosom buddy or a woman to be his confidant.

Since he was betrayed by Ian McTavish, Shayne had not trusted another soul with so much as a howdy-do. He had kept his own counsel and kept his past a secret.

Until Charlotte. She had looked at him with those soft blue eyes, and his tongue had come loose and he lost what good sense he had ever possessed. He told her about his family and Texas and the regrets of his misspent youth. Then a tiny flicker of humanity, a light that was nearly extinguished in prison, flared to life again inside him when she looked at him with compassion.

And now he was going to take her, right out here on

the open meadow like a rutting buck. Their bed would be the stubble of grass, their canopy the sky full of stars overhead.

The very thought of it made his body harden and scream to be inside her—now.

Now.

She was willing; that was plain enough to see by the way her lips softened and she made little mewling sounds each time he kissed her. Of course a woman like Lottie was bound to have had a man before, and to know what pleasure awaited them both. She was no simpering virgin—hell, she didn't even blush like most respectable women did—and that was part of her attraction to Shayne. He didn't want to spend any time wooing and deflowering a virgin.

They would be glorious together. He knew it. He could feel it pulsing in his loins like a Kiowa war drum, and each time he put his hands on her breasts he felt her own heartbeat, strong and rapid beneath his palms.

Now . . . now . . . now their rushing blood seemed to sing in unison.

It was the rhythm of a dance as old as time. And he had a partner who would match him step for step. He was hard, randy, and eager to taste Lottie's sweet nectar.

"Come here, darlin'," he said when he finally pulled away from her potent kiss. "Stand up."

She did.

Shayne flipped over on his back and took her hand, guiding her toward him until she stood, astraddle him—above him like a beautiful dream. "Now ease yourself down onto my lap."

She did.

Now Lottie was sitting on his groin with her booted feet next to his ears. His erection was pounding with each beat of his heart, her delicious weight atop him like a promise of what was to come. In a matter of moments he would be inside her.

"Give me your foot, darlin'."

She did.

He swiftly freed her foot from the half boot and turned his attention to the one on the other side of his head. Then he released her garters and rolled her stockings down, baring her ankles to him. He kissed the soft skin just below the bone where there was a tiny hollow, and again he felt the thrum of her pulse.

Lottie moaned deep in her chest.

He got harder, nudging at her body, wanting to shove inside her.

"Now raise your hips." She did. Shayne reached up and undid the waistband of the trousers she wore. He peeled them down.

Now she was sitting astraddle him, facing him, hot and willing, but she still had her drawers on. The slit in the middle gave Shayne a tantalizing view of her sweet, musky-scented privates.

"Take off that shirt," he said with a husky catch in his voice. "I want to hold those sweet tits in my hands. I want to suck those nipples and taste your sweetness."

Lottie did as he bid, staring into his eyes with the sultry, heavy-lidded look of a woman aroused. He picked up her hips and yanked off her drawers, sliding one finger over her just to feel the heat, the wetness, the welcome. He was so hot, he thought he might catch flame as he undid his own placket and wriggled his trousers down to his boot tops.

Now she was astride him, naked, facing him, with

her intimate parts open for his view, and the insistent nudge of his own erection pressed against her moist opening. He liked being able to watch her eyes and her mouth. With a little cry she yanked her soft, thin chemise over her head and tossed it away with all the wild abandon of a woman ready for loving.

She was a wonderful, blonde piece of woman. Her nipples, rose-colored in the moonlight, were hard and pointing out in a way that made him harden to the point of pain.

He put his hands on her waist and enjoyed the slender feel of her delicate flesh beneath his hands as he rubbed her body, savoring the silken slide of her soft woman's skin.

She inhaled deeply, her nostrils flaring as the musk of their arousal blended with the fresh scent of mountain air.

She was hot, willing, and ready.

And he was more than capable of obliging her, filling her, branding her with his body.

"Mount me, darlin'," he said with an eager grin.

"Show me where you want me," Lottie said, her eyes blue pools of need. Her blond curls dangled over her shoulders, whispering along his thighs at her back. It was sweet torture. Every delicate caress of those silken strands drove him higher, further into the wildness of lust.

"I'll show you that and more—more than you can imagine, honey. After tonight you won't remember another man's name. When we're finished, you'll never even think of laying with anybody else." He lifted her up and impaled her in one smooth, hot thrust of his hips.

She gasped.

He moaned.

She was tight—tighter than anything he could have imagined—tighter than any woman he ever had. And hot—hotter than a sultry-Southern August night.

He held her hips and guided her down, down. She slid, slowly, until he was in her to the hilt. The tight squeeze of her body around him was sublime torture, bringing him to a fever pitch of arousal.

"Ride me, honey. Ride me like a stallion." He began to lift his buttocks and pump into her. He lifted her. With the sweet drag and friction, he nearly lost himself. She was . . . *perfect*. As if God had sculpted her body just for him.

Faster, deeper, *harder*. He wanted her to take all of him there was to take. He was lifting her and bringing her down in a frenzy now. They were hot, slicked with sweat, lost in a fever of arousal.

She flung her head back and screamed out his name. The smooth, pale column of her throat was limned in silvery moonlight. Strands of her thick golden hair tickled him. She was nearly ready to come; he could tell by the way her mouth formed a little O when she whimpered with need.

"More, more, more . . ." Her breath was ragged and shallow.

"Yes, darlin', come . . . come for me," he said the moment before he shot his seed into her. And then the night exploded in a million shooting stars—or was that just his soul igniting?

Lottie was spent. She felt light, boneless. The world seemed to float around her. But then, slowly, inevitably, the night air began to cool her ardor. She came back into herself to find she was sitting atop him. He was still big within her.

She looked down into the face of her first lover.

Shayne was watching her with a strange, contemplative look on his face. His eyes were narrowed, his expression guarded.

"You were awfully tight, darlin'," he drawled. "Tight as a virgin, as a matter of fact."

Heat climbed in her cheeks and she started to move, but his big hands clamped onto her waist and held her there.

"You were a virgin, weren't you, Charlotte? I know now for sure because this is only the second time I have ever seen you blush."

"I never blush," Lottie said softly.

"Yes, you do—you have twice in my recollection. When you spoke of being too wild and when you looked into the eyes of the man that took your virtue. Me. I was your first lover, wasn't I, Charlotte?"

Lottie had no words for him at that moment. So they stayed as they were, with him on the hard ground and her atop him like some wanton rider. And then, remarkably, amazingly, she felt him growing inside her, hardening, thickening.

His mouth twitched. "You're the damnedest woman I ever met. I thought once I had a taste of you I would be all done with the wanting of you, but I was wrong."

She put her hands on his chest, her fingers curling into the crisp, curly dark hair that grew across the hard-muscled expanse. And try as she might, Lottie could not ignore what was happening between her legs.

She wanted him, again, more.

Lottie had been a virgin, and though she was still a little raw from Shayne's powerful entry, she found a hot coil of passion rising inside her as he began to move his body.

With his powerful hands he lifted her and then let her slide back down his length. It was indescribable.

"Yes, darlin' that's it," Shayne purred.

Lottie realized with a small shock that she was beginning to rock against him each time he moved inside her. The knowledge of this rhythm was deep within her very core, some primal drive that had lain sleeping like the wild, reckless, wanton side of her that Shayne had roused. Now the hunger and the knowledge were fully awake, demanding that she match Shayne's movements.

"Ah, yes, darlin'." His voice was raw and husky and touched her deep in her soul.

The heat swirled and flowed through her body until every nerve and muscle cried out for release. And then something happened. She began to shake and shudder from the inside out. She moaned and cried out his name.

"Yes, darlin', come to me," he roared, thrusting himself into her, touching something so sensitive and wild that she had no control over herself.

Lottie quivered and collapsed on Shayne's chest. His breathing was as deep and rough as the hair beneath her cheek.

"Oh, Lord, what have I done?" Lottie whispered as she regained control of herself.

Morning found Lottie strangely embarrassed and shy. She had never experienced this kind of inner torment before. It was awful the way she felt Shayne's eyes upon her and knew that he had touched her in every one of those hidden places.

"Coffee?"

"What?" She jumped when she found him close enough to touch.

"Would you like some coffee before we ride?" Shayne thrust a tin cup into her hands, all the while studying her with narrowed eyes. Neither one had mentioned what happened last night. She had finally pulled away from him when his eyes closed in sated sleep.

He hadn't even stirred when she left him, naked and spent.

Maybe that was the way it was for men. They got what they wanted and then drifted into blissful slumber. If only she could have been so relaxed after the deed.

Instead she had found her clothing and gone to the stream to wash herself and cry. Lottie had never been one to have regrets, but the impact of giving herself to Shayne hit like an icy wind.

She had lain with the man who threatened her sister's happiness. But it was more than that. . . .

"I'm going to saddle up the horses," Shayne said softly. He turned away from Lottie, but the memory of her tortured eyes remained with him. Why had she given herself to him, if all she was going to do was look like her heart was breaking the next morning?

Why had she, a virgin, given herself to him at all?

Now that his lust had cleared and the light of day had dawned, he found himself puzzled with no answers. He also had a cold pang of something that felt strangely like guilt lying heavy in his gut.

She had been tight—tighter than anything he could imagine—and finally, even through his desire-fogged brain, the truth had dawned.

She was a virgin—a spirited and sensual woman but a virgin nonetheless.

Shayne turned his attention to saddling Little Bit, but though his hands worked on the cinch and latigo by rote, his mind was still on Lottie.

Why?

The question hammered at his mind. He had opened up to her, trusted her with details of his life. Was her submission to his physical attentions just another way to get inside his head—and his trousers?

Why?

He turned and watched her from the corner of his eye. Her brow was furrowed and she gnawed her full bottom lip as if a great question preyed upon her mind.

A hot-and-cold tide swept through him. One part of him wanted to give her comfort and solace, but another part hardened with suspicion. He wasn't about to trust her just because he had been between her legs.

There had to be a powerful reason for a virgin to rut on the open prairie as she had. And that powerful reason made Shayne die a little inside with dread. He had allowed himself to share his childhood memories and his lust. That was more risk than he had taken with another person in a long time.

He was a fool, a man who had been too long without a woman—without a home. He knew why he had done it. He was starved for the simple comforts of freedom.

But why did *she?*

"Look, there it is." Lottie spoke the first words she had said since they broke camp. She forgot herself,

Shayne, and what they had done as her eyes locked on the sight ahead.

They traveled through a sheltered valley heavy with the scent of lodgepole, sugar pine, and juniper. Beyond the tallest tree the dark, craggy rock rose into the clouds, where a wispy halo of mist ringed its flat top.

Shayne let out a low, long whistle of wonder. "All I can say is that folks didn't exaggerate. That is a mighty big rock."

"Those do look like claw marks on the side, don't they?" Lottie murmured, her heart thumping with excitement. This was what she longed for: the thrill of discovery, the excitement of seeing new things. This was her first taste of adventure and she liked it.

"Yep, they do, darlin'." Shayne turned to her, his dark eyes causing her breath to catch. "I owe you an apology."

"N-n-no. It was my fault as much as yours. I could've stopped you—I should've stopped you, but the night—the stars—the way you made me feel inside—"

"I meant about the rock, Lottie." Shayne's face went still. "I am not a bit sorry about what happened between us last night. But since you brought it up, I'd like to know exactly why you let me take you? Why was I the first?"

Lottie swallowed hard. She had to tell Shayne. She had to tell him that Ian McTavish was her brother-in-law. Maybe then she could start to forgive herself for having given her innocence to the man who wanted to kill him.

Nine

"So tell me, darlin', why did you do it?" Shayne's voice was as hard and flinty as the tall, scarred pinnacle of rock before them. "Why did you lay with me?"

Lottie stared at the mystical Devil's Tower and tried to summon her courage. It should be easy to talk to a man she had been intimate with.

It should be, but it wasn't.

Her voice was lodged in her throat along with her hammering heart. She didn't know *why* she had done it. There had been some untamed force inside her that had swept aside her self-control and her good sense.

And there had been Shayne.

Shayne with his pain-filled eyes. Shayne with his drugging kisses. Shayne with the power to touch her where no one ever had.

But how could she tell him this?

How could she tell him that some part of her soul cried out to him? Or that she felt a responsibility to ease his sadness? Or that she had strong physical feelings for him in spite of the fact that he was a threat to her family?

She couldn't. So she simply sat on her horse in silent misery.

"We might as well make camp here and see what

else Miley packed for us," he said after a few moments of tense silence.

Lottie blinked. Shayne was watching her again with that strange light of speculation and suspicion in his eyes. And yet she found herself seeing beneath that mask. He had a heart; she was sure of it.

"Yes, let's stay here awhile." Her eyes skimmed over the towering rock again. Suddenly the excitement of discovery was not as wonderful as it had been. Her sweet moment of satisfied triumph was tainted by what lay between them. She simply could not go another minute without revealing the truth to Shayne.

"There is something I need to tell you," Lottie choked out. "Something that you must know."

Shayne's gut twisted and his heart did a painful little kick. He didn't know what Lottie was going to say, but he sure as hell knew it was going to be bad. He could tell by the way she bit her lip.

The hair on the back of his neck prickled. His mouth went dry. He had felt the same way each time one of the prisoners made that long walk to the gallows outside his cell.

"My sister Addie is married to Ian McTavish. He's my brother-in-law."

The remembered sound of the trapdoor opening echoed through Shayne's head as his belly fell to the grass below. Lottie's quaking words had the same deadly effect on him now.

Now he knew why she had laid with him. Sweet, virginal Lottie had rutted with him so she could barter her body to save Ian's life. The ugly truth forced the air from his lungs and the tiny flicker of hope from his heart. This was the last wound—the most powerful wound he would ever allow anybody to inflict upon him.

"It isn't going to work, darlin'," he said with a sneer. "You gave up your virtue for nothing, because I am going to put a bullet in Ian's head the moment I lay eyes on him."

Lottie gasped at the violence and hatred she saw in Shayne's eyes. "But you don't understand—I can't let you hurt Ian. My sister would be devastated."

"Oh, I understand all right. You thought I would be so grateful for what's between your legs that I'd give up my revenge. Well, you were wrong, sweetheart. Dead wrong. Now the question is, what punishment is fair?"

"What do you mean, 'punishment'?" She recoiled from the violence in his eyes.

"You can't really think I would let you try and trick me and let it go unchallenged—did you?" He laughed, a hard brittle sound that chilled Lottie's blood.

"If you did, then you are a fool, Charlotte Green. No, you'll pay and pay dearly."

They had left the magnificent rock in silence, the beauty and majesty of their discovery all but forgotten in the face of Lottie's confession and Shayne's hate-filled reaction.

Shayne's heart had not stopped aching. He told himself it was rage over Lottie's betrayal, but a nagging voice kept questioning him, asking if it wasn't something else. Something like him being stupid enough to have actually cared what the faithless little liar thought of him.

Each time he looked at her, the white-hot sting of

betrayal made him angry all over again, but beneath that fury there was also the pain of hurt. He wanted to deny it, but he couldn't.

Lottie had gotten to him.

And he hated himself for being so big a fool.

She turned and looked at him, and beyond reason there was pity in her eyes.

Pity.

Well, he would fix that. He would find a way to remove the pity and compassion from her lovely blue eyes and tear her from his heart in the bargain.

No matter what it cost his soul, he would cleanse himself of Lottie.

As the sunlight waned, Lottie realized through her numbness that she and Shayne would have to spend another night out alone together on the prairie.

The thought both frightened and excited her.

She wondered what was wrong with her. His words had hit with the force of a slap, and yet every time she looked at him, the memory of shared passion swept over her like a hot wind.

And his eyes . . . his tormented sad eyes haunted her.

Was there no way to heal his soul? Was there any way she could save her own?

"We may as well stop for the night." His voice was hard and gritty.

Lottie swiveled in her saddle to look at him and found his eyes trained on her. They held all the softness of a stone, but beneath his fury she glimpsed, for only a moment, raw pain.

She had done that. For a while as they traveled, she

had seen Shayne laugh and tease. His eyes had softened; he had begun to heal.

She had put that wounded look back into the depths of his dark eyes. Another betrayal in long list of betrayals. Guilt swamped her.

"Yes, this looks fine," she said softly, coming to a decision in that split second.

There was good in Shayne Rosswarne. It was buried beneath the layers of pain, hurt, and violence, but it was there.

And she was going to do whatever it took to find it.

They had eaten fried bacon, cold biscuits, and coffee. Shayne had never said a word, but he couldn't stop his eyes from following Lottie around the campfire each time she moved.

She was as beautiful and treacherous as a swift-moving river. The firelight winked off her shiny blond curls and turned her face into a lovely contrast of light and shadows.

He wanted her.

He wanted her submissive, willing, and hot beneath him. Damn him for thinking with his little head.

Shayne sipped the too-strong, bitter coffee and laughed at himself. He was an idiot—a fool in rut for a woman who only wanted to see him back behind bars or worse. How far would the little liar go to see Ian McTavish go unscathed?

"What would you do to save Ian's life?" Shayne asked roughly, startling them both.

Lottie blinked owlishly at him across the campfire. "To keep from seeing my sister's heart broken, just about anything."

"Anything, huh? That is a lot of territory, darlin'."
Darlin'.

The carelessly used endearment brought a sting of tears to the back of Lottie's eyes. Damn him for making her want him!

"And what about that other sister of yours—pretty Mattie?"

"What about Mattie?" Lottie sat a little straighter, the icy tingle of fear marching up her spine.

Shayne shrugged and his mouth twisted with cruelty. "What's to stop me from riding back into town and telling everybody that you and I are not married? And that your sweet sister was part of your game? How would folks take that news?"

"You wouldn't." Lottie rose to her feet. Her hands were trembling.

"I would." He stood up and tossed the dregs of his coffee into the fire. "I damn sure would."

In the next instant Lottie had launched herself at him. She was like a wildcat, all spit and claws. One of her nails connected with his forearm, leaving a hot trail of pain as she raked his flesh.

"I'll stop you, Shayne. I will not let you hurt my family."

She kicked him in the shin, the side of her boot skittering painfully along the bone.

"Owww!" He hopped on one foot and tried to grab her hands, but she struck out at him as fast as any Texas rattler.

"You can't hurt them just because I hurt you." She brought up her knee and connected with his privates.

A harsh groan of pain escaped his lips. He finally managed to grab her wrists as he struggled to breathe.

"Stop it," he said harshly.

"No." She struggled in his grip but it was futile.

She was breathing hard, her breasts rising and falling rapidly. Her hair was undone, wild curls dripping down her shoulders and back. Her lips were parted and her eyes were wide with fear and anger.

"God." Shayne groaned. And then he pulled her roughly to him and claimed her mouth.

The kiss was hard, demanding, and a bit punishing, but then, slowly, almost imperceptibly, it began to change. Shayne's grip loosened. His hands came up to cradle the back of Lottie's head.

Long, strong fingers tangled in her hair while his tongue plunged into her mouth. His movements were sure, gentle, and not at all what she expected from a man who threatened to make her pay.

Against her own reason she brought her hands to the sides of his face. The rasp of his beard stubble against her palms was somehow soothing. She returned his kiss.

"Hottest damned woman I ever held," he said when he broke the kiss, still holding her, staring into her eyes. "I can't get enough of you, Lottie. You are a sweet poison in my blood. I have to have you."

She studied his face, trying to read what was in his eyes. There was the smoky haze of lust, but there was more.

There was need. Raw and painful, it was there at the edge of his smoldering anger.

He needed her as much as she needed him.

"I cannot lay with you while you are planning to kill Ian," Lottie said softly.

His jaw tightened. His eyes narrowed while his gaze flicked like a flame from her eyes to her mouth and back again.

"I told you I was going to make you pay, Lottie."

"Yes, you did."

"Unless you lay with me, willingly, I will go to town and see your sister ruined. And then I will kill Ian McTavish as soon as he shows his face." His words were harder than stone.

"And if I do as you want?"

"Then I will leave Mattie alone and I will give Ian a fair chance."

"A fair chance?" Her heart fluttered.

"We will meet each other and see who is the fastest."

"That isn't much of a chance," Lottie said bitterly. "I've seen the way you wear that gun."

"It is better than what I originally planned." Shayne's mouth twisted in a grimace. "I had planned to simply put a bullet between his eyes without warning."

Lottie thought about it. Mattie's and Addie's faces flashed before her eyes . . . and little Kathryn.

"I'll do it. I will share your bed and live as your wife."

"Willingly?"

"Willingly. You will have my body but you won't have my heart or my soul."

"I'm not interested in your heart, darlin'." Shayne grimaced. "I only want to ease myself between your legs. But just for the record, I don't think you'll be holding much of yourself back."

"You're wrong," Lottie said, raising her chin a notch.

"I don't think so, but we'll find out, won't we? And let's start right now. I want you on your back."

Lottie grimaced.

Shayne's mouth twitched.

He let her go and went to where Little Bit was standing, unsaddled and grazing. With one flick of his wrist, Shayne opened the saddle blanket that was folded and tucked into the upturned saddle. Then he flipped it open and spread it on the ground near the fire.

"Come here, darlin'," he said, holding out his hand. "Let's see just how *un*willin' you are."

Lottie raised her chin, straightened her spine, and took the first step toward her own inevitable ruin.

Ten

Shayne took hold of her fingers and drew her to
him. His mouth was hot and hungry as he sipped
kisses along her neck and collarbone.

"Take off your clothes; I want to see you naked
again," he said when he finally raised his head. His
dark eyes were smoky with desire, but there was also
the guarded look of a predator beneath the surface.

Lottie's heart fluttered inside her chest. One part of
her wanted to justify what she was doing because of
the threat to her family. But another, more honest side
of herself laughed at that feeble explanation.

She wanted Shayne. The wild, untamed, unladylike
core of her being rejoiced to be in his arms. She was
a creature very like him deep down inside. They were
both not quite civilized, not quite proper.

And together they attained a passion so hot and satisfying that Lottie nearly wept with joy. At least, they
had attained that level of satisfaction once. Maybe it
would never be sweet like that again. Now she also
had been betrayed, by her own feelings and by
Shayne's desire for revenge. It bruised her heart to
think he would use the wonder of their desire as a
weapon, and she vowed to keep her woman's heart
distant from him—to give what he demanded without

giving of herself. She vowed to take his passion and physical gifts to enjoy but to keep her heart separate.

"Why don't you do it yourself, cowboy?" she said softly.

Shayne licked his lips, his gaze flicking over her body like a hot flame. His eyes narrowed. Once again she saw a flash of mingled hurt and anger melded with raw need.

But which was the greater emotion?

"No, darlin'. You made a bargain to dance with the devil in the pale moonlight. Now you must pay to hear the tune. You take your clothes off and come to me. Come with me."

Lottie swallowed hard. Shayne was hard and unyielding. A little voice in her mind warned that she might have made a mistake. Perhaps there was no core of goodness inside him. Perhaps she was playing with a stick of dynamite. He would use her and break her if she was wrong or if she was too weak to withstand the crucible of his ardor.

There was peril in what she planned—danger for her family and danger for herself.

But she had to try.

With trembling hands she undid her buttons. One by one, the pieces of her clothing and the last illusion of protection fell away. She stood motionless while he stared at her, every inch of her. When his gaze lingered on her breasts, she felt her own nipples pucker in response.

He grinned, but there was an expression of cruelty in the way his lips twisted. Her heart stumbled inside her chest with fear and anticipation.

"See, darlin', your body wants what I can give."

"No. It—it's just cold," Lottie lied feebly.

"Uh-huh. Keep telling yourself that if it helps. We'll soon see if your willpower is stronger than that wild streak in you. I'm betting the wildness will win."

And with that, he came to her and went down to his knees.

"Wha-what are you doing?"

"You said you would do what I wanted. Well, this is what I want." And with that he buried his face in the cleft of her thighs.

He kissed her.

Lottie gasped and tried to step away, but his strong, callused hands gripped the cheeks of her behind. He held her there while he kissed her—again, deeply, his tongue flicking out to slip inside her body.

"Shayne . . ." She half moaned, half screamed it.

He raised his head and looked up at her. "That won't be the only time you scream my name tonight." Then he dipped his head and began to do things to her that made her knees weaken and her face flame.

He licked her, his tongue going deep between her thighs, inside her, invading a part of her that was so private, so sensitive, she gasped in humiliated pleasure. Lottie tried to clamp her legs together, but he spread her knees and positioned himself in front of her. Shayne kissed, laved, licked and tasted her until she felt herself collapsing from the sheer pleasure of what he did. Liquid waves of delicious sensation lapped at her body. She was falling. . . .

And then he had her in his arms, laying her down gently on the saddle blanket. He stripped himself bare and stared at her for a long moment. She stared back, unable to take her eyes off his body.

He was lean and hard with sinewy strength. Here and there, he was covered with a fine, downy, dark hair, and where it was thicker—on his chest—there were creases of muscle. And lower, where it was thickest of all, he appeared to be hewn from wood.

His flesh jutted out from a nest of dark curls, but as Lottie stared, gape-jawed and astonished, the head of his shaft swelled a little more. She could see his pulse in that large phallus.

"Time to pay the piper in full, darlin'."

He slid his body over hers, leaving a trail of kisses in his wake. When his groin slid across Lottie's thigh she felt the hot, silken drag of him. The blood in her veins was hot, drugged, intoxicated with the feel of him. The size of him. The violence in him.

His head and shoulders were positioned between her legs, at her thighs.

He stared at her for one moment, in which her body throbbed and her heart fluttered. And then he bent and kissed her, opened her.

Licking, tasting, sipping at her juices while she moaned and writhed, she realized she had no defense against him. There was no armor she could erect that he could not break down. There was nothing she could do but lie there and let him wring every ounce of passion from her limp body.

And he did it with a fervor that was frightening.

She whimpered, moaned, pleaded. But did she cry for him to stop, or to plunder her more and more until she was nothing but a shell of herself?

The moon rose and drifted across the sky while Lottie lay in a simmering pool of sensation. No matter how she fought the rising tide of passion, her own body betrayed her, just like Shayne had said it would.

He knew her in every way. He knew her body in ways that she herself could not fathom, and he knew her soul. His kisses, his touch, spoke to that wild tide inside her. His violence and fury called to her and she answered in kind.

Her thighs were trembling uncontrollably. She thrashed and writhed. And Shayne had no mercy. He continued to kiss her; his tongue darted in and out of her body, and he took all she had to give.

Lottie screamed and arched. Her body spasmed deep inside while she fisted the blanket in her hands. The sensation rolled through her and over her, tumbling her mind and soul.

She slowly came back into herself and felt a wash of shame, but before she could do anything, he was there again. His fingers were stroking her hot, swollen flesh.

"No. No more. I will surely die if you do more," she pleaded, feeling boneless and wrung out.

"You won't die. It was good to see you lose control, darlin'," he said softly, taking one of her nipples in his mouth, suckling hard, stopping just at the threshold of pain.

"A woman as hot as you should never try to hold back."

"No more," she said weakly.

He laughed, a deep throaty sound that rippled over her body. "Oh, yes, darlin' there will be much, much more tonight. When I finish with you, my lying, deceitful little virgin, you won't ever want another man to touch you."

And Lottie whimpered, because she knew his words were true.

"Now, darlin', I am going to touch you and teach you the price of betrayal," Shayne purred in her ear. With amazing speed he flipped her over on her stomach. Using both hands he grasped her hipbones and raised her pelvis from the blanket. She smelled the horse scent and her own juices on the rough-woven blanket beneath her cheek.

"But wha—"

"Shhh, just be still."

His hands were all over her. He rubbed her back, sliding his palms around to cup her breasts. His hips nudged her backside and she felt him, the hot, hard part of him invading her. It was like being seared with lightning when he slid beyond a hot sensitive spot. No it was more than sensitive, that spot was where every nerve ending in her body slept.

Until now, when Shayne awakened her.

She bucked beneath him. At that moment, he penetrated her fully. He was hot, hard, and sure of his destination as he drove into her.

"Take me, darlin', take all of me."

He grunted and shoved himself home, tilting her hips upward to take him.

With a sigh of satisfaction, he settled himself deep within her.

"You are tighter than a glove, baby."

Lottie was stunned. The size of him stretched her, filled her, claimed her. The throbbing head of him nudged deep within her belly with each thrust of his hips. He did not withdraw but continued to shove against her, and unbelievably, he went deeper. . . .

"Ohhh . . ." she whimpered in a mixture of fear and sexual excitement. Her belly was tightening, her pulse quickening, and soon she found herself tilting her pelvis so he could go deeper . . . *harder* . . . *faster*.

Then he began to pump. In . . . out. He slid himself out to the tip of his shaft before he thrust it back in.

It was like dying and flying and falling out of control in a world that had no reality.

He was hot against her. She could feel little rivulets of sweat trickling between her breasts and down her temples.

Suddenly he reached out and took one of her breasts in his hand, tweaking the nipple, rasping his tough, callused hands against her flesh.

"Come, baby, come," he said as he went deeper, until she thought he would split her in two.

And then it happened again. She tensed. Every muscle in her body screamed for release.

And she screamed when he gave it to her with one mighty plunge. She felt the hot pump of his juices inside her.

"Shayne!" she cried.

Her own voice blended with his as he bellowed into the night.

"Lottie!"

She woke with the sunlight on her face.

She turned. For a moment she didn't know where she was, but the pain between her legs soon reminded her of where she was and of what had happened last night. She rose on her elbows and looked around.

Shayne was watching her. He was crouched by a cold fire with a cup in his hand.

"It's late," Lottie said, squinting up at the sun.

"I know." He tossed whatever was in the cup into the ashes and turned away. She watched him go and fought back the sting of tears.

Shayne walked away from Lottie because he couldn't stand to look at her. He had lived rough the past few years, done some things in prison he had not been particularly proud of in order to survive; but until now he had never been so completely disgusted with himself.

Even when he had disappointed his father he had never felt as low as he did now. What he had done to her, and his reason for doing it, stuck in his craw. He touched the raw wounds on his arms, left by Lottie's nails. She had come at him like a little wildcat in defense of her family. There had been a time when Shayne had felt that kind of loyalty. His father had felt as Lottie did about family, honor, and revenge.

"But that was long ago, before I turned into a genuine bastard," he said bitterly. "Daddy would be real proud of me now." He said it aloud, kicking a loose stone in the grass. "Real proud of what I've become."

He bent down and picked up the jagged stone, turning it over and over in his hand.

He hated what had happened last night at the same time that he loved every minute of it. How could he be so riddled with guilt and contempt for himself and still wish to do it all again? How could he wish he had never met her and want to tumble her all at the same time?

I want to mount her right now and ride her till I can't go anymore. I'm ready to damn my soul by blackmailing her into laying with me every day. What kind of a son of a bitch am I?

This went beyond lust, beyond having the itch to lay a woman. This feeling that gripped Shayne was bordering on obsession.

He wanted to get away from her. What he had lived for was vengeance, and to be able to go home.

And that was what kept him going. He was capable

of doing something as coarse and vulgar as he had last night because he had to do it to get home.

"But we were good," he mumbled.

They had been unbelievable together. She had more passion and lust in her than any woman he had ever met. Nothing he did was beyond her measure or capacity for pleasure.

"Can we get started?" Her voice brought him spinning around. She met his gaze unflinchingly, and wonder of wonders, the woman still did not blush. He had done to her everything a man could do to a woman to bring them both satisfaction, and yet she did not blush.

"Yes. I'm kind of anxious to get to town myself," he grated out.

What was he going to do when he got there? When all he wanted to do was kiss Lottie and get her on her back again? He wanted her, but he didn't want her to come to him because of a threat to her sister. He wanted her to be as consumed with this hunger as he was. He wanted her to be helpless to resist this madness, just as he was helpless to ignore it.

But how could he say that? No man worth his salt would say something like that to a woman. No man who called himself a man would be so weak-livered as to say he *needed* a woman.

And definitely no Rosswarne in the history of the breed had ever said he was *sorry*. Rosswarne men might have regrets that haunted their sleep and ate at their souls, but they sure as hell wouldn't give voice to such a milk-livered sentiment. That kind of softness was left to the women in the world. Yet when he looked at Lottie, that was all that ran through his head.

Sorry, sorry, sorry—I am a sorry son of a bitch.

Eleven

Lottie dragged the wet cloth over her body again. She had filled the bath with the hottest water she could stand. She had scrubbed her flesh until it was pink, and she still could not remove the imprint of Shayne's touch from her body or her mind.

She had never imagined, never dreamed that pleasure so profound could be had. But now that she had tasted it, she wanted more of what Shayne could give her.

Maybe this was why Marilee was so vocal on the subject. Could it be all the married women in town felt this bone-deep satisfaction when they lay with their men?

She closed her eyes and remembered Shayne's effect on her. Her insides tightened at the flush of pleasure that swept over her even now, when Shayne was nowhere around. Just the memory of him made her insides flutter.

Since they had returned to McTavish Plain he had kept his distance. Whenever they were alone Lottie found him watching her with the still, disapproving glance that could send her belly dropping to her toes.

It was odd, but now when he had her fully under his power, and because he held the threat of harm to her sisters, and because he could play her body like a well-worn fiddle, he seemed less happy with each passing day.

He had gotten what he wanted, and yet the raw, wounded look in his eyes returned more and more often.

"What is wrong with him?" Lottie mused, trickling hot water over her breasts. They were tender and felt fuller since Shayne had taken her innocence. It was as if she were ripening, becoming a true woman after years of being merely female.

She was nothing but a fool—a fool whose body sang like an instrument when Shayne applied his magical fingers.

What was she to do?

"Whatever it is, I'd better do it quick. Ian and Addie could return anytime," she told herself as she rose from the tub.

Tonight was the church social. It would be the first public outing since Shayne came to town.

"And I intend to be the perfect wife to Mr. Shayne Rosswarne," she said, slipping into her wrapper.

She had to find a way to reach Shayne's cold heart and convince him to leave McTavish Plain and Ian in peace.

But what was left to barter? She had given her innocence and her body. She had nothing left.

Only her heart and her soul.

Shayne heard Lottie moving around in her bedroom. Just the thought of Lottie and a bed in any proximity made him hard as a damned post.

Since they had returned to town he had kept his distance, but he wondered how long his shaky resolve would hold out.

"Not long with my pecker stiff as a rod," he said in disgust. Shayne had always prided himself on being a man who was not led around by his lower member, but here he was, standing stock-still in the middle of the parlor, thinking of crashing through that door and tossing up her skirts.

"If she's wearing any."

And damned if the woman didn't sound like a real wife the way she had told him to clean up and be ready by seven o'clock. He felt a grin pluck at his lips.

"Damned woman."

She was a caution the way she could stare him down better than any stone-cold killer he had done time with.

And damned if he didn't do what she said, just like an obedient child.

Here he was, scrubbed, shined, and polished to a fare-thee-well, waiting on her like some house-trained pet. He was pondering that disturbing fact when her bedroom door opened.

His breath caught somewhere below his gullet. Lottie was the most beautiful thing he had ever laid eyes on.

She was wearing a dress of a pale pink color. The material was some sort of smooth, light-looking stuff that made Shayne want to crumple it in his hands and bury his face in Lottie's lap.

And Lottie's bosom . . .

He licked his lips and wiped at his forehead. It had grown hot and close in the parlor as his eyes skimmed over his "wife."

The dress was cut low, real low, low enough for a man to glimpse a tantalizing swell of her sweet breasts. She had taken a scrap of creamy lace and stuffed it in the front of her dress, but viewing her flesh through the open holes of the netting only made Shayne more intrigued.

He wanted to jerk her to him and pull out that bit of lace with his teeth. Then he wanted to trail his tongue along the swell of breasts. . . .

"Are you all right?" Lottie asked.

His sexual fantasy shattered like thin ice. He swallowed and looked her up and down to assure himself this was real and not some dream.

"Uh-huh. You look mighty pretty, Lottie."

She blinked and gave him a puzzled smile. "Thank you, Shayne. Are you sure you're all right? Your cheeks are a bit flushed."

She crossed the space between them and put her cool palm against his cheek.

He nearly groaned with desire. This was the most disarming and intimate gesture he could imagine. It was the kind of thing a woman did when she loved her man.

The realization that Lottie certainly could have no love for Shayne ripped through his gut without warning. How could she have anything but contempt for a man like him?

But did he want love? Was he stupid enough to believe he could shed what prison had made of him and embrace a life with Lottie?

Because if that was the case, he had better rid himself of the notion right quick. As soon as he met Ian face to face, any slim chance he might have with Lottie Green would be dead as a doornail. That was the price he had to pay to be able to return home with his honor restored.

He was here for revenge, and after living with nothing but that goal and hunger for justice for so long, he wasn't about to put it aside for Lottie—not even for alluring Lottie.

"Lottie," he said softly, dipping his head into her soft palm, "you look like an angel."

She laughed. "Well, we both know I'm not." She took a step away from him and began to fiddle with the front of her dress. He watched her slender fingers adjust a tiny rosebud made of shiny ribbon. There were half a dozen of them scattered across her skirt, holding up a bunch of lace that looked as though it floated over the pink dress.

Shayne's throat closed up again. He felt that strange squeezing of his heart.

Could it be guilt?

"We better get going," Lottie said, lifting her gaze to Shayne. "We don't want to cause talk by being late."

The church was aglow in lantern light as Lottie and Shayne approached. They had walked, not touching, but near enough that he caught the fresh-scrubbed scent of her with each breath.

It was like being roasted slowly from the inside out to be so near her and not put his hands on her.

With each step her full, lacy skirt brushed against his leg. Fire smoldered in his gut and flowed to his hands. He wanted to turn and put his hands on her creamy shoulders. He wanted to kiss her deeply and long.

But he couldn't. Not again. Not after knowing that she had only opened herself to him because she feared him.

He hated himself for the stupid threat. Hated the way she watched him, wary and distrustful, when she thought he wasn't looking.

"Mmm, I smell apple cider on the breeze," she said.

Shayne lifted his nose and inhaled. All he detected was the sweet musk of Lottie at his side.

"Shayne, before we go in . . ." Lottie stopped and took his hand. "Please remember our bargain. My sister Mattie will be here. Please don't do anything to hurt her." She turned and picked up her skirts as she climbed the steps to the church door.

Shayne could only watch her and try to catch his breath. He felt as if he had been kicked in the gut by a mule.

But it's worth it—isn't it? To get my revenge, to be able to kill Ian McTavish and finally go home. It's worth it—it has to be.

"Swing your lady to the right . . ." A caller sent the groups of dancers swirling across the floor. Shayne watched, tapping his toes to the music.

Lottie's golden curls shimmered from the light of a dozen lanterns hung from the rafters. She was laughing and dancing with a tall mountain man. The tinkling sound of her joy made Shayne's gut tighten.

"She's a beauty, ain't she?" The voice at Shayne's back brought him spinning around. He found himself looking into Gus's weathered face.

"Yes, she is," Shayne admitted reluctantly.

"I took a special liking to those girls the moment they hit town. Funny about all of 'em not having any husbands with 'em when they got here."

"Yea, really funny," Shayne agreed while he continued to watch Lottie. The music had changed. Now the tall mountain man was holding Lottie close, his arm looped loosely around her waist.

A strange, bitter pain gripped Shayne.

"You are the only one of the girls' husbands to have survived—"

"What?" Shayne turned around.

"I said Addie's man—and Mattie's, too—died afore they got here. You're the only one to survive the journey."

Shayne turned and really looked at Gus. There was the glitter of speculation in his eyes.

"I guess I was just born under a lucky star," Shayne said.

"I would think so, with a woman like that carrying your name." Gus nodded toward Lottie. "Man would be a fool not to see that she's pure gold."

Shayne allowed his gaze to drift back to Lottie again. She laughed at something the big mountain man had said; the smooth column of her neck arched gracefully as they made a quick, twirling spin.

Shayne's belly tightened again. "A damned stupid fool, if you ask me," he agreed. Then he strode to the center of the room. Lottie's back was to him, so she couldn't see him coming. A fact, he thought wryly, that might be on his side.

"May I cut in," he said to the mountain man.

"I guess this man's got a prior claim, Miss Lottie. But save a waltz for me." He released his hold on Lottie.

Lottie's eyes were wide, her lips parted. She looked kissable. Shayne swallowed hard and held out his hand.

"Ma'am. May I have the honor?"

She hesitated for a split second, and that small hesitation cut Shayne clear to his soul. Then with a lady-like incline of her pretty chin, she stepped into his arms.

The men playing the guitar, fiddle, and mouth organ were far from expert, but suddenly the music was sweeter, the tune prettier, the light more pure. With Lottie in his arms Shayne felt cleansed and renewed.

"You're a very good dancer," Lottie commented with no small amount of surprise in her voice.

"Courtesy of my mama."

"I must admit I am surprised."

"Why, because a man who has done time in prison isn't supposed to be a gentleman?"

"Because much of what you have done since coming here has been less than gentlemanly," Lottie said honestly, though she regretted her words instantly. "I'm sorry. I shouldn't have said that."

"Yes, you should." He managed a tight smile. "It is the truth after all. I've bullied you, blackmailed you, and taken your innocence. It's only right that you should hate me."

"But that's just it, Shayne Rosswarne—"

Before Lottie could say more, Gus galloped over. With a gnarled finger he tapped Shayne on the shoulder.

"No fair hogging up the prettiest girl in town just 'cause she's your wife," he chuckled as he snatched Lottie from Shayne's arms and twirled her out onto the floor. The moment was shattered. But Shayne could not help but wonder what she had been about to say.

Twelve

"I'm telling you, Lottie, you have blossomed like a flower after a spring rain." Marilee looked her up and down with a glint of hidden knowledge in her gray eyes. "If a body didn't know better they might say you just recently became a woman—if you take my meanin'?"

"I do take your meaning clearly and I don't wish to discuss it, Marilee," Lottie said shortly.

She had danced so many dances that her feet ached, and now she was trying to cool herself by the cider bowl; but her eyes kept returning again and again to Shayne.

He stood near the wall talking with Alec Bowen. His brow was furrowed in contemplative thought. The lamplight made his black hair wink with inky lights.

"Handsome as sin, isn't he?" Marilee mused beside Lottie. "I can see why you set your lariat for that one."

Lottie's gaze settled on Shayne. Was it normal for her to have both lust and revulsion for him?

"Marilee, I don't have a mother, as you know," Lottie said abruptly.

"Mmmm. Is there something you would ask her if you did have one?" Marilee arched a brow and half-grinned. "Something of a personal nature?"

"Yes."

"Then spit it out. If I can't speak plain to my dress-maker, then what is the world coming to?" Marilee grinned good naturedly.

Lottie laughed in spite of herself. She took a deep breath to bolster her courage. "Well, when a man and a woman . . . you know . . . Is it normal, I mean is it unseemly for a woman to *enjoy* what happens?"

"Unseemly?" Marilee's mouth twitched, but to her credit she did not laugh in Lottie's face. "I can't say much about what is seemly, Charlotte honey, but to my way of thinking God gave us all these private parts and all these special feelings, and if He didn't mean for us to enjoy using them it would be an awful waste. In fact, He could've probably finished creation in five days if He hadn't bothered with the complicated parts of a man and a woman."

Lottie felt her cheeks flame. Plain-speaking Marilee had given life to her very thoughts and in some small way had justified the burning desire that was never far from her heart. She looked across the dance floor at Shayne. Had their passion touched his soul at all, or was lust the only thing involved on his part?

"I wintered with a fella from Texas once," Alec Bowen said before taking a deep pull on a jug that had been making the rounds from one man to another between dances.

He offered the jug to Shayne. Balancing the heavy crock on his elbow, Shayne tipped it to his lips. The burn of homemade liquor trickled down his throat. He didn't know if he would choke before he could swallow.

"Good, ain't it?" Miley had appeared and took his turn with the jug.

"How long have you been gone from Texas?" Alec asked.

"Texas? Is that where your people are from?" Miley jumped into the conversation, his eyes bright and cheeks flushed from the fiery libation. He leaned near to Shayne while he waited for the answer.

Shayne felt crowded by the affable men. It took a good measure of self-control to keep from elbowing his way out of the small crowd that had gathered around him. He clamped down his impulse and forced himself to answer the question.

"Yep, I'm from Texas, but I haven't been back in a number of years." Being reminded of how much he wanted to go home did not make the feat any easier.

"I wintered with a Texan . . . did I tell you that?" Alec said, his words a bit slurred. He took another pull on the jug. "Red Slovang was his name. Big, mean cuss. Tough as nails. I never could figure him out, though. He had big plans for himself in Texas. Fancied becoming something of a land baron."

"Shayne, your little woman looks lonely. If I were you I'd get over there afore those lanky twins manage to get to her first," Miley said with a drunken grin.

Shayne focused on two men who looked like mirror images of each other and who were doggedly working their way through the crush of people toward Lottie.

Lottie was talking with a handsome older woman. The soft, pale pink of her dress made her look virginal in the most sinful and arousing way he could imagine.

A hot kick of lust stole Shayne's breath away.

He knew what lay beneath those layers of lace and frothy pink cloth. He alone knew what passion and fire was housed in that soft, curvy skin.

Shayne felt the slow burn of arousal. It pooled in his groin and made his skin itch all over.

"Well, go. Don't just stand there gawking. Go claim your wife," Miley said, giving Shayne a good-natured shove.

His feet seemed weighted, his actions slow as he inched his way through the children, mamas, and fathers in the church-turned-social-hall. It seemed he would never reach her—that any moment another, more worthy man would take her hand and remove her from his life.

And then, suddenly he was there.

"Lottie, darlin', could I have this dance?"

They moved out into the center of the room. Shayne took her hand in his and lightly put the other one in the small of her beautiful back.

Then the fiddles, the mouth organ, and the guitar began a haunting strain. It was slow, mournful, and easy to move with. Shayne did not pull Lottie against him as some of the other men had. Instead there was the space of two or three inches between them. It was delicious torture to have her near enough to inhale her scent and yet not touch her.

His body strained to be nearer to her. The force of will it took to keep himself from kissing her was more intoxicating and powerful than anything that could ever come from a crockery jug. His head was spinning.

"Lottie, about what has happened . . ." Shayne's throat closed tightly. "About what I said—what I have made you do . . ."

"Yes?"

"I just wish I had known you were Ian's sister-in-law when I came to town," he managed to choke out.

It wasn't an apology, but it was probably as close as he was going to get.

"I know. So do I," she said. Then she turned her head and rested it against Shayne's chest.

His heart was beating so hard, he thought he might be dying. Lottie was in his arms, her sweet cheek against his chest while they swayed and twirled and moved to the sound of the sad refrain.

This was heaven on earth, and it was also a taste of hell. He had lived too long wanting to go home and mend old wounds to give all that up.

Shayne stared up at the stars while he and Lottie walked, side by side, to her house.

"You like the stars, don't you?" she asked.

He glanced over at her, the moonlight turning her golden curls into shimmering coils of gossamer silver. "Yep. There was a time I thought I'd never see the open sky again."

"Is prison so awful?"

"It's like being robbed of your soul. It's being chained and beaten and treated like an animal until you *are* an animal. Men to go prison, but that's not what comes out."

"Don't, Shayne." They were at her front door when she turned and trailed her fingers over his face. "Don't frown and scowl. And don't think about the past. You have your future now. You are free."

He looked into her eyes, pale and mysterious in the night, and felt his flimsy control slip. He had vowed he wouldn't force her to his bed again, but sweet Jesus, she was so warm, so inviting.

"Lottie?"

"Yes, Shayne?"

"I want you," he grated out. And then he swept her up into his arms, fumbled with the door until he got it open, and took her inside.

There were no more words, no hesitation, no thinking on his part as he marched into her bedroom and laid her down on the bed. She looked up at him with a half smile. Shayne ignored the pain in her eyes and the regret in his own heart as he tossed up her skirts.

It only took moments for him to free himself from his trousers and plunge into her. He rode her hard and fast and soon spent himself. It was what he wanted— what he needed.

But when he rose up and saw the shimmer of tears in her eyes he died inside. His blackened soul withered and curled up.

"God, what have I done?"

Shayne heard the faraway knock on a door and opened one eye. The soft, feminine hush of women's whispered voices in another room brought him up from the bed. He slipped into his trousers and crept to the bedroom door to open it quietly, creeping out, padding softly in his barefeet through the parlor.

He hesitated by the table, where a small hoop of material lay. There was fresh a needle and several colors of thread.

Lottie had been sewing. He fingered the close, tight stitches and remembered what she had told him about tamping down her spirit while she learned to sew. It touched him and reopened the raw wound of last night's deeds.

He had taken her fast and furiously and then in his

shame had left her there in silence while he went to his own bed like the skulking bastard he was.

He had wronged her again.

"It was Ian. Miley was sure of it." Mattie's voice drew his attention.

The whispered bit of conversation touched his ears, drove any kindness and remorse from his heart.

Ian was coming home.

And I'll be waiting.

Shayne turned and went back into his bedroom. He pulled on his boots and shirt. Then he found the ruby red garters and eased them up his arms just above the elbows. The black vest went on next, and finally the holster. With grim determination he tied off the thong at his thigh, snugging down the weapon until it was solid and tight against his leg.

He did a quick draw then checked to make sure the side arm was fully loaded. While Lottie was still whispering to her sister, he slipped out the front door and walked around the opposite side of the house.

He would be waiting for Ian the moment he arrived.

Mattie's face was a mask of fear. She stood on Lottie's porch whispering and trembling. "I thought you would want to know. I mean when Addie comes home and finds *him* here there's going to be a lot of fur flying. She's not going to like it one bit that you are pretending to be his wife."

"Right now Addie's disapproval is the least of my worries." Lottie pulled her wrapper tighter around her body. Fear had chilled her. She glanced toward the bedroom door. At least Shayne was still sleeping.

Maybe there was a chance she could get him out of town before Ian and Addie arrived.

"Where did Miley see them?" Lottie asked, her mind and heart racing.

"At Johnson's Wallow. Since Miley was on a saddle horse he made it to town fast. In a buggy, I guess they should be here in about an hour. Miley thought the town might want to meet them and give them a formal welcome home."

Lottie swallowed hard. If Shayne had his way it would be a welcome that nobody in town would soon forget.

Shayne kept to the alleys, working his way along the back side of the storefronts and houses. He made his way through the town without seeing anybody. The sun was a bright golden disk. He crept into the barn and saddled Little Bit.

"Easy, boy," he said. "I intend to ride hard and fast as soon as this is finished."

The image of Lottie, her lips swollen from his kiss, her eyes languid with passion, ripped through his mind. For a moment Shayne went weak in the knees. He shook his head and fought the strange, crippling emotion.

"I am not going to let my revenge be ruined by a doe-eyed woman," he said between clenched teeth. Little Bit's ears twitched and he raised his head. "I have waited years for this to be done so I can go home."

Shayne heard the unmistakable clatter of iron buggy wheels in the distance as he fastened the cinch.

"The time has come for Ian McTavish to die."

* * *

Lottie dressed with care and fixed her hair on one side with long coils of her curls trailing down her neck. If she could charm Shayne into taking her for a long buggy ride, then Ian and Addie would be in their house before he even knew they were back.

She tiptoed past his room and went into the kitchen. She put coffee on to boil and fried some bacon and eggs. When she had the breakfast done and two plates arranged on the scrubbed pine table, she brushed her hands down the front of her skirt, patted any loose curls into place, and went to his room.

She knocked softly and waited. When there was no response she knocked a little louder.

And still there was no answer.

Lottie flung open the door, knowing what she would see. The bed was carelessly made and all of Shayne's belongings were missing.

"Oh Lord, he knows!" Lottie gasped, and she turned and ran for the door.

"Please don't let me be too late to save them all."

Thirteen

Shayne crouched in the long shadows of morning light and watched while most of the citizens of McTavish Plain gathered at the edge of town. They wore the expectant smiles more often found on children than on the faces of adults. Whispers of joy because Ian and his wife were returning floated on the morning air. It was still a puzzle to Shayne that a bastard like Ian McTavish could inspire such loyalty and devotion. How could a man who let so many Indians perish from starvation end up showing care and concern for an entire town?

It made no sense.

But it didn't matter anymore.

Shayne was going to call him out and be done with it quickly. He didn't intend to ask the whys or wherefores. He was simply going to shoot McTavish and cleanse his soul in the man's blood. It was what his upbringing and family honor demanded.

It was justice. It was high time. It was the price of finally being free of the shackles of prison and betrayal and being able to go home a whole man.

Once again the image of Lottie flashed in his mind. His heart contracted with a painful pinch when he realized that after today he would never see her again.

He could never face her once he killed her sister's husband.

"Look, there they come!" a voice cried out.

Shayne raised his head and looked over the top rail of Miley's livery fence. A buggy was rolling into town, spraying little rooster tails of dust in its wake. Shayne could not make out the details, but he could see two people.

Ian and Addie—Lottie's sister.

"Now, Ian McTavish, you will pay for stealing my life and my good name," Shayne said bitterly as he flexed the fingers of his gun hand.

Lottie ran from her house with her heart pounding in her throat. The town was deserted, all the store-fronts shuttered and locked. They would all be there waiting for Ian.

"And so will Shayne. Oh, please, Lord, let me be in time."

Lottie grabbed up her skirts, hiking them high and running for all she was worth. She had to stop Shayne. She couldn't let him hurt Ian, Addie, or Kathryn—not and live with herself.

When Lottie rounded the corner near the livery stable, she stopped and scanned the crowd. Everyone was there, crowded into a tight clutch of humanity. She stood on her toes and craned her neck, but there was no sign of Shayne.

Then she saw the flash of scarlet against black. It was Shayne, dressed in black like the grim reaper, except for those satin garters.

"The color of blood," she murmured.

The buggy was moving at a good clip, right toward

the throng of people. They moved as a cohesive group, and at the edge of the mob Shayne flitted like an unseen specter.

"I will never make it in time," Lottie gasped as she began to run again.

Shayne felt as if he were walking in a fog. The moment he had dreamed of, the thing he had sought, the vengeance that had been his reason for staying alive, was now at hand.

Memories of Lottie and the cruel things he had done weighed heavily on his mind, but he had to do it. Ian's betrayal and all that had happened to him in prison justified his actions—demanded the cold-blooded murder Shayne was about to commit. Or so he told himself as he began to walk toward the buggy.

He was jostled and elbowed by the happy crowd, but he didn't care. Steadily, slowly, he inched closer to his destiny.

He had come too far, done too much to turn back now. When Ian McTavish was dead, Shayne would be free of the past. He would have regained his honor. His father would be satisfied, his name restored.

He could go back to Texas and face his father with his head held high.

That thought had driven Shayne like a rider with spurs. He had been duped, betrayed, and locked up. He couldn't go to his father and tell him the tale without being able to say he had killed his betrayer and regained the honor of the Rosswarne bloodline.

Ian McTavish had to die.

Anything less was not acceptable.

Not to Shayne's father.

Not to any man with Rosswarne blood in his veins.

Shayne couldn't see the people in the buggy over the heads of those in front of him, but he saw the black leather cover over the top of the conveyance buck and jiggle as the buggy halted and someone stepped to the ground.

He heard the rumble of greeting, the squeals of delight as the women welcomed whoever it was that had been in that buggy with Ian.

Addie.

The name popped into Shayne's head. It would be Lottie's eldest sister.

A cold fist of regret threatened to squeeze off Shayne's air, but he shoved it aside.

He had no time for softness or pity. No one had shown him pity or concern—or even friendship—for years.

Not until I came here to McTavish Plain.

Every person here had treated Shayne with respect. It hurt him in a way he hadn't expected, to know he was about to be diminished in their eyes when he did what he had to do.

"Hey, Ian, married life agrees with you," Alec Bowen said, striding forward.

Shayne pulled his gun and stepped out, planting his feet in a fight stance. "Ian McTavish, show yourself!"

The crowd parted; questioning eyes turning in his direction. Shayne scanned the crowd. He marked every face, dying a little inside as the recognition of each citizen registered in his brain as he searched for Ian.

"Where are you?" Shayne bellowed again, feeling as raw and mean as a wounded bear. "Where are you hiding, Ian McTavish?"

The townsfolk looked around at one another, clearly confused by Shayne's words. He took the time to study each face again, but Ian McTavish was not among them.

Where was he? Was this some cruel trick?

"Ian McTavish!" he yelled again. "Damn you, come out."

A tall man with dark hair stepped forward, gently pushing behind him a woman holding a baby as if to protect her from Shayne—as if he were there to harm an innocent woman and child.

"Aye, lad?"

"I asked for Ian McTavish." Shayne said, trying to look behind him to see if the cowardly bastard Ian was hiding in the buggy.

Suddenly Lottie was there. "Shayne you can't do this."

"I can; I must. Now where is he?"

Lottie glanced at Ian, who stood no more than a yard away from Shayne. The brawny Scot was hard to miss. She shivered at her own thoughts as his eyes slid to the smooth, cold barrel of Shayne's gun.

"Shayne?" she said softly.

"What?" He spared a quick glance.

"Don't you know what he looks like?" Lottie asked with a frown. Even a half-blind man would be able to see Ian.

"Of course I know the rotten, lying skunk. Now where is he hiding?" Shayne was searching every face, but there was no Ian among them.

"What do ye want McTavish for?" the tall man said in a rough, burred accent.

"I want to kill the son of a bitch." Shayne snapped.

"Then ye best be gettin' started, lad, for I am Ian McTavish."

Shayne looked up at the man in confusion. He was taller than Ian. . . . His hair was not rusty red. . . . He had no wicked scar on his cheek. . . . The index finger of his left hand was not missing the first joint.

Shayne shook his head as if he might clear the fog of confusion. He leveled his gun to force the man out of his way. Suddenly pain burst in the back of his head. Black stars danced as the world went dark.

"Oh my Lord," Gert moaned.

"If this ain't the dangedest family," Gus commented. "First Addie shot Ian and now Lottie is clubbing her poor husband to death in the street."

Ian and Addie looked at one another and then at the gunman lying unconscious on the ground.

"Husband?" they said in unison as their eyes bored into Lottie.

Lottie was trembling when she let the length of firewood slip from her fingers. It hit the ground with a thud, not unlike the sound she had heard when she hit Shayne. The magnitude of what she had done turned her knees to water.

She fell beside Shayne. "Oh, please don't be dead, darlin'. Please don't be dead."

"Honey, I think you ruined his fancy hat," Gus said dryly as he picked up the misshapen black Stetson. There was a big dent in the crown and the brim was bent down.

Lottie was rubbing her hands over Shayne's head. She felt something warm and sticky. Blood covered her fingers.

"Oh, my God, I have killed him," she moaned in misery.

"Here, a couple of you boys grab his legs. Ian and Alec, you two get his arms. Let's take him home so he can spend his last moments happy in his own home," Gus said with a wry grin.

Lottie glanced at Addie. Her sister's eyes were wide as she glanced from Shayne to Lottie and back again. She would have a lot to explain; that was obvious. But how could she tell Addie that her "husband" had vowed to kill Ian? And how could she tell her that she had just murdered the man she had given her virtue to?

"Here put him on my bed," Lottie directed.

The men gingerly put Shayne down. Lottie immediately started to unbutton his shirt while Miley and Gus tugged off his boots.

"No!" Shayne roared as he came up swinging. His fist narrowly missed Lottie's face as she stumbled back. "You bastards are not going to put me back in the box. You'll have to kill me first."

Shayne made an effort to rise, but at the same instant, as if they all shared the same thought, Miley, Gus, Alec, and Ian descended upon him in a rush. They forced him down to the feather mattress by sheer brute force.

"No. No." Shayne said, but his words were slurred and suddenly he went weak. He fell back onto the bed moaning.

"Don't hurt him." Lottie pushed her way through the men. "Oh, I didn't intend to kill him."

"Oh, he'll live," Alec said. "That ain't much of a bump. You didn't come close to killing him."

"But the blood—"

"Head wounds always bleed like a stuck hog. You ain't kilt him," Gus said with a twisted grin. "But I'm mighty curious why you thwacked him like that."

"Aye, 'tis a tale I am wantin' to hear myself." Ian said grimly.

Lottie glanced around at Alec, Gus, and Miley. Then she focused on Ian. His face was stern, his eyes guarded.

"Not now. I must tend my husband first. Ian, would you have Addie come to me when she's settled?"

"I dinna like to leave you without knowing what is amiss, but all right. I will do as you ask. But make no mistake, Lottie Rosswarne, I will be wantin' to know why your husband is trying to kill me and why you clouted him on the head. And I will be wantin' to know it soon."

"But Lottie, I just don't understand how he found you. I mean, when we left Gothenburg we also left behind our real last name. How on earth could he have tracked you down?" Addie said, frowning at the man stretched out on Lottie's bed. She had left Kathryn with Gert and had come as soon as Ian delivered the message from Lottie.

"He didn't come looking for me, Addie. He came to town looking for Ian. I just happened to be here pretending to be his wife."

"Why was he looking for Ian? He didn't even know who he was when he was looking straight at him."

"That is what I can't figure out, Addie. He says Ian betrayed him, framed him, and had him sent to jail for something he didn't do."

"Nonsense," Addie snorted. "Ian is the most honorable man I know, and you know it too, Lottie Green."

"Rosswarne. That's my name, remember?"

Lottie glanced at Shayne. He hadn't moved in all the time it took for her to bathe his wound and put two neat stitches in the back of his head.

He was pale, but even now he appeared as powerful as a dark archangel stretched out against the pale muslin bedcovers. His chest, lightly covered with a sprinkling of curly dark hair, rose and fell evenly. The white lace and pink ribbons of her pillow were at odds with the lean, dangerous look of him.

Even in sleep he was handsome and lethal.

"Charlotte *Rosswarne,* just exactly what has gone on between you and this man while I've been gone?" Addie demanded indignantly.

"Don't ask, Addie; you won't like the answer," Lottie said, bending over and touching her palm to Shayne's forehead.

"Lottie, have you fallen in love with this man? This killer? He is wild, a rake and rambler and . . . and . . ."

Lottie stood up straight and looked into her sister's eyes. "And just like me. I am not like you, Addie. I tried to be; Lord knows I have sewn a million stitches while I tried to be. But I'm not. Inside me there is a restlessness that nobody understands—except Shayne."

"But do you love him?"

"No, I don't love him, at least I don't think that I do. I would be a fool to love a man who tried to kill my brother-in-law and who only wants rid of me so he can reclaim his old life. No, I couldn't love a man like that," Lottie said softly.

Fourteen

Shayne slowly turned his head. A stick of dynamite exploded behind his eyes.

Pain—throbbing, numbing pain—swept through his head.

He raised his fingers and gingerly probed the spot where the agony was most ferocious. There was swelling and a raw sting. His hair was matted—he supposed, with his own blood.

The recent events of his life were fuzzy and disjointed. He remembered having something important to do, but no details came readily to hand.

Having no particular reason to move and cause himself any more pain, Shayne lay still and silent, waiting for the pain to subside. The sound of footsteps outside his door grew louder. Whoever it was opened the door softly. Then he heard the scrape and footfalls of at least three people enter his room.

Shayne could feel their gaze upon him. Strange how a man could know he was being looked at—sized up and measured—without actually having to see it being done. Forcing himself to lie quietly while he tried to collect his scattered thoughts made his head hurt worse, but he did it. He kept his breathing even and lay perfectly still.

"He's still unconscious."

It was Lottie's sweet voice that washed over Shayne like a cooling breeze. His body reacted to her even though he kept his eyes shut. Every muscle and nerve in his groin tingled with the happy awareness of her presence. He could picture her in his mind, in one of her fancy frocks, her golden curls pulled to the side and cascading down over one creamy shoulder like a rich, gilded fall. Another pang of sorrow and guilt gripped him, twisted his belly, brought bile to his throat as memories formed and took shape. Everything came ripping back into painful, sharp clarity.

Shayne remembered looking for the bastard Ian in the crowd.

He remembered drawing his gun.

Damn it all. She was wonderful, she was passionate and because of Ian McTavish's betrayal, she was forever lost to him.

He hated Ian a little bit more for that.

"Is he daft, Lottie? Is that what ails him?"

A voice somewhat rough and foreign-sounding raked along Shayne's skin. He had heard the voice before, but he could not take hold of the thought that flitted through his pain-fogged brain.

"Oh, Ian, I don't know what to think anymore," Lottie answered softly. "And since you say you have never laid eyes on him before today . . . I just don't know what to think anymore."

Ian. Ian McTavish? She keeps calling this man who speaks with a rough burr Ian McTavish. But why? Why would they continue this deception when they think I'm asleep?

Shayne's eyes flew open. He looked at Lottie and the two men with her. One he recognized as Alec Bowen, the mountain man. And the other was the man who had stepped in front of him while he was calling out Ian McTavish to face him like a man.

"Who are you?" Shayne hissed, damning the nausea and weakness that threatened to lay him low as he struggled to his feet.

"I am Ian McTavish, the man you claim you are going to kill." Hard eyes bored into Shayne's face. "Now if you will be so good as to tell me why you want to do me to death, I would be obliged."

Shayne staggered a foot or so from the bed. He realized in a numb, cottony way that he was buck naked. Lottie watched him, her hand extended a bit as if she wanted to touch him but was afraid. That tentative, fearful look in her eyes cut him to the quick. He felt weak, vulnerable, and confused.

"You are not Ian McTavish. I know Ian McTavish. He is short, ugly, and has the first joint missing from one finger on his left hand. Now where is the bastard and why are you all protecting him?"

The tall man turned to Lottie. "I tell you, Charlotte, the lad is daft. Addie willna like that you have got yourself a daft hoosband."

Shayne's head was pounding so hard, it felt like it would split open any moment. His vision was blurry and the room tilted crazily. He managed another staggering step toward the tall man.

"You are not Ian McTavish," he said through clenched teeth. The throbbing in his head was like a war drum.

"Yes, Shayne, he is Ian McTavish. But I know the man you describe," Alec Bowen interrupted. "The short man with red hair and a damaged finger—I know him."

Shayne swiveled his head toward Alec. The action

brought a spike of pain behind his eyes. "Of course you know him. This is his town. I want Ian McTavish. He rode in yesterday, but you all must've hid him. Where is he? Let the coward show himself."

"I am a patient man, lad, but have a care who you call coward," Ian warned gruffly.

"Shayne, this *is* Ian McTavish. The man you describe is named Red Slovang. I wintered with him once in Texas. He has a missing finger and a scar that runs right along here." Alec drew his finger along his jawbone. "As far as I know, that man never left Texas soil once in his life. He has never been to McTavish Plain."

Shayne blinked and stared at Alec. The man standing next to him was the person everyone claimed was Ian. A sick wash of dread swept through Shayne as the truth seeped into his brain.

"But—but, it can't be. He said his name was Ian McTavish. I have spent years hating the name of Ian McTavish."

Shayne's knees folded beneath him, and the lights of the world were snuffed out as a million regrets and sorrows pummeled his heart. He had hurt Lottie— turned her into his whore—and it was all for nothing.

He wanted to die.

Lottie bathed Shayne's fevered brow with a cool, damp cloth. He had been in and out of consciousness for more than a day. Now and again his eyes would open, but he didn't see her. He would swear and fight phantoms. Ian and Alec, who had not left his side, would hold him down until the madness passed.

"What do you think ails him?" she whispered aloud, not really expecting an answer.

"The lad is plagued by demons," Ian said gravely. " 'Tis plain from what he says that the lad suffered in prison. When he speaks of the box it sends shivers down my back."

Lottie realized with a pang of dread that Ian knew Shayne had been in prison . . . and if he had been in prison, then he couldn't have been trailing cattle. She supposed that her brother-in-law thought she had lied because she didn't want to be shamed by Shayne's past. Perhaps that was for the best. She would let him go on thinking that way rather than do or say something to expose her sisters.

"I heard about prison boxes," Alec's deep voice rumbled. "Like dark cages they are. Men are put in them in all weathers. They cook in the summer and freeze in the winter. Most don't live through the time they spend in those boxes. Or if they do, their minds are gone."

"Shayne's mind isn't gone. I just hit him too hard. He'll be fine. He has to be. He has a lot to answer for." Lottie was not so dishonest with herself to blame Shayne entirely. She had admitted to herself in her heart of hearts that she submitted to his attentions not because of his threats to her family, but because she wanted him.

She wanted him still. But he did have a lot to answer for, and she didn't intend to make it easy for him.

Now that Ian, the real Ian as it turned out, was not the man Shayne was after, they could have a future together. All Shayne had to do was get well and forget this nonsense about revenge. After she made him suffer a bit for his actions, they could settle down to a real life together.

It was easy. Everyone in town believed they were

married. They could go on as they were. They could be happy. And when she went on her adventure to see the world, Shayne would be at her side. He was the best companion, the one person in the world who understood her. He was her perfect mate.

But he had a little groveling to do first, and Lottie was just the person to see that he did it right.

"Don't you dare die on me, Shayne Rosswarne," Lottie said fiercely. "We've got a lot of living to do, and I intend for us to do it together."

"He's a tough Texican, Lottie. He won't die," Alec assured her with a solemn grin.

"He just better not." Lottie turned to face Ian and Alec. "Crazy man, letting some evil man fool him into thinking he was Ian. But all that is over now. Shayne just needs to get well and use the brain God gave him."

Alec raised a brow. "Once he's better and you're fully over your fear of him dying, the poor fool may wish he *was* dead."

"If I hear anymore nonsense about him wanting to track down that—what did you call him? Red Slovang?—and kill him, then you're right; he *will* wish he was dead. He near scared me to death. I can't live with that kind of fear."

Shayne drifted in a world of hellish pain. He was in the box, and then he was before his stern but loving father.

A man never stops until he has avenged his family or his honor.

Stern words that Shayne was weaned on. His father never let any slight go unchallenged, never stopped until he had obtained satisfaction. It was the Rosswarne code.

Now Shayne grappled with the memory of his hatred, his desire for revenge, and the foolish mistakes he had made.

He had been chasing the wrong man. It was like poison in his belly.

Now he had an additional reason to find Red Slovang and make him pay.

But what about Lottie?

Shayne had been taught that his value as a man was in his name—his honor and his ability to preserve it. It was who he was and what made him a man. And though Shayne never ran from a fight or a beating in his life, he was ready to run from Lottie rather than face her after what he had done to her.

He would leave her and find Red Slovang. To do any less would forever taint the name and honor of every Rosswarne who had ever lived.

Lottie hummed while she stitched a new shirt for Shayne. He was better; his fever was down and he was thrashing less and less with each passing hour. She expected him to wake clear-eyed and clear-headed. Then she would begin. It was high time Shayne Rosswarne put aside this foolish notion of vengeance and started to really live his life.

Everyone in town believed they were married. Surely Lottie could think of some story that would explain Shayne's reaction to Ian's return. It was plain that Ian and Alec would go along with whatever she said about Shayne's strange behavior.

All she had to do was wait for Shayne to wake.

* * *

Away from town in the stone castle that sat in the shadow of Redbird Mountain, Addie nursed her daughter and watched Ian pace back and forth before the fire, as he had done since his return from town.

"Ian, is there something more that you're not telling me?" Addie asked, drawing her daughter gently away. The baby's lips continued to suck, glistening with a drop of milk as she slept safe and secure in her mother's arms.

"I dinna want you to fret, Adelaide, 'tis not good for you or the bairn."

"You must tell me or I will only worry more."

Ian heaved a heavy sigh. He turned to stare at his lovely wife and daughter. "Ah, Adelaide, we are so blessed, you and I."

"Now you are really frightening me, Ian." Addie swallowed hard. "Tell me."

"I think your sister has given her heart to a man who is plagued by demons and haunted by his past. I dinna know if even her love can save him. He is driven by revenge and tortured by things he did and did not do. 'Tis not a pretty sight to see. And yet Charlotte loves him; 'tis plain as the nose on my face. I canna understand a woman's heart or a woman's mind, but in this case I afraid she is chasing rainbows and it will all come to heartbreak." He stared into the fire and heaved a great sigh.

For a moment Addie's mind was in turmoil. And then she thought of all she and Ian had survived. Not gunshots, storms or even Indian legends had been able to keep them apart.

Could her sister be given less adversity or less satisfaction in overcoming it?

"I have faith, Ian. Faith in love and the stubborn nature of any woman who carries the name of Green. My sister will meet the challenge. And if her love— *their* love—is strong enough, as you believe, they will come through."

He smiled then and came to her, gently dragging his knuckles down the side of her face. "Ah, lass, I am a lucky, lucky mon."

"Yes. I know."

Shayne kept his eyes shut and pretended sleep until he heard Lottie leave the room.

He had been playing possum for the most part since he had woken the day before yesterday. Each time he got the chance, he got out of bed and moved around, loosening up sore muscles and getting his strength back.

Lottie must have hit him hard, because he still had a bit of trouble getting his eyes to focus and seeing straight, but day by day his vision was getting better.

"And when it is better, I'll be away from here," he promised himself.

He had a man to find. And his honor to avenge.

"And from what Alec says, that lying, cheating son of a bitch will be found down in Texas." He did not want to admit that he was running as fast as he could to get away from Lottie.

Shayne had been watching the slow sinking of the sun into the west through the bedroom window. And while the fiery disk slid lower and lower, he had been trying to screw up his courage.

"I guess I am as ready as I'm going to get," he finally said aloud.

He got out of bed, and though he wobbled a bit, he managed to pull his trousers over his naked buttocks and get them buttoned after only three failed attempts to dress himself.

Finally he was wearing clothes and putting one foot in front of the other and he headed toward the door. It was not a large room, but the journey seemed long as he doggedly put one foot in front of the other. Shayne had been taught that making foolish decisions and then crying sorry was a sign of poor upbringing and weakness in a man. He had never apologized. And he wasn't about to start now. So that meant he was sneaking out—leaving before Lottie looked him straight in the eye and his courage turned to water.

He was sorry—sorrier than he could imagine being—for what he had done to Lottie. He had taken her innocence and forced her to lie with him. Just the thought brought a hot tide of shame and remorse climbing his neck.

"How can I ever look her in the eye again?"

It was just another reason why he had to leave, and soon. He had a quest and he had his shame. Both kept him from Lottie.

He had reached the door when suddenly it opened. And there she was, all soft angles and glowing beauty in a pale-blue wrapper. Her feet were bare and the sight of her small, delicate toes made his belly twist and tangle inside him.

"Shayne," she said in some surprise, her gaze flick-

Introducing Ballad,
A NEW LINE OF HISTORICAL ROMANCES

*A*s a lover of historical romance, you'll adore Ballad Romances. Written by today's most popular romance authors, every book in the Ballad line is not only an individual story, but part of a two to six book series as well. You can look forward to 4 new titles each month – each taking place at a different time and place in history.

But don't take our word for how wonderful these stories are! Accept our introductory shipment of 4 Ballad Romance novels – a $23.96 value – ABSOLUTELY FREE – and see for yourself!

*O*nce you've experienced your first 4 Ballad Romances, we're sure you'll want to continue receiving these wonderful historical romance novels each month – without ever having to leave your home – using our convenient and inexpensive home subscription service. Here's what you get for joining:

- *4 BRAND NEW Ballad Romances delivered to your door each month*
- *30% off the cover price of $5.99 with your home subscription.*
- *A FREE monthly newsletter filled with author interviews, book previews, special offers, and more!*
- *No risk or obligation…you're free to cancel whenever you wish… no questions asked.*

*T*o start your membership, simply complete and return the card provided. You'll receive your Introductory Shipment of 4 FREE Ballad Romances. Then, each month, as long as your account is in good standing, you will receive the 4 newest Ballad Romances. Each shipment will be yours to examine for 10 days. If you decide to keep the books, you'll pay the preferred home subscriber's price of $16.50 – a savings of 30% off the cover price! (plus $1.50 shipping & handling) If you want us to stop sending books, just say the word…it's that simple.

assion–
dventure–
xcitement–
omance–
allad!

A $23.96 value – **FREE** No obligation to buy anything – ever.
4 FREE BOOKS are waiting for you! Just mail in the certificate below!

BOOK CERTIFICATE

Yes! Please send me 4 Ballad Romances ABSOLUTELY FREE! After my introductory shipment, I will receive 4 new Ballad Romances each month to preview FREE for 10 days (as long as my account is in good standing). If I decide to keep the books, I will pay the money-saving preferred publisher's price of $16.50 plus $1.50 shipping and handling. That's 30% off the cover price. I may return the shipment within 10 days and owe nothing, and I may cancel my subscription at any time. The 4 FREE books will be mine to keep in any case.

Name _____

Address _____ Apt._____

City _____ State _____ Zip _____

Telephone (____) _____

Signature _____

(If under 18, parent or guardian must sign)

All orders subject to approval by Zebra Home Subscription Service.
Terms and prices subject to change. Offer valid only in the U.S.

DN081A

Get 4
*Ballad
Historical
Romance
Novels
FREE!*

**If the certificate is
missing below, write to:**

**Ballad Romances,
c/o Zebra Home
Subscription Service Inc.**

P.O. Box 5214,
Clifton, New Jersey
07015-5214

**OR call TOLL FREE
1-888-345-BOOK (2665)**

Passion...
Adventure...
Excitement...
Romance...

ll..l..lll...lll.l..ll.l.l.l.l.l..l..ll.l..llll..l

BALLAD ROMANCES
Zebra Home Subscription Service, Inc.
P.O. Box 5214
Clifton NJ 07015-5214

ing over him. "You were leaving? Without so much as a word of good-bye?"

He felt the awful kick of regret deep in his gut. And suddenly he was on his knees before her, wrapping his arms around her hips, burying his face into the warm, sensuous juncture of her thighs.

"Oh, God, Lottie," he moaned like a wounded animal. But he could not find his voice to say any more. He hated himself for what he had done. And it was too late to turn back.

He had to leave her.

Fifteen

Lottie woke with a start. It was still dark outside; only a pale line of gray marked the eastern horizon.

She had fallen asleep, like so many nights before, on the settee in her parlor with a blanket thrown over her. She had left Shayne there in the bedroom, on his knees. How could she have stayed? It killed her to see him like that, to see how he hated himself. He was such a proud man. She didn't want to shame him by watching him at such a low and vulnerable point.

Now her neck was stiff and her back cramped as she got up and stretched. Would he be his old, confident self today? Or would the impact of having chased the wrong man still be eating at him?

The house was quiet, but it was more than just the quiet of slumber. It was as if it were empty again—like it had been before Shayne had come into her life

Lottie ran to the bedroom and threw open the door. The bed was empty and all signs of Shayne having been there were gone. Without taking time to comb her hair or change her rumpled dress, she dashed from her house, heading for Miley and Gert's livery stable. The horses nickered softly in greeting as she shoved open the heavy barn door and ran inside.

The stall that Little Bit had occupied was empty.

Lottie ran outside and looked west down the empty

street, little more than a black ribbon in the weak dawn.

"Shayne!" She screamed. "Damn you for leaving!"

There was no sign of him, no telltale trace of his passing. He had left her in the night.

He had left her.

Shayne shivered and glanced at the horizon. It was still a good hour until the sun would blaze into the sky and warm the ground he rode upon. It would be hours yet before anybody realized that he had gone. Hours before Lottie would rise and realize that he had finally left her in peace—left her to pick up the threads of her life.

Little Bit was a good night horse, his footing sure, his pace steady. And he obligingly set a comfortable pace that covered a good amount of ground.

"I wish Lottie happy," he mumbled softly, his eyes staring into the dark gray of the predawn. He clamped his jaw hard, trying to ignore the voices in his head. If he lived to be a hundred he would never forgive himself for the way he had treated her.

Shayne shifted uneasily in his saddle. He had wanted to beg her forgiveness on his knees, but the words had not come. He was the product of his stiff-necked upbringing.

A man did not beg. A man did not say he was sorry. *Even when he was so sorry his belly ached with the bitterness of it.*

He had crept from her bedroom but paused long enough to stare in wonder at the placid beauty of her sleeping face. He knew his soul was damned. Not a day would go by that he would not remember Lottie and taste the bile of regret.

"But I could not stay. Not for her and not for me," he said sharply.

He had shamed her, forced her—hell, he had practically *raped* her. It was like a hard, cold stone in his gut, this guilt he carried. He would never wipe this stain of shame and sin from his blighted soul.

Lottie stared at her reflection in the looking glass. Her eyes were red and swollen from crying, her lips rough from biting back the sorrow. She wanted to howl and scream, "Damn you, Shayne, damn you for a rounder and a rake."

Her pain gave way to rage. "You think you can waltz in here, upset my life, take my virtue and just leave me? *Leave me?* Well you are wrong. No man takes from me and then leaves like a thief in the night."

With steely determination, Lottie picked up one long golden curl, rubbing it between her thumb and forefinger one last time. She swallowed hard and took a deep breath. Then with her sharpest sewing shears she lopped it off. The scissors sang with a high-pitched tone as one by one her long, carefully tended tresses fell to the floor.

Shayne had made good time. By midafternoon the landscape around him had changed enough to shake him from the strange lethargy that had gripped him. With a start he realized that he had not even stopped to water Little Bit.

"I bet you're done in," he muttered, scanning the

area for a good place to camp. Just by chance, beyond the tall fringe of a sugar pine, the silvery trickle of water caught his eye. He rode to the small stream and dismounted. Little Bit immediately buried his nose in the water and drank deeply, his thirst stabbing Shayne's conscience. He yanked off the saddlebags. With a few oaths for his careless treatment of his mount, he uncinched the saddle. When he dragged off the blanket, he saw that Little Bit was dripping wet.

Another pang of guilt seized him. Not only had his father drummed into him a code of honor, he had also had a few choice words about how a real man cared for his horse and stock.

"To make it up to you, old fella, we will camp here and get a late start tomorrow. That bastard Red Slovang has waited all these years; another day or two won't make much difference."

Nightfall came early. Summer had ripened and stretched into the shorter days of autumn without Shayne even noticing until now. He had been so caught up with his revenge and his sexual obsession with Lottie that he had not even marked the coloring of the leaves or the snap in the night air.

"Of course I slept soft and comfortable in Lottie's arms—her bed—her house," he said aloud while erotic images floated through his mind. It was odd, but he no longer was plagued by what had happened in prison; now he was haunted by a woman.

"A woman I wronged," he said with disgust. He tossed a stick into the small fire. He didn't need a campfire—hell, it wasn't even full dark—but he had wanted something to do, something to distract him from the bitterness of regret and the hollow longing that had become his constant companion.

He missed Lottie. He hated himself for missing her. Of course, he also hated himself for what he had done, but that didn't stop him from thinking about how sweet her body was and how she drove him to heights of passion he had never known.

It was like a snake chasing its own tail. Lottie had given him happiness and contentment that he never dreamed of. And now he lived with the deepest of regrets because of the joy they shared.

"And will never find again." He stretched out on his back and stared up at the sky, waiting for it to darken enough for the stars to come out. But while he watched the blanket of black and the millions of tiny lights, he did not find the same comfort or exhilaration of being free being beneath the open sky that he had when he shared it with Lottie.

The sound of a stick breaking underfoot brought Shayne fully awake. Velvet black engulfed him. His fire was dead. Night was full upon him. Now there was someone out there in the dark.

Someone coming closer.

He skinned the gun from its holster and narrowed his eyes, trying to focus as he rolled over onto his belly.

Another twig snapped nearby.

The sound had come from the right. Shayne pulled himself into a crouching position. At least with the fire out he wouldn't make any more of a target than he already was in the blackness of the night.

The scuff of a boot against the earth was close, really close. No more than three paces away from him.

Whoever was making his way loudly toward the camp was likely to step right on him at this rate.

Shayne pulled back the hammer.

A shadow loomed up before him. He raised the gun and took aim as he jumped to his feet.

"Stop or I'll put a bullet between your eyes," he growled.

Abruptly the sound of footsteps halted. Shayne squinted into the night.

"Who the hell are you and what do you mean by walking into my camp without warning?"

"I gave you all the warning you gave me before you up and left like some damn thief and coward."

"Lottie?"

"Well, do you plan on letting me into your camp, or do you plan on shooting me now?"

The fire blazed high, casting shadows over the ground and sending sparks into the night sky. But those embers were nothing compared to the sparks Lottie saw in Shayne's dark eyes. He was angry.

Well, she was angry too.

"Don't you have any sense at all?" he snarled. "I could've killed you. Came real damned close to putting a bullet into that stubborn little head of yours."

"But you didn't. So I don't know what you're yelling about."

She had found a good-sized boulder to sit on while she watched him spit and fume around his camp. With quick, angry movements, he had built the fire and was still busy gathering dried and fallen wood. It looked like he had enough to keep the fire going for a week.

"I could've. Damn, Lottie, I could've shot you." He

shook his head, never looking at her as he railed. "Lottie, you are the most reckless woman I ever met."

"So you have said five times by my last count," Lottie said in a voice that was far calmer and more reasonable than she felt. Shayne had criticized and chastised her all the while he was building the fire. It rankled her that he hadn't even spared her a good, long look.

What will he say? She wondered. *Will he now tell me that I'm less a woman than before?* Her old fears came back to haunt her, leaching off a bit of the anger that had carried her from McTavish Plain to this spot all alone. Once again Lottie worried that she was not quite proper, not quite ladylike.

But she found she cared a little less about those conventions than she had in McTavish Plain.

He frowned at the horse she had led into his camp. "Is that animal lame? Why in hell were you walking her?"

"No, she's not lame. I couldn't see the trail so I got off and walked her for a while." Lottie defended her actions with narrowed eyes and a defiant tilt of her chin.

"Guess it was a blessing you had enough sense to wear trousers for this little jaunt."

Ah, so he had noticed! He had seen she was wearing men's—well, boy's clothing.

"There, you should be warm enough till morning." Shayne stood up and slapped his hands together to clean off the dust. "And then I want to see you headed back to McTavish Plain before I start out."

"No."

"What do you mean, 'no'?"

"I mean I am not going alone to McTavish Plain."

"Yes, you are."

"The only way you can make me is to come with me, and that wouldn't work since you are hell-bent and duty-bound to defend your honor. No, Shayne, I'm afraid you're stuck with me."

Shayne stared up at the sky and sucked in a deep breath. "Good Lord, Lottie, what are you saying?" There was a hard edge of pain in his voice.

"I am saying I have wanted a grand adventure all of my life. And you are going to give it to me."

"I can't let my revenge go." He continued as if he had not heard her.

"Nobody is asking you to. A man is not a man if he doesn't defend his honor. I heard you say that so many times I'm quite sick of hearing it. Well, Shayne, you're a man, so I guess you don't have any choice but to kill this Red Slovang."

"I can't ever face my father until I settle this score with him. He's the man who duped me into thinking he was Ian. Now get some sleep; I want you to ride at sunrise."

"Fine, I don't mind traveling early." Lottie stood up and stretched, noticing how Shayne's gaze riveted on her bosom as it stretched the fabric taut across her chest. "Where are we going?"

"We aren't going anywhere," he growled.

"If you aren't returning with me to McTavish Plain, then I'm coming with you. And you might as well get used to the notion."

Shayne turned and started toward her. His movements were quick as lightning. He grabbed her shoulders roughly.

"If I have to shake some sense into you, Lottie *Green,* that is exactly what I'll do." He shook her again.

Her hat tumbled off.

He blinked and blinked again.

"My God Almighty!" Shayne gasped as he finally looked—really looked—at her. "What have you done to your hair?"

Sixteen

Lottie took satisfaction from the stunned look on Shayne's face. It was about time he paid her some mind and noticed her.

"I cut it off," she said simply.

"That I can see, but why?"

"I decided if I was going to be riding with you, looking for Red Slovang and having a grand adventure, that I would have to change my appearance. I didn't think I could have a truly wild quest with all that long hair."

"Damn, you ruined it!"

Lottie felt a sharp stab of pain at his words. Did he think she was ugly now? He peered at her as if she were some strange variety of creature. It hurt Lottie, but it also refueled her waning anger.

"Do you always do what you want without a thought for the consequences—the possible danger?" Shayne's hard voice was overloud, his features grim. His eyes flicked over her face, lingering on her lips, then returning to her cropped hair. "Why do yo have to act so rash?"

"I'm reckless," she yelled right back. "Don't you know by now that I'm wild inside, just like you?"

"I thought you had better sense, Lottie, darlin'." Though his words were harsh and taunting, the addition of *darling* at the end softened their impact. "Damn you for coming. Damn us both. But I can't let you ride with me, woman. Do you understand?"

"I understand more than you know."

He pulled her to him and kissed her. Shayne had not touched her or kissed her since she had clouted him on the head and he had realized that Ian was not the man he wanted to kill. She knew he was avoiding her because of guilt—because he thought he had forced her to do something she did not want to do.

So the only thing left was to prove him wrong. And this kiss was a good start in that direction. It was not the kiss of a man who wanted to avoid a woman. It was hot, demanding, and full of the untamed lust they shared.

He wanted Lottie; she was sure of it. No matter how much he protested, he wanted her.

Lottie tangled her fingers in his hair, tossing his hat away when it obstructed her hold. She stepped nearer to him and moaned softly when he ground his pelvis against her body. The tight-fitting jeans let her feel the hard ridge of his arousal.

No, he was not immune to her and what they had experienced, no matter what he said.

This was what she had dreamed about most of her life. This was what she had cut her hair for and what she had ridden out alone for.

She wanted Shayne Rosswarne and she wanted the danger. In spite of all the risks and all the reasons why she shouldn't, she wanted him with a bone-deep intensity that refused to be ignored.

He was like air to her. Without him she could not continue.

Suddenly he broke the kiss and pushed her from

him. His eyes were stormy and dark with passion. His breath was coming in ragged, short gasps.

"Damn it all, Lottie. I—I—I can't."

"Good, because I can't either." She said matter-of-factly.

"I-I don't understand." He stammered, staring hard at her, obviously confused by her words.

"You can't forgive yourself for what you did. Well, then, there is no reason for me to forgive you either."

"I can't blame you, Lottie. I would feel the same if I was in your place."

"I doubt it," she said softly.

He stared hard at her for a long moment; then he turned, scooped up his hat, and tromped off into the darkness.

Lottie stood with the taste of his bruising kiss still on her lips. "No, I can't forgive you until you forgive yourself, Shayne Rosswarne."

After waiting and replenishing the wood in the campfire twice, Lottie finally gave up on Shayne's returning to the spot where his bedroll was. She retrieved her bedroll and spread it out near the fire.

The stars overhead twinkled and shimmered, and though she told herself she was not tired, a heavy lethargy soon crept into her limbs.

Tomorrow . . .

Shayne knew the moment Lottie fell asleep. Her hand curled beneath her cheek and she snuggled into the rough blanket of her bedroll as if it were made of the finest satin instead of rough-woven wool.

God, she was a beauty. Even with her golden curls clipped short she was painfully exquisite to look upon.

"What am I going to do with you, Lottie?" he murmured as he stood over her. "If I send you back alone something might happen to you. And if I refuse to take you, I know damned good and well that you'll follow my trail and get yourself hurt or worse. I can't let you go chasing danger."

She sighed in her sleep and his blood roared through his body at the sound. It reminded him of the sounds she made when aroused.

His shaft hardened, tightened, and went rigid with desire. "I will not touch you again, Lottie. I can't allow myself."

Lottie woke to the smell of coffee and the brisk snap of wintry cold in the air. She burrowed under her blanket, not wishing to move from the cocoon of warmth that surrounded her.

"Get up." A hard boot nudged her behind.

"Not yet."

"Well, if you're riding with me, you're going to have to get moving. We'll be burning daylight soon."

She peered out over the edge of the rough woolen blanket. "You're letting me go with you?"

Shayne's glare could have curdled fresh milk. "Don't get any foolish ideas. I don't want to take you with me, and if I thought I could keep you from following me, I wouldn't do it. But I know you, Lottie. There's a streak of cussed willfulness in you that won't be stopped."

She hid the grin that curved her lips behind the blanket.

He glowered down at her, a cup of coffee in his hand. "Don't look so damned happy about this, Lottie. You've left me with no choice. I'll be ready to ride in less than an hour. Keep up or get left behind."

"I'll keep up," she said, scrambling from the bedroll. "You won't even know I'm along."

As if any man within one hundred miles wouldn't notice you! thought Shayne, but he didn't say a word as she snatched the cup of hot coffee from his hands. He had the sinking feeling that he had just stepped into a bed of quicksand.

Shayne set a slower pace for the day's travel than he normally would have. He told himself it was not because of Lottie. He didn't care if her backside got sore, or if her muscles cramped. It wasn't for Lottie that he kept Little Bit under a tight rein and stopped to check his hooves every few miles, or took extra time to water the stallion from his hat, or made a warm camp at noon instead of eating cold biscuits and water.

It could not be for Lottie. A man who would use a woman, force her, and defile her as he had couldn't have that much decency in him.

No, it couldn't be for Lottie. . . . He wouldn't let it be.

It was her own fault if she was uncomfortable. She should have stayed in her nice, proper, secure home in McTavish Plain instead of gallivanting after the man who had wronged her.

Didn't the woman had a speck of sense?

Nope. She didn't, and neither did he to be taking her with him.

"What cock-and-bull story did you make up before

you left town?" Shayne asked suddenly when the question popped into his head.

"What makes you think I made up any story, or that if I did, it must be a cock-and-bull story? Maybe I just told everybody the truth. Maybe I just told them all my life I had been fighting my own nature and I finally decided to give in to it."

"Uh-uh, darlin'. I was born in the day, but not yesterday. If you had told anything near the truth, neither your sisters or that big Scotsman Addie is married to would've let you out of town. Not to mention Miley and that old reprobate, Gus. I've seen how he looks at you when he thinks nobody is watching."

Lottie turned toward Shayne and grinned. "Shayne Rosswarne, are you jealous of Gus?"

"Of course not. What an infernal stupid idea. Why would I be jealous of an old fool like Gus?"

Lottie didn't say more, but she felt a warm glow simmering inside her breast. Shayne was jealous. She could read it in the taut line of his shoulders and the way his hot, dark eyes had flicked over her face when he spoke.

"Well, what lie did you tell this time?" he asked gruffly.

"I left a note saying you and I had decided to go away for a while."

"Ah, so nobody will be expectin' us back anytime soon. Your sisters won't believe a word of it."

"Probably not, but they won't follow me either," Lottie said smugly.

"Pretty cocksure of yourself, aren't you?"

Lottie glanced at Shayne. His jaw was just as hard and tense now with sun dipping low in the western sky as it had been when the sun peeked over the eastern horizon that morning. They might be talking, but beneath his teasing conversation he had not loosened up one little bit.

"I only wish that I was sure of what I was doing," she finally admitted in a whisper. She knew what she wanted all right, but she was completely unsure of how to get it.

He didn't turn to look at her, but she saw the muscles across his wide shoulders bunch up as if he had been touched—and didn't like it.

It made Lottie see a red wash of anger all over again.

She rode right up beside him and reached across the horses. Her fingers wrapped around the reins. She pulled Little Bit to a halt.

He turned to glare at her then. His eyes were snapping with fury.

"Look, I am along whether you like it or not. Now you can make that fact as pleasant or as unpleasant as you want. Where are we headed on this quest for vengeance?"

"To Texas; now get your hand off the reins and get off that horse."

"Why?" she asked defiantly.

"Because I intend to teach you how to play poker."

"Poker?" she repeated.

"Yes, poker."

Shayne had seized on the notion that if they played cards it might keep his mind off Lottie—off what he wanted to do with Lottie.

But now as he sat on the opposite edge of the blanket and watched her purse her soft, dewy lips in concentration, he realized his plan had been in vain.

How could any man breathing not be totally, completely, and hotly aware of Lottie?

"Now, you tell me how many cards you want to throw away." He was determined to get his lust under control.

She looked up and frowned. Her delicate brows beetling over cornflower blue eyes. "You just gave them to me. Why would I want to throw them away?"

"Because you want better cards."

"But these look perfectly fine." She rotated her hand, showing Shayne everything she held in her slender fingers. "I don't see anything wrong with them."

He shook his head and tossed down his hand. He snatched her cards away and folded them all together into a stack. He began to reshuffle. "Haven't you ever played cards of any kind?"

"Of course not. Playing poker and gambling is—"

"Not ladylike?" Shayne piped in without thinking.

"That's right." Lottie gave him a strange, contemplative look before she continued. "Playing cards is not exactly the kind of skill a proper young woman is taught. But I am glad you offered to teach me, because this is exactly the kind of thing I need to learn to have a grand adventure."

"Grand adventure my backside. You always wanted to learn, didn't you, Lottie, darlin'?" He gave her a sidewise glance.

She grinned and ducked her head, once again amazed that he could intuitively know her mind. "Yes, I wanted to learn. Once I sneaked behind the gambling parlor that was a few miles from Gothenburg. I earned the hiding of my life for that little stunt. But I thought it was worth it at the time. It all looked so exciting with the smoke curling around the players' heads and the money piled up in the middle of the table. I always yearned to taste that kind of excitement."

"Exciting?" Shayne shuffled one last time and started to deal. "The only thing exciting is the winning. The rest of the game is just a way to pass the time."

"I won't argue the point," Lottie said, scooping up her cards. "Just having you teach me how to play is exciting to me."

Shayne felt a kick as his heart tumbled in his chest. She was getting to him again—drawing him to her like a bee to a fragrant flower. He wouldn't do it. He couldn't give in. Not if he wanted to salvage a shred of his tarnished honor.

"Well, it's mighty evident you were watching all that excitin' smoke and not the cards being played. I can see we'll have to start with the basics."

"Such as?"

"Such as the person sitting across from you is not your friend, but your opponent." He leveled a stern gaze at her.

"You are not my friend; now you are my *opponent,*" Lottie agreed with a nod of her head. "I understand."

Jesus, how could a woman make perfectly innocent and simple words sound so deliciously sinful? Shayne wondered as he swallowed his lust.

"That's right. I am your opponent and your teacher."

"Ah, my *teacher.*" Lottie smiled and looked at him from under the fringe of short, golden curls across her forehead. "And what exactly are you going to teach me tonight?"

Shayne's breath hung in the back of his throat.
Lord Almighty!

"Well, go ahead, *teacher.* I promise I will be the perfect student: attentive, willing, and quick to try anything you want me to learn." There was not even a hint of humor in her eyes as she stared at him.

Maybe cards was not the best choice he could have made.

He had the sudden urge to run as fast as he could in the opposite direction, but he could not show himself to be so weak and cowardly.

Even if it was true.

Seventeen

The days fell into a pattern for Lottie and Shayne. They would rise before sunup, ride for a few hours, stop and eat, then ride some more till sundown.

Lottie knew he had set an easy pace for her. It made her heart swell with a feeling that was strangely akin to affection and gratitude. But at the same time, the strange, taciturn man made her furious by still insisting on punishing himself with guilt.

He clung to his misery and his guilt as though it were something precious. No matter what was said or done, he made no effort to forgive himself and move on.

He was as stubborn as a mule and as desirable as sweet sin in the dark.

She sighed and caught herself looking him up and down as he gathered the wood for the fire. Even though he growled and snapped at her at every possible opportunity, he also never missed a chance to make the journey as easy on her as he could.

Shayne made the coffee. Shayne fried the pork and whipped up biscuits to cook in the small pans he laid lip to lip in the bed of glowing coals each night.

It was he who carried water and saw to the stock. In fact, Lottie probably did less work out here on her wonderful journey than she did at home.

She ran her fingers through her short curls and watched while Shayne efficiently prepared their meal. Everything he did was accomplished with an economy of motion.

Soon the air was scented with frying pork and strong hot coffee. He used a stick to knock off the top pan and there were golden, hearty biscuits nested in the bottom tin.

"Come and get it, if you want any of it," he sang out.

She stared at him, wondering how much longer he would use his guilt and shame as armor against her. Was she a fool to continue trying to seduce a man who had vowed to never touch her again?

And then he looked up at her. In the deepset eyes she caught an unguarded look of hunger. Her heart leaped as Shayne struggled to bring his emotions in check.

He does want me!

"After we eat would you teach me some more draw poker?" she asked innocently.

"Sure, it helps to pass the time."

"Yes, it does do that," Lottie said softly. But her mind was singing with ideas—ways to make Shayne give up his guilt and self-imposed loneliness and return to her arms. Because her body ached to have him. She wanted him more than she wanted anything—except her one true, reckless adventure.

"I think I win," Lottie said, leaning near to Shayne. She had undone the top three buttons of the boy's shirt she wore, and seeing the way Shayne's gaze had flicked over her bosom all through her "lesson" she was quite certain he had noticed.

He swallowed hard and lowered his eyes to his cards. "Let me see what you've got." He reached out to take her cards, but Lottie didn't let go, making sure their fingers touched.

He jumped as if stung by a bee. A flash of satisfaction zipped through her. He might wish to ignore her, but that didn't mean his body agreed with the decision.

"Well, you have got a full house." His voice was spiced with amazement.

"See, I told you I win, darlin'," Lottie said happily.

"Uh-uh, darlin'. I told you a full house is three of one kind and two of another. My straight beats a full house."

Lottie frowned and scooted closer to Shayne. She could feel the delicious heat from his body when their thighs touched. Since she was traveling in men's trousers, there weren't layers and layers of fabric separating them now.

"Show me," she said bluntly.

Shayne cleared his throat and swiped at his forehead.

Was that sweat beading on his brow? No, the night air was cool.

"This is a straight: five cards in a row." His voice was rough and low.

"But look, some of them are those posies and others are wolf tracks." Lottie stretched over his arm until the weight of her breast rested on his forearm.

"What?" Shayne looked confused. He blinked and swallowed hard again. His gaze went to her breasts. "What do you mean, 'posies and wolf tracks'?"

Lottie reached out and pointed to the cards that Shayne held. She made sure to let her own body make contact with his during the entire process. Her nipples hardened at the slightest contact with him.

"Right there. These look like wolf tracks."

"They're called clubs, Lottie." His voice was husky and soft.

"Oh. Clubs." She scooted an inch closer. Now most of her leg was touching his thigh. She thought she felt his muscles bunch. "And these, the ones that look like a cluster of posies? What are these called?"

"Those are called spades."

"Oh. Spades."

He turned and stared at her. They didn't move, hardly even breathed. His eyes appeared bottomless, darker than usual and full of some unreadable emotion.

"So how can you have a mix of clubs and spades and still beat my full house?"

"Because, Lottie."

He was close enough for her to feel the warm whisper of his breath across her cheeks when he spoke. He licked his lips. She saw those telltale beads of sweat on his brow. He was as hot as she was.

"Why?"

"Why what?" he asked, his gaze flicking back and forth from her eyes to her mouth.

"Why does your hand beat mine?" His lips were only inches from her own. Her body had gone taut with need. Her nipples were rubbing against the fabric of the shirt with each shallow breath. She was glad she wasn't wearing a corset. She wasn't sure she could have kept from swooning if she had been laced up tight.

"I have five cards in a row," Shayne said, bringing her lusty thoughts back to the game.

"That seems like a silly reason."

"I know," he said gruffly.

"Then wh—"

Her question was swallowed by his kiss. Shayne groaned as if in pain and pulled her into his lap. His mouth was hot and hungry. His tongue invaded her mouth, tempting, swirling, mating with her own as she happily returned his kiss.

His hands were on her buttocks and then her breasts. It was as if he had to touch every inch of her body or die. Her heart trilled as her blood heated and rushed in her veins. This was what she had been waiting for.

"Oh, Shayne, make love to me," she murmured when he released her mouth and started sipping kisses along her throat.

He stiffened. Slowly, as if it required monumental effort on his part, he raised his head. He stared into her eyes.

"I—I can't—I won't," he said raggedly, and he set her away from him. He stood, rather stiffly Lottie thought, and stalked off into the dark.

"Well, so much for my skills at seduction," she chided herself aloud. Idly she picked up the cards and began to shuffle them. It was going to be another long and lonely night.

They rode side by side, but she might as well have been miles from him for all the mind he paid her.

"Tell me again what is the very best hand one may get in draw poker," Lottie asked. Though she did enjoy playing cards with Shayne, she only asked this question to get him talking to her again. He had sulked around with that pitiful expression of guilt and pain on his face for the entire day. Now she was just plain tired of watching him silently chastise himself.

"A royal straight flush." He said sullenly.

He was back to being cold and edgy and doing everything he could to avoid looking at her and speaking to her.

Suddenly her mare lurched, one foot coming up awkwardly. "Oh, my!" Lottie squeaked in surprise, gathering the reins, trying to pull the horse's head up.

Shayne was there in an instant. He swept Lottie from her saddle before she had time to think or react. She felt his strong, hard arm around her waist. Her breath dragged heavy and slow in her chest as she clung to him.

"Wh—what happened?" she whispered.

"Looks like your mount threw a shoe," Shayne said, but he wasn't looking at the horse; he was staring into Lottie's eyes. "That last nail pulled off a hunk of hoof. You'll have to ride double with me until we find a town with a smith to get her reshod."

Lottie sensed the conflict in Shayne. The last thing he wanted was to be holding her in his arms. She saw his reluctance in eyes that turned dark and shuttered at the same moment his arm tightened on her body.

"Just do me a favor, Lottie. Keep still and don't say a word—not one word."

Shayne shifted again, but it did nothing to relieve his painful erection. It was just his damnable luck to end up with Lottie sharing a saddle with him. Even though he had banished her behind the saddle, it wasn't far enough to do him any good. Every breath she took, every sigh she exhaled, touched his soul.

He had it bad, damn it all to hell, and he didn't know what to do about it. His treatment of her was unforgivable. That was the fact. He wasn't worth her spit.

It frightened him to know there was that kind of darkness within his soul, and he was determined not to let it free again.

And that just made him feel more guilty.

He didn't deserve someone as fine and good as Lottie. And so, in the way of a foolish man who has lost his heart and can't control what is in his pants, he had made himself a bargain of sorts.

He had to find a way to get Lottie to go home, whether she liked it or not. She needed to be in the bosom of her family. Maybe then he could sleep at night without the nightmares.

"Look." Lottie pointed to something beyond Little Bit's nose. Her slender wrist, so near his mouth, just begged to be kissed. He tamped down the urge and tried to ignore the sweet lure of Lottie.

"Isn't that smoke?" she said.

"Yep. Looks like we've found us a town, Lottie, darlin'."

"Oh, good I've been wanting a bath," she said with a sigh that made her breasts nudge him in the back.

"Uh-uh, darlin'. You aren't gettin' anywhere near that place. What needs doing, I will do alone."

"But—"

"No. Lottie, you may think you look like a twelve-year-old boy in that getup you're wearing, but I'm here to tell you right now that you don't."

"I don't?" She slid to the ground and stared up at Shayne. The sun showed tiny freckles that were beginning to grow on her nose.

"It would take about five minutes for every cowpoke, miner, and no-good saddle tramp to see you for what you are. I don't want to have to shoot anybody. All I want to do is find the smithy, get the mare reshod, and get back on the trail."

"But—"

"No. Lottie, this is my final word on the matter. Now stay here with Little Bit and keep out of sight."

"How do I know you'll come back?" she finally managed to ask.

"What did you say?" Shayne's voice was low and cold as he dismounted.

"You didn't want me along on this trip anyway. You think I should've stayed at home rather than have my adventure. It would be easy enough to get the mare reshod and just keep right on riding—without me. What kind of reassurance can you give me that you'll come back?"

"None," Shayne said with narrowed eyes. "I can't give you one speck of reassurance and I'm not gong to try. Now be good and amuse yourself with the deck of cards. I'm going to town—alone."

And with that, Shayne scooped up the reins to the limping mare and started walking to the town that shimmered on the horizon.

Lottie actually counted to twenty before she began yelling, questioning his parent's marital state at the time of his birth, but if he heard her insults he didn't bother to answer.

"Amuse myself with the cards," she said in a sing-song cadence as she fumed around the camp, kicking rocks. Then an idea popped into her head. "I think I'll do just that, Shayne Rosswarne. I will definitely amuse myself at cards."

She stared at the puff of dust on the horizon. "He

isn't coming back." There was a painful catch in her voice.

He wasn't going back.

No matter how tempted he was or how much he yearned for her company, Shayne had decided that he wasn't going back to Lottie.

"She will be better off. It will take her a while to realize I'm gone. I'll get the mare reshod and just ride on, like she said. Hell, she doesn't even trust me to come back anyway," he said, trying to justify the low-down thing he planned to do.

It's better for her. And he knew it was best, but the decision lay cold and heavy as a cannonball in his belly.

Shayne had found the smithy easy enough in the tiny, almost deserted town, but he had to wait while two other horses were being taken care of before the mare.

How could there be two horses needing shoeing when there weren't more than fifteen inhabitants in the whole place? Shayne wondered with a flash of annoyance.

The town, a collection of weathering buildings and deserted storefronts, had sprung up near a fort that nestled in a clearing nearby. But the fort was silent now; all the soldiers had gone to fight back East. The dying burg was little more than a cross-roads for trappers and a gathering place for saddle tramps now. A lonely collection of odd characters who shunned civilization now peopled the hamlet.

Shayne glanced up the street to the saloon. No matter how down and derelict, how empty and dried up, it seemed a town would always have a blacksmith and a saloon or two.

A whiskey would sure go down well. And maybe it would clear away the cobwebs of guilt that clouded his mind every time he thought of Lottie.

She'll be fine. The way back to McTavish Plain is straight and easy. Little Bit is sound and steady and she has all the supplies and bedrolls.

But still the voice in his head would not be silenced.

"How much longer on that horse?" Shayne asked.

The smith never looked up from the fire he was tending. "Two hours, mebbe three."

Shayne glanced back up the dusty street. A tumbleweed was growing in the rutted track, attesting to how long it had been since a wagon rolled through.

"I'm going to go find a drink. I'll be back," Shayne said.

The smith grunted and continued his labors without comment. So Shayne turned and walked up the street toward the hum and noise of the saloon. When he was closer he noticed that the double doors were wide open, allowing full freedom of movement. He idly wondered why no swinging doors covered the portal until a body came sailing out to land in the street with a thud. A puff of dust rose along with the drunk's pained groan.

Shayne stepped over the prone man and went inside. His spurs rang on the wooden floor as he elbowed his way through the crowd that had gathered to watch the abrupt eviction of their fellow.

"Whiskey," Shayne said to the bar-keep.

There was a long mirror behind the bar, but it was

too old, cloudy, and dust-covered to be of much use. Shayne hitched up one leg and rested it on the railing in front of the bar while he sipped his whiskey. He was somewhat surprised that it was good liquor—no spiking with gunpowder or chiles and snake heads in this bottle.

He studied the amber liquid and contemplated his life. He felt the dull ache of self-loathing for leaving Lottie, but it was best for her. Now he could get back on track—see to his revenge and regain his honor—and she could go back where she was safe.

And he could learn to forget Charlotte.

"Now, Miss Lottie, you just sit right here by me and don't worry about nary a little ol' thing. This next hand will be just as easy as huckleberry pie. If you need he'p you jus' say so."

Miss Lottie? No, it couldn't be. She wouldn't.

The hair on the back of Shayne's neck prickled. He wanted to turn—needed to turn—but something, some dreaded precognition, kept him frozen in place with the whiskey glass in his hand.

Lottie would not have followed him again. Would she?

"Damn right she would. In a heartbeat," he growled to his own dull, milky reflection. He tossed back the whiskey and turned, steeling himself for what he would see, and though he knew, he was still stunned by the sight of her.

Lottie sat with her back to the bar, her rounded backside snugged against the back of the battered chair. . . .

With her hat off.

Her short, golden curls shone like a beacon in the dingy, smoke-filled saloon.

Around her was a collection of ramblers, reprobates, and dust-covered wretches. They were staring at Lottie as if she were an angel come to earth. To Shayne they looked more like a pack of wolves ogling a spring lamb.

Shayne blinked and noticed one more thing about the woman and her adoring pack: Every bit of headgear, from skunk-pelt caps, to the faded red woolen knit cap of the Coeur de boise, was tossed to the floor beside the men's chairs.

Balding pates, tangled locks that had not seen a comb or fresh air in months, were now stripped naked and vulnerable in honor of Lottie.

Lottie. My Lottie.

He wanted to stride over and pull her from the chair, but he found himself rooted to the floor in astonishment. It was as if she had house-trained the group of men. When one of them used the cuspidor loud reprimands rang throughout the saloon until the perpetrator turned beet red and apologized for his crudeness.

"Now, Miss Lottie, you just let Cut-nose show you how to deal."

"Thank you, Mr. Cut-nose, that would be wonderful," she gushed.

Shayne pulled himself up to his full height. Was she batting her lashes at them? He nearly choked when he saw how she was simpering and fawning. Every man jack at the table flushed the color of new crimson long johns when she turned those lethal charms their way.

Each of the gamblers was a scarred, battered horror to look upon, and their unwashed bodies gave off an odor strong enough to reach Shayne's nostrils across the room. But Lottie acted as if each one were wearing Macassar oil and sporting a diamond stickpin in a silk neck cloth as she talked and giggled and played each hand of cards with charmingly scattered concentration.

Shayne wished he could make her smile like that.

Lottie managed the hard men like a canny shepherdess. It was both humbling and erotic to see her weave her magic.

"Well, I'll be damned," Shayne swore beneath his breath. It was like watching a mythical creature from some long-ago fable cast an enchantment.

"Ain't she a looker?" a voice behind Shayne asked. "She walked in here bold as brass asking if someone might teach her to play cards. There hasn't been a woman like that in this town since—since—well, hell I guess there ain't never been a woman like that here before."

"I don't doubt it." Shayne nearly choked.

"Yep, she is an original. I swear I never saw any of these flea-bitten galoots move so fast as they did to find her a chair and dust it off. At first I thought it was the sight of a woman in men's trousers that had them all het up. Nearly caused a stampede. But now I think it's just *her.*" The barkeep jerked his head toward the table where Lottie resided in all her splendor. "Those are not necessarily the fastest men with a side arm in these parts, but they are without a doubt the meanest."

"Mean? Those sops?" Shayne snorted.

The man grimaced. "I know it doesn't look like it now, but I've seen more than one of them kill a man for no more than belching or looking cross-eyed. That little lady has them eating out of her hand now, but old Griz there carved up a man last winter for snoring too loud. And Cut-nose there earned his name by the speed and accuracy of his knife in a fight. Those other three are just as bad."

"A true wonder," Shayne said through clenched teeth. Now he had another thought. If those men were as mean as their reputations allowed, his sudden demand that Lottie leave with him could put her in peril.

Did he want her to leave with him? Hadn't he ridden into town with every intention of leaving her so that she would have to return to McTavish Plain alone?

Funny, but right now that idea seemed stupid. He wanted to go to her, to make sure that all and sundry knew she was *his* woman.

But he couldn't—he wouldn't.

Shayne ordered another whiskey and held his tongue. He would have to watch and wait to see how Lottie handled this situation. God willing, Shayne would be there when she needed him. And he hated it, but his instincts told him that the time was not far away.

"Now tell me again, Mr. Cut-nose, what do you call this?" Lottie spread her cards in a fan on the scarred tabletop. Shayne saw every man swallow so hard that their Adam's apples bobbed like corks in water.

Mr. Cut-nose's eyes bugged out and his tongue shot through the hole where his front teeth had once resided.

"Miss Lottie, that there is called a royal straight flush."

"Oh, what a pretty name," Lottie cooed, in a way that made Shayne's blood rush fast and his heart tumble. Her voice must have had the same effect on the men at the table with her, because he heard breath being sucked in sharply as their eyes riveted on her face.

"And what do I win with a royal straight flush, Mr. Cut-nose?"

Did Lottie just lean over in a way that gave that smelly trapper a glimpse of her breast?

"You win all the pot," a mean-sounding man with a milky eye said. Shayne stiffened, ready to go and rescue Lottie, but suddenly the grim face split into a wide grin. Using hands as big and dirty as a bear's paws, he shoved a pile of coins and a couple of leather pouches toward Lottie.

"Thank you, Mr. Lefty. This card-playing is so much fun," she giggled.

The sound of her clear and unfettered laughter did something to Shayne's innards. He felt hot—restless, itchy, and mad at himself. A pang of physical sorrow sliced through him.

Why couldn't she laugh like that for him?

But he knew the answer. He didn't deserve her. He was sinful, wicked, and without honor. But Lottie didn't realize she would have been better off to have stayed in McTavish Plain instead of following him. Now she had put herself in more danger by following him yet again. She said she craved adventure, but Shayne knew the truth. Lottie craved danger and anything she wasn't supposed to have.

He clenched his jaw tight and tried to look away. But he couldn't. Lottie had him in her spell, just as she had those men around the table in her power.

"She swore she was going to have a grand adventure. I suppose this is the next step in her plan," he said glumly. He ordered another whiskey and hoped it would dull the hot throb of lust and frustration coursing through him.

Eighteen

The day dragged on, and soon twilight could be seen through the open doors of the saloon.

Shayne's head was muzzy from drinking whiskey and watching Lottie as she flirted and laughed and won at cards.

She still looked fresh and bright as a summer morning, though she had not had a break from her card-playing in many long hours. Before her was a sizeable mound of leather pouches—Shayne assumed they held gold or silver nuggets—and coins in front of her. And though she had won steadily, the men she played with still smiled and mooned and fawned over her at every new deal.

Was she cheating? Or were they letting her win for some dark purpose?

Questions and more sexual frustration twined through Shayne.

He didn't like the way the huge man called Griz looked at her. And he sure as hell didn't like the way Mr. Cut-nose managed to grasp her hand and hold it while he stared into her eyes longingly—if anyone could call that ugly cuss's gaze longing.

"Miss Lottie, where are you headed?"

"Oh, up the trail. Thought I might go to Texas," she said with an airy sigh.

"Texas? No, miss, you should steer clear of that place. Those Commanch ain't nothing to fool with. Old Lefty here can tell you." Cut-nose jerked his head in the direction of the mean-looking man with the milky eye.

"Yes, ma'am. They are meaner'n sin in Texas. They would gobble up a little lady like you." He held up his left hand and Shayne realized that he was missing the first joint of all of his fingers. "Took 'em for a necklace one of the minor chiefs had a hankering for. I was lucky to get out with my scalp. I didn't scream when they did it. So they let me go—and I got my revenge too."

Shayne wondered what the man had done to incur their wrath in the first place. There was a shifty look in that eye of his that sent prickles of warning shooting up Shayne's spine.

"Yep, those Commanch are mean. Cussed mean, Miss Lottie. You'd best stay here with us for the winter," Griz agreed with an energetic nod.

"Maybe I'll stop back by on my way through—when I'm finished with my business in Texas. How would that be?" Lottie asked, letting her stare linger on each face in turn.

They were like children being given a sugar tit. Each one grinned, blushed, slobbered, and agreed.

"Fine. Then I'll plan to stop back by here. But right now, I have to go. I intend to find myself some adventure."

To Shayne's surprise, she shoved her chair back and stood up. Every eye in the saloon swept over her body, encased in those too-tight boy's trousers.

"It has been fun. Thank you all for a wonderful afternoon. I never knew cards could be so exciting."

And with her winnings scraped into the long tail of her shirt, held like a child would hold a new-found treasure, she simply walked out of the saloon while more than a dozen men heaved an audible sigh of regret.

"I know exactly how you feel, boys," Shayne said to nobody in particular as he sloshed back his whiskey and got ready to follow her back to camp.

He cursed himself for being nine kinds of a fool but he couldn't leave her again—not yet anyway.

Shayne waited a little while before he went to the smithy, settled up on the account for Lottie's mare, and rode back to the camp, where Lottie was supposed to have waited.

He had a running argument with himself about what he was going to say to her. Or if he should say anything at all.

What could he say?

She was a grown woman. She was on this little adventure because she insisted she had to have it. He had told her to keep up with him or get left. Of course, he had also told her to stay in camp with every intention of never seeing her again, but that had backfired.

And I have no true claim on her. She can come and go as she pleases. She may have stolen my name for her use, but she doesn't answer to me.

It was a truth he did not wish to face, but an indisputable fact nonetheless. There was no guarantee she would even come back to the camp where he had left her. Perhaps she had ridden south toward Texas, toward the adventure she was determined to have.

She would be alone and unprotected.

And with that prickly awareness prodding him on, he rode the mare to a camp he wasn't even sure would even still be there.

Little Bit made good time with Lottie's lighter weight on his back. Soon she was back at the camp where Shayne had left her. With quick movements, she stripped the saddle from Little Bit and used a twisted hank of grass to rub him down and dry the sweat from his back. She wanted Shayne to know she took good care of his horse.

"But why am I bothering? He probably isn't coming back. If he had wanted me with him he would've marched up to that table and said so." Lottie's heart plummeted as the realization of her words washed over her.

She had been fearful that Shayne would not return to get her, and she had been angry that he ordered her to stay in camp as though she didn't have a will or mind of her own. That had been why she had gone to town and into that saloon. And her heart had sung with joy when Shayne walked in. It had stunned her to realize she had been aware of him on a level that went deeper than mere sight or sound. She *felt* him the moment he walked in—felt his eyes on her while she played and flirted outrageously with the nice old men who had let her win. She wasn't silly enough to think she had any skill at the game of poker, but she assumed they were lonely and happy to let her win just to pass the hours.

She had waited and waited for Shayne to come to the table, but he never did. Finally she had faced the truth.

He didn't want her anymore.

She had been a pleasant diversion while he waited for Ian, but after he found out that Ian was not the man who had wronged him, he had been ready to move on—alone.

"Damn him for making me care."

So she had come back to the camp, not knowing what else to do. She knew there was little chance he would return, but a stubborn glimmer of hope still lived inside her heart; and in spite of everything that had happened, it was not wholly extinguished.

Lottie stood for a moment and stared out into the night. It was dark, very dark.

Maybe he won't be able to find the camp. But in her heart she knew that was silly. *She* had found the camp. But she impulsively went about gathering fallen wood and dried leaves to get the fire blazing. When flames leapt high and sent sparks dancing into the night, she brushed out her tangled, cropped hair, washed her face, and waited.

Still there was no Shayne.

A hot choke of emotion clogged her throat, but she fought it, refusing to give in to feelings of despair.

"I need to fix my own supper tonight," she murmured sadly.

But before she found the makings, she took all the small bags of her winnings and wrapped them in the nightgown she had brought and never worn, hiding it all deep in the bottom of her saddlebag.

It occurred to her that she might need that money to get her to Texas, to finance her grand adventure.

Alone.

She swallowed the hard lump in her throat and refused to admit that it was fear, loneliness, and grief that choked her. She wanted her adventure right enough, but she wanted that excitement and discovery with Shayne at her side.

Lottie raised her head and squinted into the blackness beyond her fire. She heard something. Suddenly she felt it through the ground where she sat.

Hoofbeats.

Shayne had come back!

Lottie sat on a boulder beside the fire, waiting for him. Would he berate her for going to town? Or would he ignore her just as he had in town, acting for all the world as if he didn't know her in front of all those men?

"I know he saw me. A blind man couldn't have missed that show I put on for him." She fidgeted nervously and added more wood to the fire.

The blaze was big—much larger than any fire Shayne ever made. Her cheeks felt as if they were being roasted. In a few moments she was forced to find herself another perch, farther away.

She sat, stiff and awkward, waiting for Shayne to enter camp. She stared into the mesmerizing flames and tried to act nonchalant as the minutes ticked by, marked by the heavy beating of her own heart.

It was taking him an awfully long time, she thought, noticing that the thrum of hooves striking the earth no longer telegraphed through the ground. The mare was fast; Shayne should have reached camp by now.

Was he walking in?

Had he changed his mind and left her again?

A sound brought her spinning around, but all she saw was the ghost of the flames, temporarily burned onto the backs of her eyes. She blinked and tried to make her vision clear. All she saw was blackness and the phantom of the fire.

"Shayne, is that you?" she asked, reaching out in the darkness.

"You can call me Shayne if it makes it better for you," a gravelly voice said.

Lottie snatched her hand back and started to run, the echo of evil laughter ringing in her ears. Her vision was still useless as she stumbled into the dark over a rock, falling to her hands and knees. As she started to crawl, the hair on the back of her neck rose.

"No need to try and get away, girlie. It won't hurt; I promise. I know how to handle my pick."

She screamed and scrambled faster, but a hand clamped onto her ankle and dragged her backward through the stones and dried grass as if she weighed nothing at all. She kicked and thrashed, but it was useless.

"Fight if you want, honey, I don't mind. In fact I like it better when you fight."

Lottie screamed as loud as she could. But who would hear? She kicked and connected with something—someone.

"Damn you!" the disembodied voice snarled.

Then the world exploded in a blaze of pain as a fist connected to her right jaw. She tasted blood and her stomach roiled with the pain. She remained conscious and feebly struck out with her own fist, hitting something. Then another blow from a fist sent stars colliding in her head.

Lottie heard the sound of fabric ripping. The cold wash of air across her breasts revived her. With a vicious laugh, someone squeezed her left breast until she cried out in pain. She found the hand and bit it; tasting blood, she kicked and screamed.

Another slap made her head swim. She was losing consciousness, fighting weakly as she felt her trousers pulled down over her hips. . . .

Shayne rode toward the fire winking in the distance. Only Lottie would have built a fire that big. He felt a strange combination of relief and dread to know she was out there alone. He had about convinced himself that she was riding hell-bent for leather straight to Texas without him.

And I should've been glad if she was. But he hadn't been glad. He had been heartsick and miserable and he didn't know why.

A high-pitched scream floated on the night air. Shayne was suspended in time. Then he put his spurs to the mare's side and thundered toward the camp. Even from a distance he could see the huge fire.

And what was happening beside it.

Lottie lay on the ground looking limp as a broken doll. Her shirt and chemise had been ripped down the middle. The torn fabric revealed the creamy softness of her flesh. Firelight winked over her pale skin. The golden triangle of hair at the apex of her thighs was bare, vulnerable.

Someone was moving toward her.

One of the men from the card game was jerking his trousers down.

Shayne had never been so afraid in his life—not for himself, but for Lottie. He urged more speed from the mare.

Lottie moaned and struggled to sit up. The man slapped her hard across the mouth. Fresh blood splayed a dark stain against the whiteness of her face.

"Sweet little honey pot you got there, girlie," the brute said as he touched the golden hair between her legs.

He grabbed his swollen member with one hand, spreading her knees wide with the other. "I'm gonna dip into that honey right now."

Shayne roared his rage. The mare had not even skidded to a stop when he hit the ground running.

In an act of utter fury and pure desperation, Shayne launched himself through the air. He hit the man full in the chest and sent them both tumbling over and over.

Away from Lottie.

The scent of singed hair filled Shayne's nostrils, followed by the smell of burning flesh.

"Yeow."

"You son of a bitch, I'll kill you," Shayne grated out as they separated and rolled to their feet. Lottie's attacker was beating at a small flame on the sleeve of his filthy shirt. He was sickening with his milky eye and his still-erect member throbbing in the firelight.

"You got no call to be greedy. I'm more'n willin' to share her. Just give me a few minutes; I don't take very long."

Shayne lunged again. He swung hard when he was near enough to connect. His knuckles met the sharp-edged bone. Blood, warm and sticky, streamed onto the brute's matted beard.

"Now hold on a damned minute." The man staggered back, his trousers hampering his movements as the truth of Shayne's intentions dawned. His eyes took on a sharp, feral appearance.

"You don't *want* to hump her do you?" he sneered.

"And you don't want me to have a poke neither. Well, that's just plain selfish in my book."

Shayne swung again, but this time the man side-stepped. With a grunt he hit Shayne a crashing blow across the back of the neck. The blow put him on his knees. His stomach roiled. A sickening wave of un-consciousness crept from the edges of his mind.

He shook his head and fought the weakness. Lottie needed him and he was not about to fail her.

Staggering to his feet, Shayne turned toward the man. He was as big as a bear and smelled twice as bad. The look in his eyes was a mixture of hate and rage. He had managed to get his trousers hitched up and was ready to make this a real fight.

Shayne ran at him, ducking his head. He hit just below the ribs. The air left his opponent with an *oomph* and a grunt of pain.

The man went down—hard. Shayne pummeled his face over and over with his fists, but it was like hitting granite. Suddenly the man growled and picked Shayne up in a bear hug. He tossed him aside as if he weighed nothing at all. Firelight winked off the barrel of a gun.

"I ain't foolin' with you no more. I want a piece of that ass and I'm gonna have it." He raised his fire-arm and pointed it at Shayne's chest.

The shot rang out. The scent of death and cordite filled the night air.

Nineteen

Why had she thought she could fly in the face of God and convention and come away unscathed?

There are reasons why proper women can't have adventures. Addie's voice rang in Lottie's memory. For the first time in her life, Lottie understood why her sister had said those things—why Addie worried and coddled and preached to Lottie about what could happen to a decent woman who went around unprotected.

She had thumbed her nose at Shayne and ridden into town as if she didn't have a care in the world. She had pranced around in her tight trousers, flirting shamelessly to make Shayne react.

She had no one to blame for what happened but herself, and she was more than ready to lay the blame where it belonged—at her own door. She had acted like a loose woman and brought this upon herself.

Lottie stared mutely at the smoking gun in her hand. The man lying on the ground had a black hole in his chest that oozed blood, but she wasn't quite sure what the weapon in her hand had to do with his pitiful death rattle or the expanding puddle of blood around him.

Her clothes were ripped and torn. She was mostly naked; her pants were down around her ankles and she didn't remember exactly how that had happened.

She didn't *want* to remember.

She shuddered and dropped the gun. Then she began to moan. It was an animal-like sound: foreign, frightening—and she couldn't make it stop.

"Oh, God." She gave a strangled cry, feeling as if her mind and body were coming apart, splitting in half. She couldn't cope, couldn't breathe . . . couldn't bear this raw, wounded sensation.

And then there were strong warm arms around her shoulder, gathering her close, providing something solid to cling to. A soothing voice murmured and whispered assurance in her ear. She collapsed into that safe, secure haven while that same painful, strange keening sound tore from her throat. She was dizzy and her head hurt. The flesh on her breasts felt tender and bruised.

"What happened?" She choked on her own misery, wondering why her eyes were still dry when she had never before experienced such a terrible sensation of sorrow. It was like a weight on her chest, choking the air from her lungs, killing her slowly with each breath.

"It's okay now, darlin'," Shayne said in a rough, thick voice. "I'm here. Nothing will hurt you again."

"But—wh-what?" Lottie couldn't explain. She could only tremble and know a strange, sickening feeling of being lost.

The sick, tortured feeling had never left Shayne's gut or his mind. While he had taken that sorry son of a bitch's body and put it on his horse, and saddled Little Bit and strung the other horses behind him, Shayne had never managed to wipe out the image of Lottie lying on the ground, beaten, bloody, and at the mercy of an animal.

"And I didn't even get to kill him myself," he said aloud while he kicked the fire out and made sure the ashes were dead.

Lottie sat on a boulder, unmoving, unblinking.

She needed to cry, to vent her fear and her rage, but she didn't seem to be able to. She was frozen with the terror still written plainly in her tortured blue eyes.

Shayne had seen men like that in prison, so scarred and traumatized that they couldn't go beyond what had happened to them. Lottie was stuck in time.

"But if it's the last thing I ever do, I'll get her unstuck."

With his heart in his throat, Shayne went to Lottie and put his extra shirt over her torn garments. Gently he buttoned it up, then he took her into his arms and walked toward Little Bit.

He was going to take care of her, to get her through this. No matter how long it took.

They rode into town several hours later. The dark street was deserted. Only the glow of lantern light spilled from the open door of the saloon. It was a beacon to the weary, the lonely, and the lost.

Shayne rode up to the entrance and coaxed Little Bit through the doors. He had to duck and hold Lottie close to keep from being conked by the lintel. The horse clomped inside, his hooves clopping against the unswept plank floor.

"What the hell?" A gruff man asked as he scampered from Little Bit's path.

"Look, it's Miss Lottie." The man Shayne knew as Cut-nose pointed. Soon a swarm of men surrounded Little Bit, staring up at Shayne and Lottie.

"What did you do to her?" one slat-thin miner with a long blade in his hand demanded.

"Lookie right here, boys. It's old Lefty."

A murmur and clunk of boot heels brought the men to the horse where old Lefty was slung over the saddle like a bag of refuse.

"He's got a hole in him big enough to see light through."

Lottie stiffened and moaned. Shayne clamped his jaw tight and pulled her closer.

"Did you kill Lefty?" Cut-nose asked Shayne.

"No, but I wish I had. I'd have made him die a hell of a lot slower," Shayne grated out. "He attacked Lottie."

To a man, their unwashed, unshaven jaws fell open. Then the one called Griz stepped forward and lifted the left hand of the corpse.

"That's why the Commanch cut his fingers off, ya' know. He'd been mistreating squaws. Alwus felt a little sorry for old Lefty. Guess I don't feel too damned sorry for the dirty bastard now. I got no use for a low-down that will try to harm a fine woman like Miss Lottie."

"We should'a kilt him last spring," one man said, spitting and missing the spittoon. "Should'a kilt him and carved him up."

"It ain't too late for the carving up," the man with the knife said.

"I need a room where I can care for her," Shayne said, tired of hearing about how they all should have put an end to old Lefty. They all had failed Lottie as far as he was concerned, and he was the biggest failure of all.

He had left her—twice—and she paid the price for his stupidity and cowardice.

He didn't care what they did with the bastard's cold

body as long as he could have a room where Lottie would feel safe and he could care for her.

"Top of the stairs. First door on the right," the barkeep said. "I'll see your horses get stabled."

Shayne slid off Little Bit and hefted Lottie into a more secure position. He was halfway up the stairs when the barkeeper's voice rang out.

"Hey, mister, do you know Miss Lottie personal?"

Shayne turned and found them all watching him, waiting for his answer.

"She's my wife," Shayne said softly, putting his boot on the next stair. "Mrs. Charlotte Rosswarne."

Lottie woke to find herself in a soft bed with her own nightgown on her body, though she didn't remember getting undressed for bed. She'd had a terrible nightmare that had ruined her sleep, but she could not remember it now, though it had left her shaky and trembling. She blinked and tried to sit up, but her body cried out in pain.

Flopping back on the pillow, she frowned and tried to remember what had happened to make her so sore and achy. Searching her mind, she focused on the last vivid recollection.

She had been playing cards—winning, too—and taking a great deal of pleasure in knowing that Shayne saw it all. Then she had ridden back to camp and built a fire to wait for him.

That was all she remembered. There was nothing in her mind after starting the fire and seeing to the horse. She didn't know where she was or how she had gotten here.

Fear seized her.

Where was she? Where was Shayne? Had he ever come back? And if Shayne wasn't here, then who had put this nightgown on her?

The door opened and a small woman with a wizened face scuttled in. She didn't do more than glance at Lottie as she carried in a tray covered with a clean, white flour sack. She placed it on a scarred table beside Lottie's bed.

Then she was gone. That was it. No word, no greeting—just in and out before Lottie could even find her own tongue and demand answers to those questions.

"What is going on?" Lottie said aloud to the closed door, stunned to hear a strange, thick slur in her own speech.

She tried to get up again, going slower, using the bed and the table to support her weight while stabs of pain shot through her back, her thighs, and along her ribs. She touched her face. It was painful too. One of her eyes was swollen nearly shut.

"My God, what happened? Why can't I remember what happened?"

She staggered to her feet and hobbled slowly to the corner of the room, where a plain washstand held a milky-looking glass. She rubbed her hand over the film and leaned close, peering into the dirty mirror.

A scream ripped from her lips when she saw her own unfamiliar reflection.

Shayne had not stirred from her bedside until the call of nature and the need for a cup of strong coffee had finally forced him to leave. He was halfway up the stairs when he passed Rosa, the old woman who did the cooking for whoever rented rooms over the

saloon and would pay for meals. Lottie had slept fit-
fully, tossing and turning until nearly dawn, when she
finally heaved a sigh and calmed.

It had been a relief to sit and hold her hand while
she slept.

Maybe she was already eating, already healing after
a night in a real bed.

For a moment Shayne paused outside the closed
door of Lottie's room. Should he knock in case she
was awake?

But what if she is still resting? He argued with himself. Finally he gave up and slowly turned the knob
and eased the door open.

She was lying in a crumpled heap on the bare, cold
floor.

"Lottie." Shayne scooped her up and carried her
back to bed. She started to rouse the moment he pulled
the blanket up to her chin and gently moved one of
her short golden curls off her forehead.

"Shayne . . . you didn't leave me." Her voice was
shaky.

"No. I didn't leave you, Lottie," he said tightly. He
was pummeled by guilt. He *had* left her and she had
nearly been raped because of his selfish actions.

"Wh-wha—what happened to me?"

He frowned at her. "Don't you remember, darlin'?"

She moved her head gently from side to side. "No.
I don't remember anything. Were we attacked by Indians? My face—my face . . . I'm ugly."

"You could never be ugly, darlin'."

"What happened to me, Shayne? Why is my face
all swollen and bruised? And I have other bruises and
cuts. . . ."

Shayne hesitated. He had little experience with

women, and even less with women in this situation. Last night Lottie had acted as if she weren't quite right in her mind. Now she appeared to have forgotten Lefty and everything that had happened.

Was it the shock and near-rape that had taken her memory? Or was it the fact that she had killed a man that weighed so heavily on her heart that she blocked the events out?

Either way Shayne had a gut feeling that he should not tell her what had happened, but rather let her grasp the memories in her own time when she was able—if that time ever came.

"What do you remember?" Shayne prodded gently.

"I—I remember sitting by the fire, waiting for you," Lottie said softly.

Shayne smiled and tried to reassure her. "That's all."

"Well . . . mostly," she said somewhat evasively.

He let it go. Now was not the time to bring up her trip to town and the card game. Besides, Lefty had sat at that table and played with her. Any reminder might be too much for her.

"We had an accident . . . a—a landslide."

"Oh. So that's why my face is black and blue and my lip is cut and my body hurts so?" She heaved a relieved sigh that cut through Shayne's soul like a knife.

"Sure, darlin'. Now you just rest."

"Yes. I need to rest." She nodded. Her lids drifted shut, then they opened up again. "You didn't leave me," she said softly.

Shayne managed a smile. "No, Lottie, I didn't leave you."

* * *

Night brought terror and dreams to Shayne. He was locked up—confined—and Lottie was screaming his name. He was in the box, and no matter how hard he tried to reach her he couldn't break through the bonds of his wounds and guilt and conflicted emotions.

He had left her twice, and both times she had been in danger because of his actions. He didn't deserve a woman like Lottie. He woke in a slick of clammy sweat. He stood up and went to the connecting door. It was still ajar, as he had left it.

He had gone down and told the men what had happened—that she didn't remember Lefty's attack or shooting him. They all agreed to keep quiet and not mention anything.

She had won all their hearts with her smile and her courage and zest for living.

Now he was up, restless, and worried about Lottie again. He peered inside her room. The bruises and swelling had changed her face into someone he didn't know, and yet, this was Lottie—his Lottie.

The woman who had lied to make herself his wife. The woman who refused to be left behind, who wanted adventure and to see the world.

She had stolen his name and his heart.

"Oh, Lottie, how can I let you go?" he murmured.

Lottie woke to the smell of coffee and sunlight on her face. She stretched and yawned, feeling the pinch and bite of the wounds on her face.

Gingerly she put her fingertips to them.

It was strange that she couldn't remember the rock slide. And she really didn't recall that many rocks near their camp anyway. No matter how she turned the questions over in her mind, she could not imagine how she had gotten hurt this way.

"Mornin'." Shayne entered the room with a mug of coffee and a plate covered with a cloth. "How about some breakfast? And I didn't cook it, so you know it must be good."

"You're a fine cook," she said, wriggling herself into a sitting position and taking the tin plate from his hands. She lifted the cloth and found a slab of meat, two eggs, and a crust of warm, yeasty-smelling bread.

"Yep, I'm a terrific cook if you like scorched coffee, dry biscuits, and hard beans."

"I was getting used to it," Lottie said with a shy smile. Then she ducked her head as if she might blush, but Shayne knew he was being silly. There were only one or two things that ever made Lottie Rosswarne blush.

"Mmmm, I'm hungry." She dug the fork into one of the eggs and took a bite. She chewed with precise concentration, and he knew her jaw was hurting with the effort.

"Shayne," she said between bites. "I don't remember much about the rock slide. What happened, exactly?"

He hooked his boot around the leg of a chair and dragged it near her bed.

"We don't need to talk about that right now, darlin'. Tell me how you are feelin'?"

She grimaced in pain and stopped chewing. She studied his face for a long while. "Are you anxious to leave?"

"Yes—no. I don't know anymore," he said truthfully, feeling the hollow chasm of torn loyalties open up in his chest. "I lived to get revenge so I could prove something to my father, but now it doesn't seem so important."

"I'm well enough to ride today if you're anxious to go. Or are you trying to find another way to leave me behind?" she said softly.

He watched her eyes—so blue, so wary—flicking over his face. There were smudges of fatigue beneath each one, telltale signs that she had been pushed too hard for too long. And it was all because of his need for vengeance.

"No, darlin'. I am not going to try and leave you behind. You rest; we can start out when you're feeling better." Shayne realized with a jolt that he actually meant it. His revenge had become less important than she was.

For good or ill Lottie was coming with him. He couldn't leave her behind. And as soon as he did what he had to do, he was going to see she was back safe and sound in McTavish Plain.

Twenty

Shayne brought her dinner and sat while she ate; then after she dozed off, he stood up and watched her for a moment. There was a pinch of strain on her face that had not been there earlier.

What did she dream about?

Did she remember the times he had taken her passionately, with nothing but revenge in his heart? He itched to touch her again, to make up for what he had done, but the only way he could let her heal was to leave her alone and untouched.

How had he come to this?

He cared for Lottie—too much to take her to his bed again—and yet that was what he yearned to do.

She did things to him with her eyes, with her stubborn determination. Lottie had gotten beneath his skin and he didn't know what to do about it.

Sighing in frustration, he left her room. He went downstairs for another hand of cards—or a donation to the Cut-nose pot, as he had begun to think of it. The codger was luckier than sin.

An hour later Shayne was losing steadily when he heard Lottie scream.

Every man at the table thundered up the stairs. Shayne threw open the door. She was thrashing and screaming, caught in the grip of her own demons.

Shayne's heart contracted as he rushed to her side. He knew what it was to be haunted every time you closed your eyes.

"Lottie." He pulled her into his arms and held her. She hit him and kicked and fought.

"Darlin', it's me."

The miners and mountain men stood at the door, watching in round-eyed terror. They chewed their bottom lips and whispered among themselves.

Shayne knew what they were feeling because he felt the same paralyzing impotence. How could a bunch of rough geezers and a convict hope to reach a woman with a wounded soul?

But Shayne tried. He held her and whispered and let her pummel his chest until she finally quieted.

The relief that washed through him was like a gust of wind. It was as if every tortured breath that Lottie took was his. And every whimper of her misery sliced through him like the dull edge of a knife.

How had he let himself fall for her?

"Damn it all to hell," he muttered under his breath.

"Is she gonna be all right?" Cut-nose asked.

Shayne raised his head and met the man's hard gaze. "She has to be, Cut-nose. For both us, she has to be."

The night promised to be long.

Shayne sat beside Lottie's bed, touching her when she cried out or whimpered. He knew what she dreamed of: she relived the attack that her waking mind could not bear to remember.

And he didn't know what to do about that.

Should he tell her what had happened? Or should

he let her find her own way, even if it meant living in terror each time she slept?

Her eyes fluttered open and she fastened her gaze on him. There was fear and pain in her eyes, but there was also trust.

"Shayne, I was afraid."

"What frightened you, darlin'?"

"I—I—am not sure. But you were not there. I was alone."

"Well, it was only a dream, Lottie. I am here."

"Shayne?" She rose up on her elbow.

"Yes?"

"Would you come and hold me?"

He swallowed hard. It was the thing he wanted and feared most of all. But he could not deny Lottie—not now, when the specter of fear was in her life.

"Sure, darlin'." He tugged off his boots and came to the edge of the bed. "Scoot over."

He lay down on top of the blankets next to her.

"No. Not like that. I want you in here with me, where I can feel your arms around me—so I'll feel safe."

Shayne closed his eyes against the thrum of his own heartbeat. Did she know what she was asking of him?

Did she know she was killing him?

With a sigh of resignation he got up and lifted the blanket; then, fully clothed, he lay down beside Lottie and gathered her into his arms.

She was trembling.

"Don't be afraid, Lottie. I'm here. I'll never let anything hurt you."

"Promise?" she asked sleepily.

"I promise. Now sleep safe in my arms, darlin'. I'll be right here when the mornin' comes."

* * *

The days came and went with a sweet slowness of pace; the nights were sinful torture. Shayne spent his days tending to Lottie's needs and talking with the strange collection of men that made up the town. The place had no name; it was just one of many ramshackle communities that had sprouted outside the walls of a fort—in this case Fort Walker—where wagon trains could get supplies, information, and protection from the hostiles.

But now with the biggest hostilities taking place in the Southern states, the Indian problem was secondary. Any travelers had to depend on themselves for protection. The fort was empty.

Shayne did not feel the biting urge to hurry to Texas. He was confused by that reticence and by the fact that the more time he spent caring for Lottie, the less he heard his father's strident voice in his head.

But the lessons of his youth were well taught and hard learned. He couldn't just set aside his quest for vengeance.

Or could I? While the question hammered at Shayne's mind, Lottie's sweet body pummeled his manhood.

Lottie could not sleep unless he held her, so that was what he did. The toll upon him was devastating. Her body was warm and soft and he wanted her. He wanted her with every nerve and fiber of his being.

When she moaned softly, he would hold her close and whisper words of reassurance in her ear until she stilled. For several nights she had snuggled deep against his neck and sent a frisson of chills down his back with her own breathing.

He wanted her.

And he didn't dare give in to those feelings.

Tonight was worse than usual. Lottie clung to him and by doing so she put her sweet, luscious body tight against him in places that ached and throbbed.

He wanted her.

"Shhh, darlin', it's all right," he said, rubbing her back in big circles, trying to soothe her.

And soothe her it did. But while Lottie quieted and started to inhale deep, even breaths, Shayne felt himself tense and stiffen.

He wanted her.

His own body was his worst enemy.

She snuggled near and sighed in contentment. His sack got thick and heavy with want. His breath dragged in and out of his lungs painfully.

"Oh, Lottie, I want you."

"Then why don't you take me?" came the unexpected question. "You're here with me, so why do you hold back? Haven't you forgiven yourself yet?"

He froze. Shayne had not realized that she was awake. But here she was, snuggled up against him, her breath fanning at his neck, asking why he didn't do what he wanted to do.

"No. I haven't," he admitted into the darkness.

"Don't you think it's high time?" She slid her hand down his chest and stopped with only inches separating her fingers from the part of him that throbbed with need.

"I—I—" Shayne couldn't say the words. He just couldn't.

"You are a fool, Shayne Rosswarne," Lottie said with a sigh. "Don't you think I know how you feel? Don't you think I've seen your eyes beg me to forgive you? Just because you haven't said the words doesn't mean I don't know what's in your heart and your mind."

He stiffened in more places than just his manhood.

"I have forgiven you. Now will you please forgive yourself?"

He was torn, at war with himself. He wanted this woman with every fiber of his being, but his father's words were playing like a tune in his head.

A man had to be strong. A man was not a man unless he defended his name and avenged his honor. A man never shows weakness. A man never admits he is sorry for the things he does. If he doesn't like his actions, then he doesn't repeat them.

Easy to say, harder to do when Lottie made him crazy with want.

Shayne kissed Lottie's forehead. And then, though it took more strength of purpose than he thought he possessed, he slowly slid from the bed.

"I can't, Lottie. I can't."

Shayne felt like a wounded animal when he left that room. She was offering herself to him. He wanted to take what she offered, but he couldn't.

She said she forgave him, but she didn't remember his latest failure. No, she would not feel the same if she was in her right mind and could recall what had nearly happened with Lefty. Lottie surely could not forgive Shayne for nearly letting her be raped.

Shayne went in search of the diversion of a card game and found the odd collection of men eager to oblige.

"That wife of yours is quite a woman," Cut-nose said abruptly in the middle of dealing out a hand of draw poker.

Shayne looked up to find the man studying his face with single-minded intent. Did they somehow know how things were between them?

"Yes, she is. One of a kind Lottie is."

"You sound proud as a whitewashed pig," the old man chuckled. "Where'd you meet her?"

"Our paths first crossed in a little town called Gothenburg, Nebraska, in a sheriff's office," Shayne lied, recalling what Lottie had told him about seeing the old outdated "wanted" poster with his face on it. Only a woman like Lottie would look at a "wanted" poster and pluck a man's name for her own use.

He smiled at the thought. "She kind of set her sights on me, so to speak." She was unique. Scrappy and sultry as sin. She was special in a world populated by the ordinary.

She deserved so much more than a convict with no honor.

"Yep, quite a woman," Cut-nose said as he revealed his hand to the disgust of the other players. With a toothless grin he raked a pile of coins to his side of the table. "Ready to play again?"

"I can see I'm going to have to watch you closer," Shayne said with a lifted brow. "You are taking unfair of advantage of me while we talk about Lottie."

For a while Lottie never believed it would happen, but slowly, her face began to heal. The bruises changed colors. From black and blue to yellow and green until finally they were gone. The puffiness in her eye went away, and when she looked at herself in the mirror she recognized the face looking back.

But something was still not right.

Shayne was different. He watched her with a quiet stillness as if he were waiting for something. And she still had no memory of the landslide that had nearly killed her.

It bothered her, puzzled her, and kept her lying awake, staring into the dark and trying to figure out why.

And then there were the dreams.

She could never remember them, but they always left her shaky and afraid. Only Shayne's presence drove the horrible empty fear from her soul.

Had she been hit in the head so hard that she wasn't right? Or was there something more? Something that Shayne was not telling her?

There seemed to be something more when Shayne was around.

Something there just out of her reach— some elusive thought or memory that she couldn't quite grab hold of—and the more she tried, the more the elusive thoughts slipped through her hand.

And besides that odd, niggling notion that she needed to remember something, she had not managed to get Shayne back into her bed. He still avoided her as though he were fighting his personal demons, but there was also a sad, melancholy longing in his dark eyes.

Like now.

He had come upstairs. Lottie had recognized his unique catlike tread on the stairs before she ever saw him. He stood just outside the door. She was fairly certain he didn't know she was aware of his presence.

He was watching her intently through the crack. And she could nearly feel his eyes on her skin beneath her night rail. He had insisted she do nothing but rest and remain in bed so she had not even dressed since she woke up here.

She watched Shayne from the corner of her eye. His hands flexed at his side. He acted for all the world like a man who wanted to say something but was afraid to speak. But Lottie knew that Shayne Rosswarne had never been afraid of anything or anyone in his life—except for saying he was sorry.

"Come in and talk to me," she said, watching him control his features before he lifted his boot and stepped into full view.

What was it? And did it have something to do with the accident? Or was it the same old guilt he was carrying?

"I haven't seen much of you today. . . ."

Shayne's head came up abruptly and her words stuck in her throat. He was bristling, on the defensive; in fact, he looked as if he might bolt from the room at any moment.

She was going to have to take a different approach in order to achieve her goal.

"What have you been doing?" she asked, walking to the small, narrow window and peering into the empty street. A gust of wind broomed dust down the road.

"Playing cards," he said softly.

She turned to him and saw his eyes flick over her body—only once, and so quickly that she would not have noticed if she hadn't been watching him so intently.

He's not immune to me.

Suddenly the way was clear. She would have to seduce Shayne Rosswarne.

Twenty-one

Lottie stretched, bringing her arms over her head and arching her back. With the window behind her she was certain Shayne would see every inch of her form in silhouette.

His jaw tightened.

"I am so stiff from doing nothing but laying in bed."

His eyes flicked from the bed to her and back again.

"Let me tell you, it's no fun to lay in bed . . . all alone."

His hands tightened into fists at his side. "Lottie . . ."

She wrapped her arms around her waist and hugged herself. The action pulled the thin fabric taut across her breasts. Shayne's gaze riveted to her bosom and stayed there.

"I'm tired of being alone," she said softly.

He had not moved, but his body had tightened with every suggestive move and word. Now he was as taut as a bowstring, watching her warily.

He knows what I want.

"Shayne, I need you—"

She thought she heard him groan.

". . . to rub my back. I'm still so sore, from the rock slide."

He looked stunned, a little off balance. He blinked and she could see the confusion in his face. Now he wasn't so sure of her intentions, and it made him even more vulnerable.

Lottie's heart leaped with hope.

"Will you do that for me, Shayne?" She looked at him and licked her lips, taking a deal of satisfaction when his eyes followed her tongue's course around the edge of her mouth.

"Fine. I'll rub your back."

"Oh, good," she sighed. Lottie moved to the bed and lay facedown.

"What are you doing?" His voice was gruff and thick.

"I'm laying down so you can rub my back, silly."

For a moment there was only the sound of Shayne's breath, deep and ragged as he inhaled. Then he heaved a great sigh. She heard his footfalls as he approached the bed where she waited.

He hesitated by the side of the bed. She could feel the tension in his body. It was answered by her own. Her nipples hardened against the fabric of her nightgown. She relaxed into the feather mattress. She felt warm, and the itch of anticipation thrummed with every beat of her heart.

"My back, Shayne," she said, hoping he would put his hands on her.

He did.

The warm weight of his palms was pure pleasure to her, though he still stood by the side of the bed. He was stiff, and bending over the bed in order to reach her must have been awkward. Lottie waited to see what he would do.

His hand was warm and a little rough through the

fabric. He made a big circle and then she heard him draw in a raspy breath between clenched teeth.

"Where does it hurt?" he said in a voice gone low.

"Down low, near my hips. I think I'm still bruised."

His hand stilled for a moment. It seemed as if time itself waited with her. She hardly breathed until finally, his hand began to move again, slowly, deliberately.

She moaned.

He snatched his hand away.

"Are you hurtin'?" There was concern in his voice.

"Yes. No." She turned over and looked up into his face. "I *am* hurting, Shayne. And you can make it stop."

"Lottie—" he warned.

"No. I said I wouldn't forgive you until you forgave yourself, but damn it, I am tired of waiting. I have forgiven you, Shayne. Now can't you do the same? Can't we start over?"

He wanted to. God knew how bad he wanted to skin off his clothes and climb into that bed with her. He was near the end of his strength in denying what he wanted—what she asked.

"Stubborn man." She sat up and reached out to him. Without meaning to, he was with her on the bed, holding her, kissing her.

Lottie's mouth was as sweet as summer wine. He held her close, careful not to squeeze her ribs or apply pressure where she might still be sore and hurting.

She kissed him with all the abandon she had ever shown, and with a warm rush he realized in the deepest recesses of his heart that she had forgiven him.

Truly. Completely.

His heart kicked painfully inside his chest. Maybe . . .

"Ow," she said.

He pulled away, afraid that he had hurt her. "Lottie?"

"Something hard is poking me." She grinned.

Relieved, he grinned back, understanding her playful words and warming inside at her boldness.

"Isn't that the idea?"

"Yes, but in this case it felt like cold iron, not hot steel."

He grinned wider and stood up. He unbuckled his gun belt. Her eyes were riveted on his hands. And then he saw her expression change, shifting to one of pain, fear, and memory.

"Th-the—g-gun." She stammered. "I remember holding the g-gun. It jumped in my hand. There was a shot. . . ."

Shayne set the gun belt aside and grabbed her shoulders. She had started to tremble like an aspen leaf in the wind.

"Lottie?"

"I sh-shot him," she screamed. "I remember now. It wa-wasn't a rock slide. I was . . . I blew a hole in him." Her body was rigid with the memory, her eyes glassy and full of terror.

"He put his h-hands on me, Shayne." She said in a pleading voice that ripped at his insides.

"He was going to rape me."

"I know, darlin'. The bastard hurt you."

"Bu-bu—but I killed him." Her body was shaking so violently that her teeth clacked together. "Dear God, I shot him like an animal. It wa- was hor-horrible."

She slumped forward and he caught her in his arms.

Shayne didn't know what else to do but hold her. He brought her to his chest and simply provided the safety of his arms and the warmth of his body while she trembled.

"Easy, darlin'. I'm here."

"But, I took someone's life. How can I live with that?"

He knew her pain; he lived with it every day of his life. This was the bitterness of regret. Shayne would have done anything to keep Lottie from knowing that feeling.

"Remember what you told me?" he asked softly.

"About wh-what?"

"You said you wouldn't forgive me until I forgave myself."

"So?"

"So, I feel the same way. You did nothing to be ashamed of. I want you to let it go, Lottie. You did what you thought you had to do. Hell, you had no choice. If he had killed me he would've raped you."

She stilled. Then she raised her head and looked at him. "I was afraid he was going to kill you."

"You did what needed doing, darlin'."

"Like you, Shayne. Haven't you done what you thought needed doing. Even when you came to McTavish Plain?"

He stared at her tear-filled eyes. "No, Lottie, there's a big difference. I hurt you, humiliated you. I had no excuse to do that just because I thought Ian had wronged me."

"But at the time, you thought you had to do it, Shayne. When will you let it go?"

He shook his head. "I can't."

"Then I guess I'll be the same. I'll cling to my guilt. Is that what you want?" A tear trickled down her cheek.

Shayne remembered how she was after she shot Lefty. Her eyes had been dry that night. The thought of Lottie torturing herself for the rest of her life sent a lance of pain through him. He would do just about anything to keep her from that hell.

"Well, Shayne? If you think it's so damned important to carry your guilt around like a weight, how can I do any different—anything less?"

"Lottie—"

"No. If you want me to let it go, then you have to do the same."

"All right," he said fiercely. "I let it go. Now are you happy?"

"Prove it," she challenged.

"How in hell can I prove it?" He raked his fingers through his hair. The woman could get to him quicker than any other person on earth.

"Make love to me, Shayne. If you make love to me now I will know that you have finally forgiven yourself."

"Lottie, this is blackmail."

"Call it what you want. I know you, Shayne. You say you have let it go, but you'll keep right on hating yourself for what has gone on. Now you can prove it. If you can make love to me, then I'll know that you have forgiven yourself. You say I need to let what I did go. How can you ask me to do something you're not able to do yourself?"

She stared at him with the challenge shining in her clear blue eyes. Damn it, he did want her, badly.

With the pad of his thumb he captured a tear that was clinging to her lashes. He held it there, staring at it. It sparkled like a jewel against the dark, rough skin of his hand.

"You never cried for yourself that night, Lottie. But you're crying now."

"I'm crying for you, Shayne, for us . . . for what we could have if you can just put aside your guilt. Are you so strong that you can just give up what we shared?"

A strangled moan escaped him. Hell no, he wasn't strong. He was weak and foolish and had no defense against Lottie.

"Damn it, Lottie." He kissed her fiercely. All the pent-up lust and frustration drove him on. He picked her up and set her in his lap, letting his hands roam over her body, touching her like a blind man who wanted to learn every inch of her skin by heart and commit it to memory.

If it was possible, holding her felt even sweeter than it had before. There was a poignancy that Shayne could not ignore. They were not destined to be together and he knew it. This coupling, this joining of bodies and souls, was a fleeting joy that might never come again.

She thought it could be so simple, but Shayne knew better. He knew that their love could not sweep away the obstacles between them. He still had a man to kill and his honor to restore, but for this one fleeting moment, he could have heaven with Lottie.

And so Shayne grabbed at the moment of happiness like a thirsty man reaches for water. He fondled her breasts, taking extra care not to hurt the sensitive flesh. He kissed her and suckled on her bottom lip until she made little mewling sounds of pleasure in the back of her throat.

Shayne stripped her bare and laid her down in the center of the soft feather bed while he shed his own clothes. Her eyes skimmed over his body, leaving a wake of hot skin and aroused passion.

He had never known a woman like Lottie. She had more passion in a glance than many women had in their entire bodies.

He went to her and climbed onto the bed, feeling the mattress give and creak against the ropes beneath. He straddled her. She still had a few pale bruises on her lower belly and thighs, and these he kissed as if he could somehow soothe her body and his soul with the action.

"I have missed you," he said truthfully as he spread her thighs and positioned himself between her legs. She smiled at him as he trailed his finger from the triangle of golden curls toward her naval and higher. Then he took her breasts, soft, firm handfuls, in his palms and kneaded them gently, bending to suckle first one hard nipple, then the other.

She moaned softly and grabbed his hair. She tugged gently, lifting his head until his lips met her own. Before he could think, she plunged her tongue into his mouth and challenged him with bold movements.

"Lottie, Lottie, Lottie," he moaned.

Being with her was like coming home.

A part of him was still conflicted, but the greater part took what she offered, rejoicing in the feel and scent of her beneath him. This was what he had dreamed of during endless nights. This was what he wanted.

And though it would change nothing between them, for the moment being in Lottie's arms was his reason for being.

"Shayne." Her hands kneaded the flesh of his buttocks and she was rubbing one soft, curved instep up and down over the muscles of his calf.

"Lottie, you're about to set me on fire." He sipped at the tender skin of her throat, nipping at her collarbone.

"Then let's burst into flame together."

Boldly she grasped him in her hand. He bucked in surprise. She slid her palm over the rigid length of him, exploring with her fingertip when she reached the rounded tip. He was softer than doeskin, and yet there was a pulsing strength in him that had nothing to do with softness of any kind.

He was a man—a strange, exotic contradiction of gentleness and savagery . . . of hardness—and yet within his body of tendon, sinew, and bone, she had witnessed and been the recipient of tenderness beyond imagining.

He was Shayne: flawed, scarred, and frequently wrong. He was the man she wanted.

And now, after he made love to her, they could finally begin again.

Lottie wanted Shayne to put aside his silly quest for vengeance and live with her in McTavish Plain. When morning came they could pack their belongings and point Little Bit and the mare north. Her house, her business, and her family would be waiting for them.

They would have peace and happiness.

She squeezed his shaft and he moaned, reaching between them and unwrapping her fingers from him.

"Stop torturing me, darlin'."

"Is it torture?"

"Uh-huh."

"Terrible, awful, torture?" she teased, kissing at his chin, nipping his earlobe.

"I can't hardly bear it," he said huskily, wondering

if she knew how truthful he was being. She was so hot and he was so ready, he was half afraid he would shame himself like an untried youth.

"Then maybe you'd better do something to end this terrible torture." She grasped him and guided him into her.

They sighed in unison.

Lottie raised her pelvis and pushed hard against Shayne, settling him deep inside her. This was how they were meant to be. Surely God had created them for each other. Surely he was her soul mate, the one man intended to be with her like this until they were old and gray.

"Lottie, darlin'," he growled, and he pulled himself almost completely out, then rammed into her hard. "You . . . are . . . so . . . hot." Each word was punctuated by his body. She moaned softly and grabbed his hair. She was hot, and so ready.

He plunged deep. Her body began to quiver and convulse around him. He spewed his seed into her, and she took him all, pumping him, squeezing him dry.

He was spent: weak as a kitten and satisfied beyond reckoning.

"That was wonderful," she purred, rubbing her palm over his back.

"Uh-huh. Perfect, Lottie."

"And we will have many more perfect times like this, Shayne. Once we're settled back in McTavish Plain we'll start every day just like this."

He stiffened at her words. He had known this was only a temporary bliss, but he had hoped it would last longer. He had to tell her.

"Lottie, I am not returning to McTavish Plain."

"What?"

"Nothing has changed. I'm for Texas to find Red Slovang."

"You can't mean that, Shayne," Lottie said softly, searching his face.

"I do mean it, Lottie. This was wonderful, but nothing has changed." He rose from the bed and dressed.

"So now I suppose you'll try to leave me again," she said sharply.

He didn't answer as he walked to the door. He simply walked out of the room.

"Are you sure about this?" Cut-nose asked, looking at Shayne as if he had lost his mind.

"I'm sure. I've got something to do and I can't let Lottie keep putting herself in danger while I do it."

"She ain't a'gonna like it."

"No, I suppose she won't, but you don't let her sway you. Keep her until tomorrow and then take her back up north. She has family that are probably worried sick about her."

"What about you?"

"What about me?"

"Aren't you worried sick about her?" Cut-nose narrowed his eyes.

"Look, Lottie is a fine woman. She deserves a home and an upright man she can depend on."

"A man would be mighty lucky to have a gal like that to come home to."

"The right kind of man." Shayne swallowed hard. "But not me. I haven't got what it takes."

"Isn't that something you should've thought about before you up and married her?" Cut-nose snapped.

Shayne had told them Lottie was his wife. He had been so scared for her, so afraid of losing her after she was attacked, the words had just slipped out.

"I—I married Lottie because she wanted it." Shayne wasn't about to tell them that she had picked his name from a wanted poster. They thought too much of her to hear that. "But I have something to do—something important."

"What is so all fired important that you have to send your wife back to her people alone?"

"I want you to take her so she isn't alone."

"And you'll be doing what?"

"I have to kill a man. I have to regain my honor and face my father. It's past time I stood on my two feet before him like a man."

Twenty-two

Lottie had no intention of being left behind. In fact, she was sick and tired of Shayne *thinking* that he could leave her.

"It's time he learned who I really am," Lottie said through clenched teeth as she laced her boots. She had packed her belongings into a saddlebag.

"And now *I* am ready to leave."

She opened the door, grateful that the hinge did not squeak. Then she crept out onto the landing. She could hear the rumble of men's voices below.

It was Shayne, Griz, Cut-nose, Dobbs, Estes, Frank and Billy playing cards below.

She flattened herself against the wall and moved ever so slowly, hoping that they would be concentrating on their cards and not on her.

When she was halfway down the stairs, Griz looked up and met her eye. She froze while he watched her, chewing his plug of tobacco like an aging bull. Silently she willed him not to say anything.

His eyes bored into her, but there was no change in his expression. The grizzled mountain man could have been hewn from stone, so still was he.

Suddenly he erupted from the chair with a blistering oath. He began to jump around, swatting at his body.

"What the hell?" Shayne said.

"Are ye' tetched, you old coot?" Cut-nose asked.

For one fleeting moment Griz's eyes met Lottie's again. She read the message in them clearly.

Run.

And she did. As quietly and silently as she could, she came down the stairs and slipped out the door that was always wide open.

The night air was cool on her cheeks as she sprinted toward the stables.

"Thank you, Griz, I owe you one," she said beneath her breath. "And I will repay you somehow."

Lottie took Little Bit, since he was more accustomed to night trailing. She made good time in spite of the fact that parts of her body still ached. Clamping her gloved hands tight on the reins, she tried to ignore the stinging ribs and her aching back, but they would not be ignored.

Whether she wanted to or not, she found herself reliving the night Lefty had come to her camp. No matter how hard she tried to forget, the memory of his hands, his breath, and his body would not be erased.

She was surprised to find one hot tear snaking its way down her cheek. Impatient with herself for being soft, she swiped it away and kicked Little Bit to greater speed.

"Come on, boy, it's a long ride to Texas."

Shayne played until nearly sunrise. He told himself that he was fattening his stake, but he knew deep inside he was simply avoiding the inevitable.

"Well, boys, it's time I hit the trail," he said finally,

pushing his chair back. He glanced toward the dark stairs.

"Go ahead," Cut-nose prompted. "She'll be sleepin' sound."

Shayne nodded, taking the suggestion too easily, too quickly. He told himself it was for the best; leaving her was the only solution. She had been in too much danger by being near him. She needed to go home to McTavish Plain, to the safety of her dress shop and her family.

He crept up the stairs and turned the knob silently. Then he opened the door a crack and peered inside. Even in the darkness he knew the room was empty.

"Lottie!" he bellowed as he threw the door open and stomped inside. The bed was smooth, the room bare.

"Son of a bitch!" he swore as he turned on his heel and headed for the stairs. He met the men coming up as he was going down.

"What's happened?" Dobbs asked.

"She's gone and left without me." Shayne said, breaking into a run as he headed for the stables. Cut-nose was laughing, his eyes winking with amusement.

"Where do you think she went?" one of the men yelled at his back.

"The little fool has gone on to Texas." Shayne said with absolute certainty. She had up and left without him.

Lottie made camp and saw to Little Bit. She built a small fire, just big enough to nest the frying pan full of bacon. Her mouth was watering from the smoky scent that mixed with the snap of evening air.

The landscape had changed drastically, though it was now little more than shadow and darkness beneath the fingernail moon. But she no longer smelled the perfume of trees. Now there was a dusty taste at the back of her tongue, and the wind felt different.

She shivered a little and looked into the shadows. Unbidden memories of Lefty filled her mind but she pushed them aside. Lottie was determined not to be a shrinking violet. She reached deep inside herself for courage and faced her fear. She knew she was free of the paralysis of terror when she realized with a start that the bacon needed turning.

"Damn it, you are going to burn my dinner. And I hate the taste of burned bacon."

Her heart kicked inside her chest when Shayne stepped into the glow from the campfire.

"You came."

"Just what in hell did you think I'd do when you left me?"

"See how it feels?" Lottie quipped as she swished the pan and turned the bacon with a fork. "Now, tell me, Shayne. Exactly where do you think you will find Red Slovang?"

"What did you say?"

"Look, you have been trying to get rid of me for a long while because you have your revenge to see to."

"That's right," Shayne said defensively, jutting out his jaw and glaring at Lottie. She looked too good, too *kissable* with her tight trousers and long-sleeved shirt. He knew her flesh was soft and uncorsetted beneath the fabric. It was mighty distracting.

"I finally decided the only way to deal with you is to see you finished with Red Slovang. Maybe then you'll be able to put the past to rest and get on with your life."

"Lottie—"

"No." She held up her hand to silence him. "I refuse to talk about anything with you until Red Slovang is dead and buried." She plopped down on the bedroll she had spread out earlier. "Now, tell me where it is we'll find the weasel that framed you and got you tossed in jail."

Shayne stared straight ahead at the vista of the western horizon and tried to figure out a way to get rid of Lottie. She was like a burr in a horse's tail: stuck fast and hard to remove.

And he wasn't sure he wanted to.

Every time he closed his eyes there was the memory of her body, so perfectly fitted to him it was as if God had measured her to fit him.

But just because she was hotter than the gates of Hell and twice as pretty, stubborn, and tough was no reason he could ever have a life with her.

He was a convict—a man who had spent time in jail, run with the wrong kind of men, and given up any claim he might ever have had to a normal life in a straitlaced town like McTavish Plain.

"We're being followed," Shayne said tightly under his breath. "Don't turn around and don't act like you know it."

"I didn't know until you said something," Lottie quipped. She did as he said, but that didn't stop the hair on the back of her neck from prickling. She shifted uneasily in the saddle and gathered her reins, ready to kick Little Bit and head for tall timber if Shayne said to do so.

The thought came to her suddenly that she trusted him with her life. A funny situation, considering the man had been trying to get rid of her for the better part of their acquaintance.

"It's Indians," he said, drawing her thoughts back to the present with a jolt. "They're coming. Let me do the talking."

A band of a dozen nearly naked men rode boldly up to them. The men were well muscled, long-limbed, and mean-looking.

Lottie swallowed hard.

Shayne and the Indians eyed each other critically. Then, in a series of grunts and hand gestures, they began to communicate. She sat frozen with fear while the odd conversation progressed.

Then suddenly, one of the men kicked his horse, let out a whoop, and rode hard at her. In a flash he had her hat off her head.

A strange, tense silence descended over them all. Shayne's jaw was tight, his hand hovering near the gun strapped at his hip while the men all stared at Lottie.

Another spate of unintelligible words were exchanged between Shayne and the man Lottie assumed was the leader of the small band.

One of them reached out and touched her short, cropped hair. She dared not move, hardly even breathed.

A series of rapid-fire words and shared gestures passed among the Indians. Then they turned to Shayne as if waiting for something.

A sharp bark of laughter was his answer. Soon all

the men—both the Indian warriors and Shayne—were laughing heartily.

And though Lottie couldn't understand what he was saying, she got the drift of his conversation. They were laughing at her—making a joke of her clothes, her short hair.

Of the fact that I'm not a conventional woman.

She hated it, but what she hated even more was the burn of humiliation in her cheeks.

"Damn it," she said under her breath.

"Why, Lottie, darlin', I do believe you are blushing," Shayne said with a wink. Then he leaned across the mare and Little Bit and kissed her soundly.

The Indian who had taken her hat gave it to Shayne, and with a few more garbled words, the hunting party whooped loudly, raised their fists to the sky, and rode away.

"Well, darlin', you have done it now. You have single-handedly ran off a band of Comanche warriors. And all it took was your haircut!" Shayne doubled over, holding his sides and laughing.

"I have only just now realized what prompted my sister Addie to shoot her husband," she snapped.

Then she pointed Little Bit south and kicked him soundly. He covered a lot of ground in a short space of time, but she could still hear Shayne's laughter ringing in her ears.

Once again the same old fears and insecurities were dogging Lottie's every waking moment. The incident with the Comanche hunting party had hurt her deeply.

Now she wondered if Shayne's determination to be rid of her was simply because she wasn't woman enough to keep him interested.

She suffered the tortures of a million doubts and a hundred self-deprecating thoughts as she rode. Had she cut her nose off to spite her face when she took the shears to her own hair and donned men's clothing?

Would she have been more tempting to him as the dressmaker of McTavish Plain instead of an independent woman determined to have one grand adventure in her life?

The rain came at sundown.

It was a hard, cold, driving rain, borne on a northerly wind. It stripped leaves from the trees and filled gullies and arroyos to overflowing.

Lottie was wet, sore, and miserable. The weather matched her own dreary thoughts. For the first time she thought fondly of her cheery parlor in McTavish Plain and how her windows would steam up when she had a fine fire going in her hearth.

Maybe that was where she belonged. Maybe she had been a fool to think she could have an adventure.

"We've got to find shelter from this." Shayne turned to her with rain dripping off the tip of his nose and a steady stream running from the back of his wide-brimmed hat.

"Wh-when—where?" she stammered; her teeth chattering together made it difficult to talk.

"Over there. In the last flash of lightning I saw what looked like a barn."

Lottie nodded and let Little Bit follow the mare. It was a barn, but half of it was gone, torn away by some long-ago event. There were still two walls at right angles and a partial roof that did provide a small corner of dry protection.

The horses seemed as glad of the shelter as Lottie when they rode into the rickety structure. An old layer of straw had been covered over with blown-in dirt, but at least it was dry.

Shayne dismounted and shook his body, shedding water off his slicker as neatly as Ian's hound, Darroch, might shed it from his coat. A strange stab of home-sickness lanced through Lottie at the thought of the dog that shared her sister's home.

A hard, dry lump had formed in her throat. She was sad, lonely, and near tears.

"Lottie?" The sound in Shayne's voice caused her to look up.

"What is it?"

She met his gaze. His hard, dark eyes were, as usual, unreadable. What was it that drove this man? Was it only his need for revenge or was it something deeper?

With a heavy sigh she realized that she knew nothing about him. He was still as big a mystery to her now as on the day he walked into her dress shop.

And he always would be.

A strange, placid feeling folded over her. She was done with chasing him. It came to her like a bolt of lightning.

"I will go with you to find Red Slovang. I'll see this through to the end with you. But then I'm going to give you what you want, Shayne. You won't have to run from me anymore. I'm going back to my life in McTavish Plain."

"You're what?" He frowned at her, his eyes narrowing.

"I am through chasing you. I'm done. I see it's pointless. Whatever demons are driving you are yours alone. I understand you now. I can't make you want to be with me; I realize that now. I was a fool to even have tried. But you can rest easy now, Shayne. Soon enough I'll be out of your life forever. I'm giving you exactly what you want."

Twenty-three

Shayne stared at Lottie's back in stunned silence. He should be feeling like a range bull who slipped a rope. It had taken a while for her to see the truth. He should be jumping for joy. He should be glad that she finally realized that he was a rambling rogue.

But he wasn't.

In fact, he had never felt so strangely abandoned in his life. Whatever this hollow dark feeling was that crawled inside him, he didn't like it—not one bit.

It was like being alone in the dark of night without stars, without hope. The prospect of life without Lottie was a bitter, icy stab of regret that squeezed all the air from his lungs. It hurt to breathe.

But that can't be. He had been trying to get shed of her almost since the first.

Lottie was a sweet hunk of woman—he never denied that, or that she made the best love of any woman he had ever lain with—but he certainly didn't have any illusions about a lifetime with her.

No. He didn't deserve her. He had been trying to get it through her head that she belonged in McTavish Plain.

"And I finally did it," he whispered under his breath, trying to ignore the cold fist crushing his heart.

There was a sharp pain in his chest. He felt as though his soul was being ripped in half.

How could Lottie's simple decision do this to him? She was giving him what he wanted—that was how she put it.

Giving me what I want . . .

He had to pull himself together. . . . He had to be a man.

Lottie and Shayne tended the horses and made a crude camp. He built a fire at the edge of the ruined roof. Random raindrops found their way to the wood with sizzling plops and tiny bursts of steam as the water encountered the flames. Mist rose in an eerie cloud around the fire.

Lottie sat close to the blaze and rubbed her arms. Her slicker had kept her fairly dry, but she shivered as if she was chilled to the bone.

"I wish I had a cup of Mattie's tea."

"I wish I had a jug," Shayne said glumly. His strange, melancholy mood had gotten worse. Now he sat opposite Lottie and yearned for the oblivion of a good drunk, the kind that obliterated thought and hammered all the sharp, painful edges off his emotions.

He glanced at the ruined barn, his eyes drifting to the portion of the loft that remained.

"When I was a boy we lived near a fella that had a barn like this. Jacob Smithers. He made the best brew in the county. Used to bury it in the corner by his corn crib. Biggest corn crib I ever saw."

"Like that one over there?" Lottie nodded to the ruins of a corn crib that no doubt housed a large colony of rodents.

"*Exactly* like that one over there," Shayne said, striding over to kick several of the broken boards aside. Mice went scurrying in all directions.

He fell to his knees, and using his hands as a shovel he dipped out the soft blown-in dirt and old straw. "This is Jacob's place."

He drew out a crock, dusty but with the cork still in place. "No wonder it looked so familiar to me. Looks like the place has been abandoned for years. I wonder what happened."

Lottie shrugged. "Places change; folks move. Maybe he died."

"Naw, Jacob was a crusty old fart like my Pa. He was too ornery to die." Shayne used his shirttail to wipe the jug clean.

"Is there anything in it?" Lottie asked.

He shook the jug, smiling at the hollow tune of sloshing liquid. "Sounds like."

He blew off most of the dirt and dust and used his teeth to pull the cork. It left the bottle with a thick *pop*. Shayne sniffed the neck of the crock. Then he used his elbow to support the jug and tipped it up. Liquid heat trickled down his throat and settled in his belly.

"How long have you been gone from Texas, Shayne?" Lottie asked with a frown.

"Five years and four months." He glanced up at her. "Want some?"

She hesitated for a moment. Then she shook her head. "I don't think so. I'm not much of a drinker."

"Well, I am. Here's to you, Lottie darlin' and the fact that you have finally come to your senses." Shayne nodded in her direction and then took another long swallow. "I intend to sit and drink as long as it rains."

It rained for three days. And Shayne's word was good. He found firewood and made sure the horses got watered and fed, but beyond that he drank.

And drank some more.

And when he was sure the crock was finally empty, he dug up another one and continued to drink.

Lottie had never seen this side of him. He didn't talk; he didn't eat. He simply kept the crock between his thighs and every little while he took another swallow until he finally slept.

But his sleep was not peaceful.

He thrashed and cursed and fought his demons. Once or twice he even called out her name.

Lottie did not go to him. She was done. She had made her decision. Even though she loved him with all her heart, she had finally come to realize that Shayne Rosswarne was a force of nature. He was wild and free like the wind.

And she couldn't rope or tame the wind.

She had thought they were alike in their wildness, but she had learned that wasn't true. Lefty had taught her that painful lesson.

But it wasn't so easy to watch Shayne grappling with unseen forces and wallowing in his own private hell.

What was eating at him?

He should be over the moon since she had finally agreed with him that she would be better off in McTavish Plain. She had quit fighting to stay with him, and now he seemed more unhappy than before.

He was a complex man—a man she would have run rivers and climbed mountains with. He was the other half of her soul, but she could not fight him to be with him.

Shayne was lost in a world of fear and regret. His father had told him about revenge and being a man, and he couldn't have his honor restored and have a life with Lottie.

That bitter yearning was tearing him apart. He craved a life with Lottie.

A life. Not a lonely existence riding from one town to the next, one scheme to the next. A life where he could put down roots, plant a tree, and plant his seed—and shape a place for himself and his children, if God should bless him with sons and daughters.

He had allowed himself to consider a future—a normal life with a woman. *With Lottie.* And now he was suffering for his folly.

Lottie was through. She had made up her mind. She was giving him exactly what he wanted. He had never really expected her to quit—not Lottie.

He had thought she would keep on coming, her stubbornness never waning. But he was wrong.

And he had never been so alone in his life.

The sun was hot and red through Shayne's closed eyelids. His tongue was thick, his mouth dry and cottony.

He sat up. His head nearly fell off. He put both palms on his temples and tried to hold the throbbing melon on his shoulders.

It didn't help.

"Do you feel as bad as you look?" Lottie asked sweetly. She was frying bacon over a small fire. The smell of the pork was turning Shayne's stomach inside out.

Shayne blinked and focused on her face. She looked at him from curious blue eyes that held a measure of humor and curiosity in their depths.

"Don't enjoy my misery so much," he snarled.

She shrugged. "Then you shouldn't take so much pleasure getting yourself this way."

He growled and staggered to his feet, but his head suddenly was wanting to explode. He leaned over, bracing his palms on his knees to steady himself while he dragged in lung-fulls of breath, trying to calm his stomach and make the world tilt upright.

"You are a cruel woman, Charlotte."

"No, I'm just ready to get on with it, Shayne. All I have heard from you since we met is that you *had* to find the man that wronged you. Funny, but it doesn't appear you're doing very much to locate him all of a sudden."

Shayne's head snapped up. He managed to focus until there was only one Lottie staring at him. Her eyes were cold and calm as a frozen mountain lake.

She was right.

He had gotten drunk and felt sorry for himself. He had wallowed in his misery and loneliness, but why?

Because she said she would only stay until it was finished.

Shayne shook off the thought. He couldn't be avoiding his destiny just because Lottie was going to leave him when it was done.

He couldn't be. No real man would do such a thing.

He wanted to find Red Slovang. He wanted it finished; he wanted to see Lottie head back to McTavish Plain.

He did.

"Then saddle up, darlin'," Shayne sneered, fighting the pain that clawed at his insides.

"Where are we going?" she said, gaining her feet in one smooth motion.

"We're going to find Red Slovang. You're right. It is time I finished this and put to rest the ghosts that are haunting me. And then you'll be able to get back to your life in McTavish Plain."

"When will we be in Texas?" Lottie asked, weary of riding. The sun was strong, the air full of dust borne on a steady westerly wind.

Shayne died a little inside, knowing she was anxious to leave him.

"We've been in Texas for two days, darlin'." Shayne pulled Little Bit to a halt and scanned the horizon. "I couldn't wait to leave this country when I was a boy. Now I wonder why I was so foolish."

"It is beautiful. Wild and untamed, but beautiful," Lottie said softly. "That sky seems to go on forever."

Shayne swiveled to stare at her. "I craved adventure just like you, Lottie. I couldn't see the beauty in front of me because I was sure my destiny was out there somewhere. It is a pity that a big chunk of my life is gone and I'm only just now realizing that what a man wants and needs can be right in front of him."

Lottie didn't know what to say to that. Lately at night she had the same odd kind of notion as she found herself growing homesick for McTavish Plain.

She hadn't been able to put it neatly into words the way Shayne had, but that was how she felt.

Maybe she had been yearning for adventure, dying to see what was over the next mountain for so long that she had thrown away a happy future that was right in her own small town.

Could that be true? Had her destiny been in McTavish Plain all along?

"Your hair is starting to grow a bit," Shayne said with a crooked grin. "It's curling around your neck now."

Lottie swept off her hat and ran her fingers through her curls. They were indeed longer than the last time she had really taken the time to notice.

"I don't think I told you that I admire you, Lottie."

"Admire?" she repeated, slapping the hat back onto her head.

"Yep. You've got grit. It takes a real, genuine lady to tame a town full of reprobates the way you did."

A lady.

His words made her throat contract. Did he really think of her as a lady after she had worn men's clothes, cut her hair, and chased after him like a wanton woman?

"I haven't said a lot of what has been in my mind, Lottie. I've known girls and women but damned few ladies. You are a lady. Whether you're in skirts and ribbons or trousers and boots, you're a lady. Don't ever think otherwise. When you go back home, you hold your head high and you make sure that you don't forget what I say."

"Damn you, Shayne." Lottie swiped at her eyes. "Just when I think I'm past paying you any mind, you find a way to get to me. Why are you saying this now?"

He scanned the horizon again. "Over that rise is the Tipton spread, and ten miles beyond is my family's ranch. If anybody in Texas will know where to find Red Slovang, it'll be old man Tipton. His family fought for Texas independence and there have been lawmen in every generation of Tiptons since. I figure he'll point me in the right direction. With a little luck, you'll be headed back to McTavish Plain by morning."

Lottie rode beside Shayne beneath the tall wooden gate. "T-Bar Ranch" had been seared with a hot iron into the wood deep enough to let all who entered know that the man who had built the place intended to be around for a long, long time.

A weathered rocker and a straight-backed chair sat empty on the wide porch running the length of the front of the house. A short-haired yellow dog snarled from under the steps.

"It doesn't look too friendly."

"It isn't supposed to. This is Texas," Shayne said cryptically.

A gray-haired man stumped out the front door. He stood tall on one flesh-and-blood leg and one appendage carved from wood. He peered up at Shayne.

"You're that Rosswarne boy, ain't you?"

"Yes sir."

Lottie had never heard Shayne address anyone in that manner. Shayne pulled himself up straighter in the saddle. For a moment she had the feeling she was glimpsing a bit of the boy he had been before prison and life had hardened him. Her heart pinched a bit and she fought the lure of Shayne Rosswarne.

"You've been gone a long time," Mr. Tipton said.

"Yes sir."

"Stopped here afore goin' home, eh?"

"Yes sir."

"Why?"

"I'm looking for a man and thought some of your sons or nephews wearing badges might know of him. Are any of them around that I might talk to, Mr. Tipton?"

The man's hoary brows rose to his thatch of silvery hair. "All my boys got het up about the fracas back east. They saddled up and went to fight in the secesh business. Ain't no Tiptons left in Texas but me."

"Sorry to hear that, sir." Shayne murmured.

"Danged fools'll probably get theirselves shot up or killed. You'd think seeing me lose a leg to the Commanch wars would've taught 'em something." He tapped his knuckles against his artificial leg. The hollow sound vibrated though the air.

"Well, I thank you kindly for the information, sir," Shayne said. "I'd best be on my way."

"You headed home now?"

"Yes sir. It's long overdue. I have a few things to settle with my pa."

The man frowned and stumped closer to the edge of the porch. The snarling dog came out and sat obediently at the bottom of his wooden leg. "You don't know, boy? You didn't get word?"

"Know what?"

"Your pa has been dead for near two years now."

Twenty-four

Shayne rode in silence, but his mind was in turmoil. All the years he had been in prison, all the time he had plotted his revenge against the man who wronged him, he had never once considered that his father wouldn't be at the ranch when he came back.

Joss Rosswarne was a big, hard, forbidding man. Death was not something Shayne had considered would ever touch his sire—not for many, many long years.

It seemed there was a battle Joss hadn't won.

Shayne struggled to hold himself together as the foundation of his beliefs shifted like loose sand beneath his boots.

He had eaten, slept, and lived vengeance. Plans of murder had been his bread and water—the air he breathed. He had wronged Lottie, left the promise of a new life in McTavish Plain, and turned his back on his own future.

And for what? What had it all been for? The man he had to prove something to had been dead and buried for two years.

Shayne had wanted to have his revenge because he wanted to be able to stand before his father and assure him that the honor and name of Rosswarne had been avenged. He had needed his father's acceptance, and the only way he knew to buy it was with Red Slovang's blood.

Now that would never happen. It was too late. And in chasing this foolish notion of buying his good name back with Slovang's blood, he had driven Lottie away.

She had ridden in silence since they left the T-Bar. Shayne wondered if Mr. Tipton's words ran through her head in an endless tune the way they did through his.

She had done nothing to give him any indication of her opinion, but his belly knotted with apprehension. He wanted to ask her, but his throat was clogged with his own words.

Did she think him less of a man? Were her opinions now weighted by his inability to accomplish his goal and heal the rift with his father? Did she perceive him to be as stupid as he felt?

He had been so anxious to leave Texas; did she now feel the same anxious urge?

Shayne had been a rebellious, foolish youth, hell-bent for trouble and determined to show his father that he was a man in his own right—not just by virtue of being Joss Rosswarne's son. Joss had cast a mighty big shadow across Texas and had left a footprint that Shayne had been chafing to try and fill.

What a fool Shayne had been—still was, for that matter. He had let the poor judgment and mistakes of his youth dictate more mistakes now that he was a man.

Lottie was beautiful, sweet, and passionate. She was the kind of woman a man searched for all his life. God had seen fit to put her right into Shayne's hands. And what had he done about it? He had abused her, shamed her, tried to leave her at every possible opportunity.

He hated himself and didn't blame her if she felt the same way.

"How much farther to your home, Shayne?" she asked quietly, bringing his thoughts to an abrupt halt.

Home. So many emotions wrapped into one small word.

"Over that next rise. My father ran his spread like he did everything else, with narrow-minded, tight-fisted control. His cattle were the best in the county—hell, they didn't dare be anything *but* the best. Just like his wife and his son and everything that bore the brand of Joss Rosswarne," Shayne said bitterly.

"You loved him."

"And I hated him, too," Shayne said with choked candor. "He had such high expectations of me. I made sure I could draw faster, shoot straighter, and ride better than any man his sight fell upon. I spent all my awkward youth stumbling over my eagerness to please my father. It was my own cussed determination to be a better man than he was—a man he would have to respect on his own merit. And in the end I managed to disappoint him at every turn and lose my own self-respect.

"And now it's too damned late to show my father anything." Was it also too late for him to salvage any kind of a life with Lottie?

"My mother always took a deal of pride in our fat cattle and lush fields. She used to tell anybody that would listen that my father squeezed the prosperity out of each inch of Texas soil with the strength of his hands and his will."

"Shayne, about your father—"

"Look, Lottie, there it is." He stood in his stirrups and pointed.

Lottie followed the line of his arm into the gently rolling valley beyond.

There were a few cattle, but they were rangy, thin, and gaunt. And the fields looked parched and dry. Brown grass and withering trees met her eye.

The ranch house appeared to be sagging in depression, its windows staring out like vacant eyes from a skin of peeling paint.

"Oh, my God. What has happened?" Shayne croaked out. But before she could offer any explanation of her own, he put his heels to the horse and thundered past Lottie. For a moment she thought she spied the glisten of tears in his dark eyes.

Shayne rode to the house and leaped from Little Bit. He took two steps before the front door opened and an old woman stepped out onto the porch with a rifle in her hand.

"I told you I'd put a bullet in the next man that came here demanding that I sell out." She lifted the barrel of the gun. "Now leave before I put a hole in you."

Shayne shuddered to a stop. He stared at the old woman in silence.

That voice . . . those eyes . . .

"Mama?" he asked softly, his heart at war with his eyes. His mother's hair had been a dark, glossy brown, her skin smooth. This woman was old. Ground down by pain and work, she looked barely able to hold the rifle in her work-worn hands.

"Shayne? Oh, my sweet Jesus. Is it really you, Shayne?" The rifle fell from her hand, clattering to the warped dry wood of the porch. Then her eyes rolled up in her head and she sagged into Shayne's arms as he closed the distance between them.

"Yes, mama, it is me. I've come home."

"At last, Shayne. Your father said you would come, but I had nearly run out of hope."

And then she fainted dead away.

Lottie dipped a cloth into the basin of tepid water. She gently bathed Shayne's mother's face. They were in the front parlor, which was clean but threadbare. There were traces of finery still evident in the gilt frames that held portraits and in the piano that sat near a window, but everything was showing the wear of time and poverty.

"She looks so old and frail," Shayne said from the shadowy corner where he had stood vigil, his face a mask of pain and worry. Lottie saw his hands clench and unclench. She read the tension and impotent rage in the taut lines of his body.

He wanted to hit something. He wanted to make someone pay for the ruin of his home and the destruction of his memories.

She felt the same way. A part of her, the part that was connected to Shayne with gossamer threads of affection, cried silently for him.

"Someone is going to pay," he said, giving life to the words in Lottie's own mind.

"But who, Shayne? Maybe she's simply grief-stricken over your father . . . and you."

"You know how to kick a man when he's down, don't you, Lottie?" Shayne said softly. "But you're right. I bear most of the responsibility. I was hell-bent for destruction and my family is paying the price for it."

"No. It wasn't you, Shayne." The woman's voice was a crackly whisper. She reached out and Shayne came to her. He went down on his knees beside the settee where she lay. Her hand covered his dark hair, the dry, cracked fingers curling into the strands with love.

"I missed you, boy, but your papa knew you would come back. On his deathbed he told me not to give up hope. He knew you would come back and avenge him. He knew you would put things right. Your papa had a lot of faith in you."

"What happened, Mama? Where are all the hands and the stock?"

"Run off or killed. Things changed after you left, Shayne. We got ourselves a mean neighbor. He wanted your daddy to sell. He thought he would sell out cheap since you, our only son, had up and left. But Joss didn't know the meaning of 'give in' and our neighbor didn't know the Rosswarnes."

"What killed him, Mama?" Shayne's eyes were awash with unshed tears, his voice harsh and filled with pain.

"A bullet in the back."

Shayne's entire body stiffened. He glanced up at Lottie; his eyes were blazing with hatred and dark fire.

"Who shot him, Mama?"

"Our neighbor. I knew it; everyone knew it, but nobody could prove it. The murderin' sneak is slippery as a snake. Got the law in his breast pocket—paid them all to look the other way."

"Who? Who, Mama?"

"A man by the name of Red Slovang."

Lottie gasped. Shayne's face hardened, his hand flexed near the hilt of his gun.

"Don't worry, Papa was right. I'm home now and I'll have my revenge. Tell me exactly where Red Slovang lives."

Shayne sat atop Little Bit and stared down at the ranch house below. There was a bustle of activity as hands ambled between the barn, bunk house, and corrals.

Those corrals were full of fat cattle and fatter horses, and Shayne could not help but notice the telltale signs of his daddy's own bloodlines.

Joss Rosswarne had been partial to a particular kind of splashy oxblood paint. The corral below sported more than thirty paints with that unusual hue in their hides.

And the beeves also bore his father's mark. Joss Rosswarne had been one of the first ranchers in the area to import polled breeding stock from the East. It was possible those curly heads had once sported horns, but Shayne didn't think so. They were naturally polled and some of them probably wore Joss Rosswarne's brand as well.

Shayne thought back to the time he met Red Slovang in the guise of Ian McTavish.

The man had approached him in a bar in Austin. He had a winning smile and a sweet line. Shayne's gut twisted with rage as he thought about how easily he had been taken in. Like a fish seeing a fancy lure, Shayne had swallowed it all as Red played on his foolish dreams—and on the chip that Shayne had worn on his shoulder.

It had been easy.

And the bastard did it to get me out of the way. The truth was clear as water now. Red Slovang wanted the Rosswarne spread and stock. And to get it he had made sure Shayne was locked up.

"I have been the biggest fool ever born." Shayne heard a sound and turned to see Lottie riding up to him. He rode to meet her, shielded by a hillock, not wanting to announce his presence to the ranch below.

Not yet.

"Shayne, what are you planning?" Lottie asked when he reached her.

"I don't know yet, but I intend to find a way to avenge my father and break Red Slovang in one blow." He focused on her face. "But this may take a while, Lottie, so if you decide to go back to McTavish Plain now, I'll understand."

They stared at each other for a full minute while his heart ceased to beat. Her leaving was the last thing he wanted, but it seemed even more important now to be a man—to stand on his own two feet without needing anyone.

"I'll see you back at your mother's house. She's fixed a big meal—said it was your favorite," Lottie said tunelessly.

Shayne could only stare in silence at her ramrod-stiff back as she galloped away.

Why couldn't he just spit out his pride and tell her that he wanted her to stay?

"Mrs. Rosswarne, you set a fine table." Lottie was touched by the pride Shayne's mother took in setting his favorite dishes before him. There was fried chicken, thick gravy, and fried okra with yellow corn-bread.

"I take a deal of joy in my cooking when there's someone to eat it." She sat down near Shayne, her eyes drinking in the sight of him.

"I haven't had a meal like this since I left Texas," Shayne said, folding his large brown hand over her work-worn smaller one.

"Oh, go on with you. Lottie probably sets a fine table."

Lottie laughed. "Sorry, but sewing is my only feminine skill. I'm not much of a cook. I rely on my eldest sister to keep me in victuals."

"It must be fine to have sisters and family close by," Mrs. Rosswarne sighed.

"Are you lonely, Mama?" Shayne asked abruptly, bringing Lottie's gaze to his face.

"Very lonely, son. You and your papa left a mighty big hole in my heart. But you're home now. Things will be different." She smiled.

"Not until I find a way to bring Red Slovang to his knees." His eyes narrowed and he toyed with the cutlery beside his plate. "Tell me what happened. Tell me all of it."

Lottie sat curled into a big old leather chair. Her head rested on an ancient quilt as she listened to Shayne's mother recount the incidents that led to disaster.

"He came one day offering to buy this place," Mrs. Rosswarne said. Now that she had her son back, some of the strain had left her face. The traces of her former beauty were evident in her thick lashes and dark brows. Lottie could easily see the evidence of her Spanish heritage as she spoke softly.

"Your father declined his offer—civilly at first. But he came again and again. And then we started having accidents around the place. The windmill in the lower pasture was pulled down one night. With no water we had to shift the cattle to the other pasture. That was where most of them were rustled from."

"What about the men?"

"The war has taken the best of Texas's manhood, son. What was left tried as hard as your pa to keep watch, but if they were in the south pastures, fires were set in the north. It wasn't long before we were selling off the best stock to make ends meet."

"The bastard was manipulating you."

"Yes, and though we were sure it was him, there was no proof. He offered to buy us out again—at a lower price, of course. Your father threw him off the place. You had been gone a few months by then, but we thought you'd be back."

"Red Slovang knew I wasn't coming back."

Mrs. Rosswarne swiped at a tear. "I see that now. He was cocky—arrogant—telling your father that he had no son to leave the place to and that he should sell. It broke your father's heart, but it also stiffened his resolve. He was managing to keep the place together and then we were hit by rustlers. The best stallions and mares disappeared."

"What about the law?"

"As I said, Shayne, the best of Texas is fighting back east. Those left are cheap and easy to buy. The law turned a blind eye. Your father swore he wouldn't be driven out by some fast-talking crook."

"How—how did he get shot?"

Shayne's mother drew in a shuddering breath. She was trembling. "Joss had the notion he would be best served by watching the place where Red Slovang had set up camp. He had bought that broken-down Spencer farm that butts up against our eastern line and was fixing it up. He went out one night to watch. . . . They found him back-shot and half dead the next morning. The bullet had hit his spine. He wasn't able to talk much."

Shayne stood up. His body was vibrating with rage as he stalked to the window and stared out into the darkness. "I want to kill the bastard."

"If you do that the law won't turn a blind eye. Red Slovang has greased the palms of powerful men. You'll have to find another way, Shayne. You'll have to be smarter."

"You need to appeal to his greed, Shayne. His greed and his vanity are his soft spots," Lottie offered. "And I think I know a way to use both."

Twenty-five

Lottie turned before the looking glass, critically surveying the seams of the fancy gown. "I don't know; what do you think, Mrs. Rosswarne?"

"I think I am mighty tired of you calling me that. Please, call me Isabel."

Lottie smiled. "Fine, Isabel. Can you see the stitches? It has to look finely done and freshly made— not like a dress that has been made over." Light played over the emerald green watered silk of the bright full skirt. It and a dozen others from Isabel's youth had been brought out of a cedar-lined chest and cut down to fit Lottie.

"It's beautiful, Charlotte. And beautiful on you."

"But do I look like an Easterner? I have to make Red Slovang think I am fresh from the East, with a hankering to settle down and marry."

"He'll believe it." Shayne's voice brought them both spinning to the doorway. He lounged there, his dark eyes skimming over Lottie's form in a hungry fashion. "You look pretty enough to convince the man that you hung the moon, if that's your intention."

She felt the warm flush of arousal begin low in her belly. It had been a long time since they had made love and she wanted him still—wanted him even though she knew that when this was finished she would leave him. How could she crave a man that she was so determined to leave—to make him a sweet memory, a secret pleasure of her past?

He licked his lips and Lottie gripped the back of a nearby chair to keep from swaying. He made her weak in the knees with his hunger and her own answering need.

"Oh, my, I completely forgot that I have apples soaking for a pie in the kitchen." Isabel stood abruptly, her gaze darting between Shayne and Lottie. "You children excuse me. I'll be busy for some time." She hurried away while Shayne grinned.

"She did that on purpose."

"I know," Lottie said awkwardly. She should be embarrassed to know Shayne's mother could feel the current of arousal arcing between them—she should have been, but she wasn't.

Strangely, she felt very comfortable in the big, rambling Texas house. The ceilings were too high, the furnishings too fancy yet at the same time threadbare, but it felt *right* to be there. Shayne's mother had accepted her immediately. They had settled into a nice friendship almost from the start.

Shayne's eyes skimmed over her body in unashamed appreciation. "It's been a while since I saw you in women's finery."

"And what do you think?" Lottie grabbed a handful of her skirts up in each hand and did a little quick turn. She winked at Shayne when she stopped.

He pushed himself away from the doorjamb and came to her. With one finger he traced the fine old lace at her bosom. "I think I want to unlace your bodice and see what's hidden beneath all this satin and ribbons."

She sighed. "Not a bad idea, cowboy. You'll get no resistance from me."

How could they be so in tune with each other physically and so far apart on every other level?

"Lottie?"

"Mmmm?" she asked, enjoying the hypnotic rhythm of his finger as it left a trail of chills and burning desire. Her nipples had gone hard, her lower belly all soft and needy.

She wanted him.

"Lottie, my mother was giving us some privacy. What do you say we put it to good use?"

She smiled at him and wrapped her arms around his neck. "What took you so long?"

With a throaty growl he pulled her against him. The thick petticoats and layers of skirt whispered as he moved her slowly back and forth against him, grinding his arousal into the cleft of her thighs.

"Lottie, you are under my skin . . . in my blood. You are sweet poison."

"Poison, am I?" She nipped at the soft skin beneath his ear.

He growled in response. "You must be poison. How else can you explain what we do to each other?"

"I stopped trying to explain it, Shayne. What happens between us is some sort of magic." She was limp in his arms, awash in the joy of having his hands and his mouth on the bare flesh above her bodice.

"I kind of like you in all these petticoats." He ran his hand up her leg, his fingers light as the touch of a butterfly's wing as he made her tremble with desire. "It takes a lot longer to get you out of this kind of rigging."

"And you want to take a long time?" she asked suggestively.

"Darlin', I want to take so long with you that our lovemaking never ends."

Lovemaking. The word hung in the air like the sweet perfume of a flower.

Shayne covered her mouth with his. He kissed her hard and long, probing deep into her mouth with his tongue while one hand continued up her leg. He gathered ruffles and petticoats as he reached higher.

She felt his fingers slip into the slit of her drawers. And then, a heartbeat later, his fingers slipped into her.

She moaned in delight.

His fingers were slightly abrasive against her tender flesh, but his touch was whisper light and tender as he stroked her and set her blood on fire.

Shayne knew her. He knew where to touch her, how to tempt her.

He did so now. Her knees buckled and her back arched as he teased, pleasured and tickled the most sensitive part of her.

Soon her breath was coming in ragged gasps. She clung to his shoulders, suspended in his arms, suspended in time while he brought her to a shuddering climax.

Lottie's body was not her own. It and all her nerves, sinews, and will power belonged to Shayne. At moments like this he owned her fully, completely, and she wanted it that way.

Soon, while she was still spiraling in time as her body convulsed and shuddered, he scooped her up in his arms. She was barely aware of being gently deposited on the settee. And only marginally cognizant of him stripping off her clothes, a layer at a time, until she was naked.

He looked at her—a hot, licking glance that started at the cleft of her thighs and ended with her eyes. Their gaze locked, and in that thrilling moment they knew.

There could never ever be another person on this earth that would complete either of them as the other did. They were two halves of the same whole: perfect together.

He quickly shed his own clothes and came to her. His erection was jutting out, pulsing, throbbing, the head dark with need.

She grasped him and gently drew him upward to her until she could reach him with her tongue. Then she licked him, delighting in the way his buttocks tightened and he tensed above her.

"Lottie, you are killing me," he grated out, his hand gripping hard into the back of the settee as if he feared he might fall without that support.

"No, I am giving you pleasure." She did it again. And finally, when he had arched and bucked and tightened every muscle in his body, she took him fully into her mouth.

His skin was moist velvet against her tongue. She explored the small opening, the slick, taut hardness of him.

He groaned.

She suckled him.

"Damn, woman. You *are* killing me."

He pulled away from her. He lifted her hips and thrust hard into her. He was big, pulsing with life and need. He stretched her, filled her, brought her to the point of blissful pain.

Then he slowly withdrew. With a grunt and a grin he drove into her—hard. She took him, her body closing about him in a way that went beyond mere physical need.

They were connected, part of each other. They were a perfect fit. Like horses that had run in tandem all their lives, they knew what the other wanted and gave it. Every movement was answered in kind.

She dragged her nails down the hard, rippled flesh of his back and smiled with satisfaction when he closed his eyes and leaned into her like a cat being stroked.

This was bliss; this was fire and ice and things beyond words.

She reveled in their shared ability to bring each other satisfaction, but in the back of her mind a little voice cruelly reminded her that if their plan worked she would soon be on her way back to her life in McTavish Plain.

Morning found Lottie, Shayne, and Isabel sitting at the table with cups of hot coffee in their hands. They had spent the night preparing their plan, making sure they all knew what was to happen.

"I still don't like it, Lottie; you could be in danger." Shayne scowled across the table. He had been voicing his objection loudly all night long.

"Nonsense. Red Slovang isn't going to expect me to be his enemy; therefore I won't present a threat—at least not right away."

"What do you think he'll do when you tell him?" Isabel said, her brow furrowed but her dark eyes twinkling with eagerness.

"I hope to have charmed him so much that, by the

time I tell him who I'm supposed to be, he'll be completely off guard." Lottie focused hard on Shayne.

"You have got to stay out of sight, Shayne. In order for this to work, you must let Red Slovang believe you're still rotting in jail."

"Do you think he'll believe you're my niece?" Isabel asked, her eyes darting to Lottie's golden hair.

"Why not? A long lost relative come to claim the family property is not so far-fetched." Lottie shrugged.

"And while you sweet-talk him I am going to give Mr. Slovang a dose of his own mysterious accidents."

"Yes. We'll break him down a bit at a time, and when he's confused and off balance, then you can reveal yourself," Lottie agreed.

"And after I settle the score for my pa, you can get back home where you'll be safe."

The old buggy shone from the cleaning and waxing Shayne had given it. Lottie's little saddle mare held her head and tail high as she cantered smoothly over the rutted, dusty Texas road.

Lottie was going visiting, setting a trap she hoped Red Slovang could not resist. Her jaunty hat was sitting at an angle on her curls that had been smoothed and tamed into a cluster at the side of her head. She was corsetted and buttoned, and between her and Isabel, Lottie was fairly sure she could pass for an Eastern spinster looking for a man to marry as soon as possible.

The look on Shayne's face as she had driven the buggy out of the barn nearly ripped her heart from her breast.

He was a proud, angry man. When he looked at

Lottie like that, she could hardly ignore the pain and hunger in his eyes.

"Soon, when Red Slovang has been brought to his knees, you will have what you want, Shayne," Lottie had told him. Then she straightened her back and tightened her gloved fingers on the lines. Soon it would be over and she would leave, just as he wanted. Shayne would finally have his honor, his revenge, and his all-important freedom.

Red Slovang's ranch was what Lottie had expected to find at the Rosswarne spread. The house was small but well kept; a new coat of white paint gleamed against the dark-green shutters at the lower windows. Dove gray fretwork ran around the edge of the low porch.

The corrals were full of paint horses, and beyond that, fields of fat cattle in the company of a huge red-and-white bull. He ambled to one cow and mounted her, doing his best to increase Red Slovang's herd and his wealth.

Little puffs of dust rose up from the wheels and settled on Lottie's burgundy velvet pelisse. She coughed a little as the buggy came to a halt in front of the house.

Her stomach was in knots as she waited for someone to come and acknowledge her presence. She didn't have to wait long.

The door opened and a man with small, mean eyes came out. His rusty hair was going white at the temples. His body was lean, strong, and without any trace of softness to it. An old scar lay along his jawbone.

"You must be lost," he said gruffly.

"No, I don't think so," Lottie said in her sweetest voice. She brushed at the fine dirt on the nap of her skirt. Her dark gloves had a powdery sheen when she extended her hand to the man who had come to glare at her from the side of the buggy.

"I am your neighbor and I wanted to get acquainted." Lottie batted her eyes. "I am the new owner of the old Rosswarne spread."

"Would you say that again?" Red Slovang's voice was harsh and gritty. Lottie ignored his manner and acted as if he had just offered her a cool drink and the hospitality of his home. She rose up and extended her hand, and finally, with a blink of his eyes he took hold of her glove and helped her to the ground. One joint of a finger was missing.

"I said I'm the new owner of the Rosswarne place. I am so bored sitting there with my ailing auntie that I thought I might just as well get acquainted with my nearest neighbor." She took a deep breath and sashayed past the man, whose mouth was gaping open.

"My, you have quite a place here." She whirled to look at him, shading her eyes with her hand. "I am planning on making a lot of improvements; would you mind sharing some of your expertise, Mr. . . . Gracious, here I have barged in on your hospitality and not even heard your name."

"Slovang, Red Slovang." He looked confused. "What do you mean you're planning on making improvements?"

"Oh, my auntie Isabel is not well. As her last relative she has deeded the place to me. I was tired of living in the city. Mama always said the best men were in the West anyway. And my mother was a very shrewd woman."

Lottie scanned Red Slovang quickly, then averted her eyes in what she hoped was true maidenly fashion. "I am hoping to marry a Texan, you see."

Even from the corner of her eye she could see the hot glaze of speculation. Red Slovang pulled himself up a notch, rolled back his shoulders, puffed out his chest. "Come inside. I'm sorry I didn't get your name either, Miss." He slid his hand to the small of her back.

"Oh, I'm Lottie Green. My mother was Auntie Isabel's second cousin."

"Pleased to make your acquaintance, *Miss* Lottie Green. Come inside and let me offer you some true Texas hospitality."

Lottie smiled sweetly. The fish had taken the bait.

Twenty-six

"Mr. Slovang, I do declare, you must be what we Easterners call a cattle baron. You own some of the finest stock I have seen in this country."

"I have worked hard to build my herd." He said pridefully.

"Did you bring in stock from the East?" Lottie asked, plastering a false smile on her face while her anger threatened to undo her. She knew from what Isabel had said that the bull now servicing Slovang's herd had been the last real asset Isabel had. It had disappeared right after Joss died. The law had been quick to say it had probably been lost to wolves or Comanche raiders or any possible source except Red Slovang.

"No, I found some ranchers in the area that had mismanaged their spreads and were obliged to part with their best stock."

Obliged. Another word for swindled and stolen.

"Well, gracious me, look at the time. I must get back. Auntie Isabel will be needing her medicine."

"In a bad way, is she?" He barely suppressed his glee.

"Very bad. I doubt she'll hang on for more than another month," Lottie lied smoothly.

"You will be needing a friend, Miss Green. I would be honored if you would consider me such."

"Thank you." Lottie smiled. "I will definitely call upon you for assistance when the time comes."

Shayne bit down hard on the inside of his jaw. He was hunkered down in a copse of wild pecan trees watching. It was taking every ounce of control he had to keep from riding down into Slovang's yard and shooting him.

The way the bastard handed Lottie up into that buggy nearly undid him.

"Son of a bitch," Shayne said softly. He had not been in favor of this part of Lottie's plan, and it did him no good at all to watch her bat her lashes and smile prettily at the man Shayne hated beyond reason. "Just get out of there, Lottie. You should be on your way home."

But she lingered, smiling, talking. Once again her zest for adventure was putting her squarely in the path of trouble.

She finally got into the buggy and lightly flicked the reins. Soon she was out the gate and down the road, little plumes of dust marking the wheels' progress.

Slovang watched her departure for a long time.

Shayne rolled over on his back and sucked in a breath of sweet, Texas air. Tonight he would begin his part of the plan.

"And I am going to enjoy every minute of watching Red Slovang squirm."

The next day Lottie was at the breakfast table with Isabel and Shayne when they saw the cloud of dust.

"Too much for a horse and rider. Must be a buggy," Shayne said, his eyes squinted over the rim of his coffee cup.

"It's Slovang," Lottie said, leaping to her feet.

"How do you know?" Shayne asked, his expression darkening quicker than the Texas sky. "Did you invite that bastard here?"

"No, of course not."

"Who else would it be?" Isabel rose from her chair. "Come on, you and me have to make ourselves scarce." She grabbed their cups and tossed the coffee out the back door. Then she washed them and put them in a cupboard out of sight. On her way by the table she brushed the tablecloth and made sure the oil lamp was positioned squarely in the middle.

Shayne watched all this with a growing expression of ire. Lottie could feel the anger emanating from him.

He was a handsome cuss when he was on the dangerous side of fury.

"Come on, son. He will be here any minute," Isabel urged, picking up her skirts and heading for the staircase.

"And we're sure it is Red Slovang?" Shayne snarled.

"Sure enough for you to mind what I am saying. If you want Lottie's plan to succeed you are going to have to help her." Isabel met Shayne's dark-eyed glare with one of her own.

Lottie nearly smiled at the obvious clash of wills. She found herself wondering what Shayne had been like as a boy. In her mind's eye she could well see him testing Isabel at every possible juncture.

"I'll be right upstairs if you need me," Shayne told Lottie. He took a step and then halted. He turned and came back and pulled her into a crushing kiss. He branded her with his lips, his tongue, and when he was done he set her from him and said, "Now I am going."

She barely had time to gather her wits and straighten her bodice before she heard the footfall of boots on the warped front steps.

When Lottie opened the door, Red Slovang was standing there, hat in hand, with a wide grin on his face. His eyes skimmed over her and she could see his eager curiosity as he tried to examine the rooms behind her.

"Mr. Slovang, what a surprise," she said airily, opening the door wider. She was willing to feed his curiosity as long as it went no farther than the ground floor.

"Do come in. May I offer you coffee? It is quite a treat to see you; having one's coffee alone can be a trial day after day."

"Uh, is Mrs. Rosswarne not able to come down?" His gaze flicked up the stairs.

"No, I am afraid she's too ill. I must carry on alone. Meal times are the worst." Lottie sniffed and turned away.

"There, there. I told you I'm ready to offer you friendship, Miss Green." He patted her shoulder in a manner that made her flesh creep. She wondered if Shayne was watching from above.

"I am honored." Lottie lowered her gaze. She was repulsed by the man, but she hoped her aversion to looking at him was being perceived as maidenly shyness.

"Miss Lottie, I am here to invite you to dinner at

my ranch tonight," he said with the practiced slickness of a snake-oil salesman.

"I—I hardly know what to say." She glanced at the stairs. She could almost feel Shayne's eyes on her.

"I'll send my buggy for you at six o'clock," he said forcefully. He took a step toward her.

Lottie steeled herself for his touch. He grasped her hand and brought it to his lips. "I hope, Miss Green, that we are going to become particular friends."

"I don't like it." Shayne paced like a cat while Isabel attended to the finishing touches of Lottie's attire. They were upstairs in Isabel and Joss's bedroom. Lottie was enchanted by the fireplace and the heavy carved pecan furniture, made from trees from their own grove.

"Shayne, this is the perfect opportunity for you to do more mischief," Isabel told him with a patient smile.

"I don't need Lottie keeping company with that bastard in order for me to administer justice."

"Justice? I thought we were out for revenge," Lottie said dryly.

"In this case it's the same thing. I took a deal of pleasure cutting his back fence. Unless he has some cowboys worth their salt, half his herd will be in Miller's canyon before he misses them."

"I'm sure that's how he got most of our stock," Isabel said softly, fastening an old silver-and-turquoise necklace at Lottie's throat. "I wasn't able to go looking. The fences were down and Horace just wandered off to find some new cows."

"Horace?" Lottie asked.

"Joss's prize bull."

"Red and white polled?" Lottie asked.

"You've seen him?" Isabel's hands froze. Her face was a portrait of emotions. Lottie could see that Shayne got a lot of his fire from her.

"There was a very eager bull doing what God intended with a herd of contented cows when I was at the Slovang place." Lottie wondered why she felt such heat in her face. She had never been one to be shy about what went on naturally between animals or people.

Then she realized Shayne was watching her. The heat in her face was her own body's response to him. She didn't even have to be looking at him to have her own body react to his scrutiny.

He made her hot; he made her randy.

She cleared her throat and focused on the task at hand. "I will keep Slovang busy with parlor talk. What are you going to do tonight?"

"I'm going to pull down the windmill in his back pasture," Shayne said coldly. "It's time he had a taste of his own poison."

The buggy came a few minutes before six. Lottie walked down the steps, pulling Isabel's elegant black lace shawl around her shoulders. She was wearing a dress of scarlet satin covered in fine, tiny open-worked lace of deepest ebony. Her feet were in Isabel's best slippers and her toes pinched a bit as she reached the buggy.

"Mr. Slovang. I thought you would send one of your ranch hands," Lottie said, genuinely surprised. She hoped that Isabel and Shayne had not been standing

at a window watching as he drove up. If he saw
Shayne now and realized what was going on, their
plan would be ruined. And if Red Slovang had the
law in his pocket as Isabel said, Shayne could be in
real trouble.

They were going to have to be very careful.

"I tend to the important details of my life person-
ally." He handed her into the buggy, holding her fingers longer than was necessary.

Tonight she would play another card from her hand.
And if she had learned anything from Cut-nose and
Dobbs, Red Slovang would call her bluff and raise the
stakes.

Shayne rode east. He had all night to accomplish
this bit of business, but the thought of Lottie keeping
company with Red Slovang made him put the spurs
to Little Bit as if the devil himself were on his trail.

There wasn't much of a moon in the night sky, and
what there was had been covered by thin, high clouds
when he reached the windmill.

It took only moments for Shayne to toss a rope high
up into the wooden frame and catch hold of a loose
board. Once caught he made a big circle round the
windmill, anchoring the lariat tight. With the rope dal-
lied round the saddlehorn, he turned Little Bit. One
prick of his spurs and the stallion bolted. The windmill
collapsed with a splintering of wood, a creak, and a
groan.

Dust filled the air as the wooden structure settled
to the earth. Shayne undallied the rope and left it tangled in the wreckage. He secretly hoped Red would
know it was his, but that was silly; all ropes looked

alike. He pointed Little Bit toward home but soon found himself on the knoll overlooking Slovang's house. All the downstairs windows winked with lamplight, the only brightness in the dark night.

Shayne shifted uneasily in his saddle. It was lonely on the hill, watching that house and knowing that another man was enjoying Lottie's company.

"But Lottie wants one more adventure before she goes home." That nagging thought chewed at Shayne's mind. He knew the clock was ticking and their time together was growing short.

She was a strange, headstrong woman. He didn't understand her any better now than he had the first day he walked into her dress shop. Shayne's unwilling thoughts turned to McTavish Plain. More than a dozen men would be willing to comfort Lottie on cold nights once she returned. Shayne didn't know what she planned on telling folks, but the upshot of any story was going to be that she was free to find another husband.

Another man to share her bed and her life.

The thought made his belly clench as though an icy, iron fist had grabbed hold and was twisting it.

"She'll be better off," he told himself, and even though he knew that was true—that she deserved a better man than him—his heart pinched with sorrow to think of facing a single day without Lottie.

He climbed out of the saddle and sat down on the hillock with his legs crossed. With Little Bit ground-tied beside him, he watched the house below and felt his heart break clean in two.

There was no way to see Lottie settled back in McTavish Plain and save himself from a lifetime of grief.

* * *

Lottie sipped the wine and tried to pretend she was listening to Red Slovang. He was a big bag of wind who could talk for an hour and never say one thing of interest to anyone but himself. They were on a settee that seemed way too small and confining. She battled the urge to rise to her feet and cross the room.

"What do you think, Miss Green?"

His question brought Lottie's mind plummeting to the present. She didn't have a clue what he had asked her, so she smiled sweetly and said, "Now, Mr. Slovang, I am just a woman and can't keep up with a man as sharp as you. Say that again, please?"

He preened. He actually inhaled so deeply and puffed up so big, the buttons of his fine, dark-charcoal satin vest pulled taut across his middle.

"I said I can't believe a woman like you is not married."

Ah, at last.

"I came west to find the right kind of man," Lottie said with a sigh. "I didn't want a merchant or a banker. In fact, I must confess, I am somewhat fascinated with men from Texas." She paused and batted her lashes.

"There is something so *appealing* about a man who can tame a land—harness the weather, tame the wilderness and Indians to build a place . . . well, like *this*." Lottie held out her arms and indicated all her surroundings.

Once again Red Slovang responded with a puffed-up arrogance that both sickened and thrilled Lottie. She had showed him her cards and he was ready to do the same.

"Could I be so bold, Miss Green—"

"Call me, Lottie."

He smiled wider and scooted closer on the settee. "Could I be so bold, *Lottie,* to hope that you might be wanting to marry?"

She smiled and averted her eyes. "I should be honest and tell you I am here to find a husband, Mr. Slovang."

"Call me Red."

"All right, Red. I have given up on ever finding the right kind of man back east, so when my auntie Isabel told me of her dilemma I knew my course was set. I am here to take over her ranch and to find a man who will assist me in restoring it to its former prosperity." She looked up and met his gaze. "Do you think I have set an impossible goal for myself?"

"No, Lottie, I don't. In fact, I think you have found the right man—in me."

Lottie closed her eyes and let the cooling breeze blow in her face. She was seated next to Red Slovang in the buggy, and the heat and scent of him was nauseating.

She had thought this would be easy: tempt the man into courting her; lure him into a trap while Shayne chiseled at his empire accident by accident.

Now she realized how difficult it would be.

He had already started holding her hand, rubbing at the soft middle of her palm in a way that made her flesh crawl.

Now he was sitting so close, he was crushing her skirts. She could feel the brush of his shirt against the

bare flesh of her upper arms when he handled the
lines to guide the horse.

Unbidden, the memory of Lefty ripped into her
mind. She hadn't thought about him for a while. When
Shayne was near, it was easy to forget what had happened. But now, here she was again, with a man that
she didn't want—a man whose greed and lust were
as obvious as the bulge in his pants.

Lottie shifted her weight and realized that a part of
her had insisted on helping Shayne because it offered
adventure. Once again she had thumbed her nose at
convention—at his warnings—and set herself straight
on a course to disaster.

*No. Not this time. I will be the one in control.
Shayne won't have to rescue me this time.*

"Well, here we are, Lottie," Red Slovang said, tugging the lines until the buggy shuddered to a rolling
stop.

"Oh, I hadn't even realized," Lottie said honestly.

"That is quite a compliment, that you enjoy my
company so much the trip passed quickly."

Her gaze darted to him. He was sincere. The man
was so sure of himself that he took everything she
said and bent it to his liking, making every statement
into a compliment.

"I—I had better go in. Auntie Isabel will be waiting
up for me, the poor dear."

His hand covered hers and he gripped tightly. Even
through the glove she could feel the heat, the lust.

"You are a remarkable woman, Lottie. I hate to see
you working yourself so to take care of an invalid.
Perhaps—perhaps if you and I came to an understanding—"

"Mr. Slovang—Red. I think I had better go. I wouldn't

want you to think I was a woman of questionable virtue. I am anxious to have a husband and home, but I think it is best if we do not rush this." She scrambled from his grip and stepped to the ground. When she turned back he was studying her with a frown. Lottie dragged in a breath of night air. It was flavored with the scent of juniper and Texas wildflowers, and Red Slovang's displeasure.

"Tomorrow?" she asked sweetly.

He finally smiled tightly. "Of course, Lottie. I'll come by tomorrow and we will continue this discussion."

"Good night, Red," She said, backing away from the buggy. As soon as he picked up the reins, she ran up the steps and into the house. She closed the door behind her and leaned against it.

"Just what in hell did you think you were doing sitting so close to him and letting him paw you like that?" Shayne's husky whisper demanded from the shadows. And then he was there, pulling her into his arms, claiming her mouth, staking his territory.

And she was happy to let him.

Twenty-seven

He carried her up the stairs and nudged open the door to his bedroom.

"Your mother—"

"Knows I am a grown man. I am hot for you," Shayne growled as he laid her on his bed. Lottie had not been in his room, and though she too was hot and ready, she found her gaze flowing over the walls, the furniture.

This was the room where Shayne had grown into a man. There were the treasures of youth still in evidence: a curl of wicked-looking barbed wire, now rusty and old, beside a broken spur. On a dusty shelf in the corner, a small miniature of a young couple who Lottie assumed were Isabel and Joss in their early years together. The woman had dark hair and snapping eyes and the man was another version of Shayne himself.

But the bed dominated the room. It was a massive thing with a high, plain headboard and squat posters at the foot. Shayne's hat adorned one finial; his gun belt was draped over the other. And in the middle of the bed was Lottie, with her heart pumping hard and her loins itching with want.

Shayne stood at the foot looking down at her with all the possessive desire of a healthy male in full rut.

Just the flick of his eyes over her face and body got her primed and ready.

It was amazing what he could do to her with no more than a smile and a suggestive lift of his brows.

"Damn it all, Lottie, I have got to find a way to get you out of my system. I tried not touching you to see if that would drive you from my mind, but that sure as hell didn't work, so I have come to the conclusion that I have got to do the opposite."

"The opposite?" She ran her tongue over her lips, her blood heating when his gaze followed its path. She wanted his lips on her body, on her mouth.

Now.

"Yep, I'm going to make love to you until you are out of my blood."

She shivered at his words.

"I'm going to do everything a man can do to a woman to bring her pleasure."

"And then?" The hot flush on her skin made her eager to shed the heavy gown. She was restless with need. Almost involuntarily her legs shifted beneath her skirt.

He watched their outline.

"And then I may do it again just to be sure the cure took." With quick, impatient movements he stripped off his shirt and then his boots and trousers.

"Because if you're leaving me soon, then I have got to find a way to remove you from my mind or I won't be any good to myself or anybody else. You're all I think of, Lottie. You have bewitched me."

He came to her then. With sure movements he began to unlace, unbutton, and unfetter her. His eyes licked hotly over her flesh. Shayne's hands were tender and gentle and too slow for Lottie. Impatiently she started to help him free her from the bondage of fabric.

"Damn it," he hissed when she was half undressed.

"What?" she asked, feeling hot, itchy, and impatient with Shayne's throbbing erection so close that she could touch it. She did reach out and trail one finger down the shaft, watching with delight as he stiffened. She ran her finger around the tip, toying with the soft head and the small opening there.

"I hate corsets," he growled and leaned near. With his tongue he dipped beneath the boning and flicked his warm, wet tongue over her nipple.

She groaned and squeezed his flesh in her hand.

He growled.

Together they began tearing at the laces of the corset, and soon the boned contraption was off. Now she was in her slitted drawers and gartered stockings.

"Stand up, Lottie."

She gained her feet, eager to see what splendor Shayne had in mind.

He led her to the center of the room. An oval braided rug covered the wooden floor and on this Shayne kneeled. "Now come here, darlin' and spread your legs."

She did, positioning herself in front of him. His head was at the level of her belly. He kissed her stomach, laving his tongue over her naval as he bent lower.

And then he wet her curly hair with his moist tongue, parting it, opening her. She watched in heated fascination, grabbing his dark hair in both her hands, guiding him, holding him to her when he might have moved from her.

She spread her legs wider and tilted her pelvis toward him.

He obliged her by gripping her buttocks and bringing her wholly to him. He delved deeply, pleasuring her in a way that was almost magical.

Lottie rose up on her toes, trying to offer herself to him more—to give him her innermost part so he might touch, caress, and bring her to greater heights of ecstasy.

"You taste sweet as honey and stronger than good wine, Lottie."

She looked down at him, the faint light from the sliver of moon casting his eyes in deep shadow. Her fingers were tangled in his hair.

The room smelled of their lust.

"Shayne, take me," she said, tugging at his hair.

But he did not do as she asked. Instead he returned his mouth to her body, kissing her, probing with his tongue, sending ribbons of fire snaking through her body. It flowed like liquid flame through her legs and pooled in her belly.

Her breasts were hot and heavy. She wanted to feel his hands on her.

"Shayne. Please," she begged like a wanton, feeling her body tighten and coil. She was weak, trembling. Her legs no longer seemed capable of supporting her.

She moaned and felt herself falling, but Shayne was there. Shayne with his hands, his body, his ability to turn her into a mass of molten need.

He scooped her up, bringing her legs around his body so she was both held and impaled by him in one smooth motion. She was hot and slick and he slid into her like a hand into a custom-fitted glove.

"Ah, Lottie, take me." He nudged his shaft into her, and in response her own body seemed to stretch, welcoming and milking him into her cavity until he was seated there deeply.

He was big and hard. His member moved something deep inside her. He filled her in a way that went beyond the physical.

"Nobody could be better than we are together," he growled, and nibbling at her earlobe.

She trembled inside and she knew her climax was coming. He knew it too, and he settled her back on the rug, him on his knees, his hands moving to her nipples.

He plucked at them, teasing her, taunting her as the trembles of her body turned to shudders.

And then she was flying, her body no longer hers; she was a creature of sensation, controlled by Shayne and his body. He moved inside her, thrusting hard, nudging her deeply again until she came apart.

She splintered into a million shards of light, each one a different shape, sound, and color. She left her body, unable to speak or think or do anything but *feel*.

She was aware of Shayne stiffening. Through a glaze of passion she watched him rear his head back and thrust hard into her. Then his body shuddered and he moaned, low and long.

They lay locked like that for several shared heartbeats. Then his eyes opened and a feral grin broke across his face.

"Well, darlin', that was perfect, but I guess we'll have to do it again, because you are still in my blood."

Lottie was amazed when she felt him thicken and grow inside her again. She smiled and yanked on his hair, pulling him to her.

"Come here, cowboy, I need a kiss."

Morning was only a few hours away. They were tangled together, exhausted, but no nearer to getting each other out of their systems than when they first started.

"Shayne, I have to get up and wash and get to my room. What will your mother think?"

"She won't think anything—she'll know." He grinned unrepentently.

"You have no shame." Lottie swatted the round muscle of his buttock as she climbed from the bed, scooping up her clothes as she went.

"I have nothing to be ashamed of, darlin'. You're a lot of woman and I'm man enough to know it and do something about it."

She paused at the door and stared at him. He was also a lot of man, and deep in her heart she knew his like would never come into her life again.

Too bad they couldn't find some way to span the distance between them. But Shayne was sure he was unfit to be loved, and Lottie had better sense than to batter her head bloody trying to convince him otherwise.

It happened, she supposed, that a man and a woman might suit each other like hand and glove in the physical area and still not be able to make things work in any place but a bed.

Still, it made her a little sad. But she had made up her mind. Though they were fantastic in bed, nothing had happened between them to change their situation.

He was staying in Texas and she was going home to McTavish Plain.

"I'm going to wash and fix a pot of coffee."

"I'll be down in a bit," Shayne said, rolling over and stretching his body. He grinned as her gaze slid down his form in appreciation.

"Stop it, darlin' or you won't make it out of this

room before noon," he threatened with a throaty chuckle.

Lottie closed the door and felt a corner of her heart seal itself off.

She would never forget Shayne Rosswarne.

Lottie had washed and dressed and had shared one cup of coffee with Shayne. Isabel was still in bed. Shayne's head came up abruptly. His gaze swung toward the road leading to the ranch.

"Son of a bitch," he cursed.

"What?" Lottie asked.

"I'll give you two guesses who that is riding up to the house." He took the stairs two at a time while Lottie patted her cheeks and smoothed her clothes. Red Slovang's visits were coming earlier and earlier. She was going to have to be very careful. At the same time, she realized her heart was beating in her chest wildly. Lottie had to admit that all this intrigue gave her a thrill of excitement. She was still having her grand adventure—and it was still all the sweeter because she was sharing it with Shayne.

Lottie stepped outside into the wash of dewy air, as yet unwarmed by the rising sun.

"Red. You're here early."

"I hope not too early, Lottie." He had an extra horse that was saddled and trailing behind his. "I brought you a mount."

"Did we have an engagement to go riding?" Lottie asked coyly.

"No. But I wanted to ride with you to take a look at your spread." His eyes twinkled. "I know more about this land than anybody around these parts. I can tell you exactly what you need."

I'll bet you can, Lottie thought, but she said, "Let me change into something more appropriate. Would you mind waiting here on the porch, Red? Auntie Isabel is so easily upset."

"Not at all," Red said, his eyes roving over the house. His expression was a mixture of avarice and anger.

Lottie shivered slightly. He could be dangerous. She was going to have to be very careful to spring the trap without getting snared herself.

Lottie was amazed at the size of the Rosswarne spread. It seemed they had been riding for hours and she had yet to see a fence or a cow.

Red Slovang had done his work well when he began to steal from Joss.

"There's the fence you share with me. You know, if our spreads were combined I—I mean *we* would be the biggest landowners in the county."

"Really?"

"Uh-hum. Beyond that fence is my land. If the two pieces were joined together you could see the sun rise and set and never reach the end. Any woman who shared such a position would want for nothing."

Lottie ignored his obvious sales pitch and squinted at the fence ahead. She saw the rubble of some structure not far off in the distance. "What is that?"

"Oh, that's an old windmill that once watered the stock on this end of the Rosswarne place. Wind must've blown it down a few years back," he lied smoothly.

"Really? Does this area get violent storms?"

He turned and leveled a gaze at her. "Things are

unpredictable. Some folks seem to be hit harder than others by fate and nature."

Lottie clenched her gloved hands tighter on the reins. She couldn't wait for him to discover what it felt like to be hit by calamity.

"I had better get back now, Red. Thank you for showing me around. I see there's a lot of work to do," Lottie sighed meaningfully. "I only wish I had the ready funds to begin."

Red Slovang squinted at her and leaned his weight on his saddlehorn. His eyes were flat and hard as a still lake. "If you and I could come to a formal arrangement, Lottie, I would be willing to see a nice settlement on you right now."

"What kind of formal arrangement?"

"If you will agree to be my wife, then I'll be more than happy to advance you a considerable amount to do what you wish. If you want new paint and wallpaper in the house, or if you should decide you want a new wardrobe for a honeymoon, the money would be there for your use."

"Red, this is sudden. I never dreamed—"

"Nonsense, Lottie. I can see you are a realistic woman. You and I are both capable of seeing what an advantage it would be to both of us if we were to marry."

"Let me think about it."

"Fine, I'll ask for your answer tomorrow."

"Tell the bastard to burn in hell!" Shayne bellowed. He tossed a log into the big cookstove in the kitchen. "You can't be meaning to go along with this."

"Of course I'm not going to marry him, but I could

let him think that I will while you're executing your part of the plan."

"I don't like it, not one bit." He growled.

"Son, that is fairly evident, but I'm starting to wonder what it is you dislike so much." Isabel leveled a gaze on her son.

"What is that supposed to mean?" he asked, glaring at Lottie and then her. "I want revenge on Red Slovang, not to see him hitched to Lottie. And besides, when this is over she's returning to McTavish Plain."

Isabel gave Lottie a speculative look that made Lottie wonder what Isabel had meant.

"Your revenge is only possible if Slovang no longer has the means to simply dust himself off and start over. Think about that, son."

Lottie focused on Shayne. "I have to let him think we're to be married if I am to get into his pockets," Lottie told Shayne reasonably.

Shayne's jaw twitched as he clamped his mouth shut tighter than a trap. He knew Lottie and his mother were speaking the truth, but the more he saw Red Slovang courting Lottie the more he was plagued by some strange, hot sickness. He lay awake at night because of it and spent most of the day puzzling over it and fighting off the effect it had on him.

He didn't know what it was, but he didn't like it.

"All right. But I am going to be watching every chance I get."

"You won't be watching this evening. Tonight you're going to relieve Red Slovang of some of the stolen Rosswarne stock."

* * *

Shayne cut the fence and eased Little Bit through. There was no moon, so the landscape was only shadows of varying darkness.

He kicked the stallion and let the animal pick his way to the herd. Shayne knew the minute he neared the cattle by the earthy scent and the heat coming from their bodies. The cattle lowed. Soon the ambling sway of a dark object told Shayne the big bull had come to investigate the disturbance to his herd.

Using his lariat to drive the docile creature, Shayne easily headed Horace toward the break in the fence. He smiled as he thought of Red Slovang discovering his prized moneymaker had been stolen.

Just as Slovang had stolen the animal from Joss. Of course, Shayne had no intention of going back to prison for rustling, so he had made arrangements to put the bull somewhere besides on Rosswarne land. He headed for the Tipton place, grateful that the old one-legged survivor had been willing to listen to his tale, and even more grateful that he was willing to help.

"Never could abide that damned Red Slovang," Mr. Tipton had said. "Man's got shifty eyes and a weak handshake. You can keep all your stock in Miller's canyon. Nobody will look there, and if they find 'em on my property I can plead my bum leg as an alibi." He had laughed and they had shared a stiff whiskey.

Now Shayne herded the bull into the canyon and dragged the gate constructed of woven chaparral and thorn bush in place behind him to close the entrance.

"And now, Little Bit, we need to go back. I intend to keep Lottie in sight whether she likes it or not."

* * *

By the time Shayne reached the hill overlooking Slovang's house it was late. He wondered if maybe Lottie had already been taken home, but then the door opened and he saw her.

The lamplight behind her bathed her in an angelic glow. She was a beauty, her golden curls nearly brushing her shoulders now, the made-over dress of burgundy hugging her curves to perfection.

She laughed.

Shayne's gut clenched painfully as she turned and said something to Red, who followed her out onto the long porch.

They sat down in chairs side by side and Shayne saw the man take Lottie's hand and bring it to his lips.

He wanted to kill him, but not because of his time in prison, or even for the deeds against his mother and father. He wanted to kill Red Slovang for touching the woman he . . . *he loved?*

Was that it? Had Shayne gone and done the unforgivable? Had he fallen in love with Lottie?

I would be nine kinds of a fool if I have.

She had told him from the start that she wanted no part of marriage. She wanted her independence and she wanted one big adventure to last a lifetime.

"No. I couldn't be dumb enough to have fallen for Lottie."

But as he continued to watch her in the dim light from the lantern on the porch, he wondered if he wasn't lying to himself.

Twenty-eight

The days wore on and Lottie became more and more embroiled in Shayne's revenge.

Red Slovang had pressed her for an answer, but she had put him off.

And she didn't know why.

Why didn't she simply lie to him and tell him that she would marry him? Why did that lie stick in her throat when it had been so easy to lie about being Mrs. Shayne Rosswarne?

Lottie had told that lie over and over in McTavish Plain before Shayne ever got there. And she had no trouble repeating it, and behaving as his wife in every way, when he arrived on her doorstep.

What was one more lie? Why was this lie any different?

Lottie didn't understand why the thought of telling Red Slovang she would marry him seemed like some sort of betrayal against Shayne. After all, this elaborate plan to milk Slovang of money and ruin his life was all for the Rosswarne family. And yet each time Lottie thought of Red Slovang thinking she would be his wife, a sharp pain of some unnamed sorrow ripped through her.

She didn't want any man ever to think of her that way.

"No man but Shayne," she admitted softly to herself. And that frightened her.

She had wanted a grand adventure to keep in her secret heart of hearts. And she had given up on having Shayne as a part of her life.

"I have to let him go," she said fiercely. But she knew that was the biggest lie of all.

"I want your answer, Lottie." Red Slovang had her trapped on the settee in his house. His eyes bored into her; he gripped her hand so hard, it was just short of being painful.

Lottie swallowed hard. Why couldn't she just say the words? After all the lies, why choke on this one? She closed her eyes and summoned her strength. Surely just one more lie . . .

The explosion rocked the house. Lottie jumped from the settee as Red Slovang released her and headed for the front door. She could see men spilling from the bunkhouse, running with buckets toward the blaze that was devouring the barn.

Shayne.

She picked up her skirts and ran out onto the front porch. Slovang was mad with rage as he stood there and watched the barn disintegrate into a pile of ash.

"I want you boys mounted and ready to ride. Somebody burned down that barn and somebody is going to pay," he bellowed before he spun on his heel to face Lottie. "I'll have Cooky take you home, Lottie. We'll continue this discussion tomorrow."

"Or the next day," she said with a sigh of relief. Once again Shayne had saved her.

The next two days were eventful. Red Slovang became aware of the theft of his bull and the destruction of his windmill—and all of it on the heels of the burning of his barn.

"Somebody is going to pay for this." He slammed his fist into his palm as he paced back and forth in front of Lottie at the Rosswarne ranch. Red was no longer smoothly in control. Now he had dark smudges of fatigue beneath his eyes, and his formerly impeccable suit showed signs of wear and travel stains.

"I've spoken to the sheriff over in San Saba. They are going to be on the look out for any drifters or men without a good reason to be here."

Lottie shivered slightly. She could feel Shayne's eyes on her from above. She silently prayed he would keep himself hidden. Each day he became more sullen, more determined to reveal himself and call Red Slovang out to face him down the barrel of a gun.

"Do you have any idea what happened?" Lottie heard herself ask.

"Someone put a torch to my barn. It's probably whoever rustled my bull."

"You don't think it's all just coincidence?"

"No. I don't. In fact, if I didn't know better . . ." His words trailed off as his eyes flicked around the room. Lottie could practically hear the wheels turning in his mind.

"If you didn't know better about what?"

"Oh, nothing. It doesn't matter. There was a man—but no. He's far away." Red blinked and focused on her face. "All this has interrupted our plans, but now that the law is on it, I'd like to pick up where we left off."

He moved across the room and picked up Lottie's left hand. She wondered if the slim, pale ring of smooth flesh, where her fake wedding ring once sat, was evident.

"I'll send Cooky to pick you up. Come to my house for dinner. I want us to come to an agreement tonight."

Shayne paced like a cat. Lottie had left an hour ago, dressed in a pale blue gown that was cut too low and too tight. His palms had itched to mold themselves against her body. He had left the room to keep from stripping her bare and burying himself inside her hot, wet sheath.

He was tired of hiding, tired of skulking in the shadows. And the more he tried to even the score with Red Slovang, the less satisfied he became.

There was something very wrong with all this revenge, but he couldn't put his finger on what it was that clawed at his insides and made him so restless that he couldn't sleep, couldn't eat.

Soon it would be over. Soon he would have his vengeance.

"And Lottie will be gone," he said while misery folded over him.

He looked around and everywhere he looked he saw traces of Lottie. She was burned into his brain and his flesh like a brand.

"She owns me," he said in anguish, raking his fingers through his hair.

He had never felt like this before.

"And it has to end. Tonight has to be the finish of it all. I can't go on like this."

Shayne scooped up his hat and headed for the door. It was time he finished this dance. It was time to pay the devil for playing the tune that he had stepped to for so long.

There was a half moon in the sky as Shayne rode boldly through Red Slovang's gate. He saw the men posted and he didn't care. Tonight it would be finished.

One way or the other.

"Stop right there." A man stepped forward, cocking his side arm as he spoke.

Shayne pulled Little Bit to a halt.

"State your business."

"I'm here to see Red Slovang," Shayne said, the hair on his neck bristling as half a dozen men readied their guns.

"He's entertaining tonight. Come back tomorrow."

"Can't do that. I've waited too long as it is," Shayne said reasonably.

"I said—"

"Tell him that I have come to settle accounts for Ian McTavish and Joss Rosswarne."

The man's face worked as he stood trying to make a decision. Whether it was Shayne's determination or his own fear of Red Slovang, the man finally holstered his gun and walked to the house. His knock echoed in the night. When the door opened, Shayne saw Lottie inside, seated like a queen.

His belly pinched with some strong emotion he dare not name.

"Come on up, but leave your gun," the man said.

Shayne dismounted, flipping his gun from the holster and into the air. The man caught it awkwardly.

Shayne's rowels chinged as he took the steps two at a time and stepped through the open door.

He found himself looking down the barrel of a gun as Red Slovang closed the front door behind him.

"I should've known when the bull came up missing." He had a cigar in his teeth. "So Joss Rosswarne's pup found a way out of jail."

"Ian McTavish sends his greetings," Shayne said dryly, casting a glance over Lottie. She was sitting so tense, Shayne had the notion that if he touched her she would fracture like fragile glass.

"So you finally figured it out, did you?" Red Slovang moved to the sideboard and poured himself two fingers of brandy. "Pretty smart, wasn't I?" He chewed the cigar back and forth as he spoke.

"Slick as snot," Shayne said. "When I got out of jail I went looking for the wrong man."

"How is it that you're still standing? I had it on good authority that Ian McTavish was not a man to trifle with."

"I had a little help from his sister-in-law."

Red frowned and turned to Lottie. His eyes glittered with malice.

"You. I should've known that you showing up here was a little too neat. That story about being Rosswarne's niece was too good. Who in hell are you?" Red asked.

"I'm Shayne Rosswarne's woman," Lottie said with a small, tight smile.

"No, she is not my woman," Shayne said, taking a step forward.

"Don't take another step or I'll shoot her, your *woman* or not," Red said, waving the gun wildly. It was then that Shayne leaped at him. They went down together in a heap of legs and arms. The gun went off. The bullet went wild, embedding in the wall. Lottie got to her feet. The gun went off again, hitting one of the lamps on the side table. Kerosene spilled out onto the thick carpet.

Lottie picked up her skirts and dodged the liquid. Then suddenly, as if time had slowed down, she saw the cigar fall from Slovang's lips.

Shayne hit him and broke free, his gaze going to Lottie at the moment the liquid ignited. Flames shot up from the carpet, fire licking in a line up the spilled kerosene to the table. It took only moments for the fire to block the way to the door.

"Lottie, the window." Shayne grabbed her elbow and dragged her with him. He ducked his head and used his forearm to shield his face as he leaped through the glass with Lottie in tow behind him.

The pop of glass and a burst of flame marked another lamp igniting.

"Slovang must be unconscious. I have to go back for him." Shayne touched her cheek, trailing his fingers down her jaw.

"Don't you want revenge?" Lottie asked.

"I only want my soul back," Shayne answered.

"Be careful," Lottie said, and then he was gone. He dived back through the same broken window. The whole room seemed to be engulfed in a hot, raging inferno.

She stood with her knuckles in her mouth and watched in horror. Shayne was gone.

The smoke was black and choking. He yanked the kerchief from around his neck and tied it over his mouth and nose. Seeing was not possible, so he fell to his knees and crawled, feeling his way. Finally his hands collided with a leg and a boot.

Blinded and choking, Shayne managed to get Slovang up and flopped over his shoulder like a bag of grain. Shayne wondered if he was already dead.

He didn't know or care. All he cared about was getting the bastard out and returning to Lottie.

Lottie. Her image floated in his mind. Cool and golden, her eyes the soft blue of a summer sky. She was all woman.

His woman.

He had some talking to do, some questions to ask.

And all he had to do was get out of the fiery furnace that was cooking him alive.

Shayne felt a blast of heat coming nearer. He shied from it. The only way he could go was up. And up he climbed, staggering, stumbling up the stairs. He was completely blind, his lungs seared from the smoke and the smell of fabric and wood burning. He felt along the wall until his fingers touched a doorknob. He tried it.

Locked.

Like a blind man Shayne groped, one door after another, finding them all locked until at last one opened. He stumbled through and went straight to the window.

He didn't know what lay below. He didn't care.

He used his elbow to break the glass, hearing the roar of the fire behind him as the hungry beast of flames followed him to the flow of oxygen—more fuel to feed the ravening monster.

He dived through, with the weight of Red Slovang bearing him down, down, down until the impact with the hard earth below took all thought away. The last thing he saw in his mind's eye was Lottie.

Lottie. Lost to him forever.

* * *

"He's going to be fine," Isabel told Lottie with a sympathetic smile. "The doctor said that broken leg will mend quick enough. He's young and strong."

"Yes, he'll be fine," Lottie said. "And since Red Slovang's neck was broken and his dealings revealed for the whole county to see, I know you'll be all right now, too."

"I can't thank you enough, Lottie. You helped Shayne and me more than words can tell. But are you sure you have to leave?"

"Yes." She was all packed and ready to go. Isabel had insisted that Lottie wait until Shayne was conscious before she left, and she had waited but now that she knew he was out of danger, she was anxious to get on the road back to McTavish Plain.

He had said he wanted to regain his soul, and with his family name restored, she was sure he had done just that.

His denial of her as his woman to Red Slovang had hurt her more than she thought possible. Now she wanted to salvage what dignity she had left and go home. Home, where she could be safe with her memories.

"I—I have to get back where I belong."

"Go to him, Lottie," Isabel said, patting Lottie's shoulder with a dry, thin hand. "Say good-bye to him if you must."

"Yes, it's time to say good-bye." Lottie drew herself up and opened the door to Shayne's room. Immediately she was assaulted with memories of their lovemaking. He was sprawled out on the bed, his swarthy body a contrast against the white linen sheets. His leg was splinted and propped up on a makeshift sling tied between the short posts of the footboard.

"Shayne?"

His eyes flickered open, his gaze sliding over her face to the man's shirt and trousers she wore.

"Why are you dressed like that?" he asked.

"I'm leaving today."

"Anxious, huh?"

"I have had my grand adventure," she said from her position by the door. She was afraid to move, afraid if she took one step she would fling herself into his arms and beg him to let her stay.

Her pride would not let her do it.

"Was the adventure everything you hoped for?" Shayne's eyes flicked over her face, lingering on her mouth.

She fought her body's response to him, but it was no use. She wanted him. She would go to her grave wanting him.

"It was more than I ever hoped for."

"What will you tell folks back in McTavish Plain?"

"I don't know. Maybe I'll tell the truth," she said with an awkward shrug. "I'm tired of telling lies."

"The truth. And what would the truth be?" Shayne asked, licking his lips as if he had gone parched with thirst.

"I guess the truth is something different to everyone." Lottie backed up a step, fighting the invisible pull of Shayne. She touched the doorknob, turned it, and slowly opened the door behind her. "I—I have to go."

"Lottie."

She didn't answer, was afraid to answer, afraid to

shame herself by letting him know that she had foolishly fallen in love with him.

"Lottie." He said again.

"What?"

"Don't go."

She froze with her hand on the knob, her heart in her throat. "What did you say?"

"I said don't go. I don't want you to leave."

She turned and looked at him. He looked just the same, his dark eyes unreadable, his chest rising and falling evenly. "Why?"

"Because I don't want you to leave me."

"But you told Slovang I wasn't your woman."

"I don't want you to be my woman. I want you to be my wife—my *real* wife, with a ring and a preacher and witnesses. I want to carry you over the threshold of this house. I want you to cook my meals, warm my bed, and bear my children."

"What?"

"I have done it, Lottie. I have done the unthinkable. I have fallen in love with you and can't live unless you say you will let me spend the rest of my life with you. If it has to be in McTavish Plain, fine. Or if it's chasing around the world looking for danger and excitement, then that's fine too."

"Strong words from a man flat on his back," she said with a trembling smile.

"You always liked me best in this position—admit it." He wore a wicked grin. "I love you, Charlotte Green. Will you marry me?"

"And be a real bride?"

"Yep, a real wife and a real bride. Not some bogus one made up for your sisters or for a town. I want you with me, Lottie. Forever."

She went to him then, and she did shame herself with her tears. She wept on his bare chest; she wept while he kissed her. She wept when he pulled her onto the bed beside him.

"Shayne, I have to tell you something."

"What, darlin?"

"You remember the leather pouches I won in the card games with Dobbs and Cut-nose?"

"Yes."

"Well, one of them contains a map. It shows the way to a treasure of silver in Mexico. Just think how exciting it would be to go in search of a treasure. It isn't all that far from here to Mexico, is it, Shayne?"

"No, darlin', not far at all. In fact, no place is too far with you at my side."

Put a Little Romance in Your Life With
Constance O'Day-Flannery

Discover the Romances of
Hannah Howell

The Queen of Romance
Cassie Edwards

BOOK YOUR PLACE ON OUR WEBSITE AND MAKE THE READING CONNECTION!

We've created a customized website just for our very special readers, where you can get the inside scoop on everything that's going on with Zebra, Pinnacle and Kensington books.

When you come online, you'll have the exciting opportunity to:

- View covers of upcoming books
- Read sample chapters
- Learn about our future publishing schedule (listed by publication month *and author*)
- Find out when your favorite authors will be visiting a city near you
- Search for and order backlist books from our online catalog
- Check out author bios and background information
- Send e-mail to your favorite authors
- Meet the Kensington staff online
- Join us in weekly chats with authors, readers and other guests
- Get writing guidelines
- AND MUCH MORE!

**Visit our website at
http://www.zebrabooks.com**